FATE'S END

JERRY AUTIERI

1

Yngvar stood at the base of the path, gazing up the thin line through rocks and brush, and knew his life would change forever. Long shadows cut a lattice into the golden light of the dying sun that skimmed across the path. A black lizard stood, frozen at its center, stared back at Yngvar, then finally darted away into the scraggly bushes growing lining the way ahead.

He licked his lips in anticipation. His heart beat against his ribs so hard he expected the men behind him would discover it. Everything was as he remembered. The map had been true.

"Don't look like much," Bjorn said from behind. "You sure this is a king's grave?"

Yngvar nodded, studying the path. It crawled up what might seem a steep hill, but had revealed itself as a burial mound to an ancient king. Now that he knew what it was, its shape was obvious. To another, it might seem little more than the highest hill of a tiny, deserted island in the middle of the Midgard Sea.

"The Byzantines sure believe it is," Thorfast said. His voice was closer, as he stood directly behind Yngvar with the Greek slave who would read the runes of the dead king's grave and reveal his name.

"Lord, we should go before the sun sets." Alasdair stood by his side, shielding his smooth, bright face with one hand. His other hand rested on a wooden crucifix hanging from his neck by twine.

Yngvar turned to face his crew. Thorfast held the Greek slave by a rope tied to his neck. The man hunched over as if carrying a heavy burden, though all he owned was a gray shirt and brown pants. His head and eyes were oversized for his rail-thin body. Bjorn was a huge shadow against the setting sun, but his shouldered ax gleamed with the light. Gyna stood beside him, looking out to sea to where a Byzantine ship sat at anchor.

A line of six Franks stretched out behind them toward the beach where his ship lay. He considered these men his crew, though they nominally followed Bjorn as they were his father's men. One of the Franks was their leader, Nordbert, who now sported a fresh scar down the cheek of his proud face.

"None of you need fear anything," Yngvar said. He wrapped his wrist in one hand behind his back. This was how his Byzantine officers had stood, and he liked the authority it imparted to them. Only Thorfast seemed aware of his affectation and gave a faint smile for it.

"I just think it'll be hard to carry away treasure in the dark," Alasdair said. "There can't be more than an hour of light left."

"Don't worry for it, lad," Bjorn said with a rough laugh. "I don't want to be mucking around a grave in the dark. Spirits or fucking worse things will come for us. We'll get this treasure on the ship and be gone before then."

Yngvar shook his head.

"It's too much to carry off at once. We'll take some, then guard this spot to claim the rest in the morning."

"Can our ship carry so much?" Thorfast asked. He gathered the rope tighter to his hand, drawing the Greek closer.

Yngvar shrugged and turned back to the path.

"This is what the gods promised me—promised us. All our suffering, all our dreams, are buried beneath this mound. Gold as you have never imagined. We left Frankia as poor boys. We'll return as rich lords. This is what we've sought all these long years."

Gyna groaned. "Well, you'll be a fucking toothless old man before then if you keep prattling. Let's go."

Yngvar picked his way along the path, each step steeper and rougher than the last. At the top, he came to the crack he had excavated, which was the long-hidden entrance to the burial chamber. The bones he and Alasdair had found were still there. The skull with a crack radiating out of its eye socket seemed to study him. Yngvar imagined it offering a slow, knowing nod. Of course he would return. What man could stay away from such treasure for long?

The Greek moaned when he saw the bones shoved aside from the entrance.

"A curse hangs here," he said. "Men who know the legends are wise enough to stay away. The fools like this one come to leave their bones to the demons of this island."

"Not a curse for you, Theodoros," Yngvar said. "You tell us who is buried here and you will have earned your freedom."

"What good is accursed freedom?" The slave, Theodoros, raised his hands to hold his fat head. But Thorfast tugged on his rope as if bringing a dog to heel. The slave fell silent.

"I don't understand Greek, but I'd say he's worried," Thorfast said. "I can't say I'm not, as well."

"Both Alasdair and I saw what is in there." Yngvar set his hands to the crack in the earth, feeling the warm, rough stone glide beneath his palms. "Whatever risk we take, it will be worth it. Curse or no."

"Bold words," Thorfast said. "We can defeat anything that bleeds. But we can't defy a curse."

"If it's our fates to be cursed, then we cannot avoid it." Yngvar pressed his arm through, feeling the instant change to cool air beyond. His body would slip through easily, as would all the gold and silver he would carry away. "Besides, is it not the desire of every king to be known in every land? The one buried here couldn't have been any different. He has been forgotten, and he cannot be remembered as long as men fear a curse. So I have vowed to bring his name to the world again. Then he will withhold his curse and grant us his gold. What good is gold to him in his ancient grave? We will be fine."

"Lord, this place does not look the same. The entrance has changed. Some of these rocks have fallen." Alasdair leaned down and set his hand on a rock like he was comforting an old friend.

"You've a better memory than mine," Yngvar said, withdrawing his arm back to the warm, humid air. "Though, I suppose I dug the opening wider. I can't remember exactly."

"What's that all mean?" Bjorn asked. "You can't agree on what you remembered. Won't be the first time for that. Come on, now, there's still plenty of sunlight. Gyna's got the torch ready to go."

Yngvar scanned the high rocks that framed the entrance. From here he could see all around the island and out to sea. The black shape of One-Eye Petronius's ship was sharp against the sparkling water. Fool Byzantine was too frightened to set foot on the island but more than willing to help himself to a share. Yngvar needed the security of the larger, sturdier vessel, though, and so had made his bargain with Petronius.

He sucked his gut in as he shimmied through the crack. Bjorn might struggle to pass through it. He decided the entrance was narrower than his first visit.

Beyond was cool and dark. The light did not reach inside, slipping past the door as if too afraid to follow him. Yngvar had to stoop to prevent his head from touching the ceiling. He reached back through the crack.

"I'll need that torch," he said to Bjorn. "And I think you must wait outside until we can dig open the entrance. It has fallen in since I was last here. Now, Theodoros, come with me."

Yngvar waited in the cool darkness for the torch and his captured Greek. Poor Theodoros had been a simple scribe working with merchants at a dock on western Sicily. But a quick raid had led him into Yngvar's hands. He had been treated well, and Yngvar was sincere in freeing the man. But not until they were well away with their treasure.

"Theodoros," Yngvar chided as the thin slave joined him inside. "You're about to become a rich man. I know my kinsmen have a reputation. But when we give our word, it is better than gold."

Yngvar turned away and held his torch aloft. He had in fact broken too many vows to consider, most recently one to his lord, King Hakon. The gods were stern in their punishment of oath-breakers. He wondered how much of his suffering had been for the false words he had made.

The short passage led to earthen steps down into the darkness. He started down, probing ahead with his feet to be certain the stairs would not crumble beneath him.

"Ah! Something touched me!" Theodoros shouted, leaping against Yngvar's back. He shoved him away with a grunt.

"Webs, you fool. There will be roots as we go deeper. Don't piss yourself just yet."

Alasdair and Thorfast had filed in behind him. He could hear Gyna's voice as she argued with Bjorn at the entrance. The other Franks, led by Nordbert, were pushing inside. These Franks loved gold as much as any Norseman. In fact, many were the descendants of Danes who had come to Frankia even before the time of Yngvar's grandfather, Ulfrik Ormsson. Neither Nordbert nor his men would let a chance for gold and glory escape them.

Steps crumbled, but Yngvar moved with care and never lost his footing. His torch ranged ahead, casting a flutter of shadows into the cramped passage. There were pictures showing along the walls of its narrow length. Yngvar had not studied them before, but now ran his hand over the crumbling art. Flakes slid to the floor, but the picture was clear. Ancient men with spears and shields clashed with each other. They massed into huge armies, but grime and darkness obscured the details of how they fought.

"It seems the old people were not much different from us," he said to Theodoros. "Any clue to the king's name here?"

The shadow of the Greek slave shuddered and offered no reply. They pressed downward until Yngvar felt the footing become smoother. His heart raced. He was nearly at the burial chamber.

The sharp decline stretched on longer than he recalled. The ancient builders had dug deep into what must have been a natural hill at one time. They set their king to rest beneath heavy stone and earth, never to be disturbed until this day.

The burial chamber entrance appeared before him as a dark rectangle in the way ahead. Yngvar spotted writing around it and gestured at Theodoros.

"Read those words," he said. "And tell me whose grave this is."

He left the Greek blocking the way for everyone else. He stepped beyond the opening into the chamber.

"It's all here," he said, his words breathy and low.

The scent of wet rot and earth filled his nose. The air was clammy and still. His torch burnt away cobwebs and scattered weak light across the small chamber.

The happy gleam of gold and silver blinked back at him.

A black stone coffin dominated the center of the room. Dirt and fallen rocks covered it, untouched since Yngvar had originally found the place. To his left, shattered skulls and broken spears he had knocked over when he first discovered the chamber covered the floor. Of the ten original skulls only one remained, spun around on its shelf, staring at its destroyed companions.

"Gold and silver," Yngvar said, nearly laughing. His torch lifted higher. There was no light here, as he had found during his initial visit. The hour was late and perhaps the sun no longer struck the crack. The air was stale and did not move. The smoke from his torch quickly filled the small room and left his nose raw.

"Lord," Alasdair called back. "Are you safe?"

Yngvar snorted at the question. Why would he be in danger? His eyes could not leave the piles of gold coins spilled out from long rotten chests and sacks. Some of these remained intact. Great earthenware jugs sealed with wax lined the room. More scenes of glorious battle clamored for his attention along the walls.

But Yngvar only had eyes for the treasures covering the floor.

"It's all that I remember," he said. He crouched to lay his hand on gold. The cold, hard coins jolted his memory.

"Theodoros," he shouted. "Name the owner of this grave for me. There are more words here on this coffin. Surely you must know what they mean."

The slave slunk into the chamber, protecting his sides with his arms as if expecting a blow. Yet when his eyes set upon the gold spilled out on the floor, he spun around with mouth agape.

"That's right," Yngvar laughed. "There must be a thousand

pounds of gold here. More treasure than any living king. And you may have a share, if you do as I have asked."

Alasdair now stepped in, but the chamber was only large enough for the three of them. Thorfast's white hair was still visible in the low light as he peered over Alasdair's head.

Yngvar stood beside the black coffin, stretching his torch over the spoils.

"You see, I did not exaggerate. The floor is of gold and silver. It fills every corner of this chamber. What might yet be in these sacks and closed chests, I cannot say. But I would expect it is more gold and jewels."

"Lord, the air here is foul. I can hardly breathe."

"Look at that," Thorfast exclaimed. "So much gold!"

Yngvar laughed. "You thought me a liar. Now, we must take what we can tonight, enough to encourage the men to hard work tomorrow. But first, Theodoros, recover your breath and speak the name of this king that we may remember him."

Theodoros blinked at the gold coins. But Yngvar's command filled the chamber and drew him back to his thoughts. His huge eyes reflected the torchlight. He turned to the walls, running his hands along the frescos as if it would aid him in seeing them better. He shook his oversized head.

"You have the name, don't you?" Yngvar stepped closer, pulling him by the shoulder. "If not, then you need to keep digging through here until you find one."

"I have found a name," he said. His voice was as dry and rough as the bones littering the floor. "But I must be sure of it."

"I won't hinder you there," Yngvar said, releasing the slave and patting his shoulder. "Be certain, for it is of great importance. Now, while you do that, I'll start figuring a way to carry off these coins."

He found what he had sought. A stack of old shields like bronze plates rested where the spears had fallen. Snatching one up, he weighed it in his hands. Though coated in verdigris, it was sturdy.

"We'll shovel up gold with these," he said. "It'll be tricky getting them up the passage and outside with gold in them. But tomorrow we will return with sacks and chests."

"I have prepared sacks, lord," Alasdair said. He unfurled a small leather sack and offered it. His hand wandered, as he could not look away from the gold spilled at his feet. Yngvar smiled and accepted the sack.

"Of course you would be prepared. I was too eager to reach this place to plan more. Now, let's fill these sacks and be away before the sun sets. I would like to find a golden cup for tonight. I think I see one."

Yngvar waded into the treasure piles. As he moved deeper into the room, he stole the light from others. Theodoros hissed at the sudden darkness.

"And what have you learned?" Yngvar asked as he plucked his prize. Coins spilled out to clink merrily back into the pile. He held a silver cup that had reflected gold in the poor light. Still, it was treasure, though tarnished.

"I am certain of the name." The slave's voice was hushed and reverent. He was little more than a gray shadow at the edge of the torchlight. He ran his thin fingers through his dark hair.

"Then let us hear it." Yngvar polished the cup against his white shirt sleeve. Once cleaned, it would do to drink from it tonight. Perhaps a real golden cup remained to be discovered.

He realized Theodoros had not answered. He stuffed the cup into the sack and frowned in expectation.

Theodoros cleared his throat, then went to the coffin. He ran both his thin hands over it.

"He was the King of Mycenae, son of Atreus, brother of Menelaus, and father of Orestese. He was a great general, slayer of hundreds by his own sword. We stand in the tomb of Agamemnon."

Theodoros's eyes seemed to gleam beyond the light reflected from the torch. He stared balefully at the black stone coffin as if his own father lay within it. At last, he looked to Yngvar, lips quivering.

"Well, now we know his name," he said. He leaned down to scoop coins into the sack. "After we are away with the treasure, you'll have your payment and be set free. You've done well, Theodoros."

The Greek slave inhaled as if to speak.

But the words never passed his teeth.

The earth lurched and the shuddering boom of stones crashing together filled the chamber. Dirt and rocks dropped from the ceiling. The coins exploded up from the floor, creating a spray of gold and silver.

Yngvar collapsed back as screams filled the chamber. The torch and sack fell from his hands.

"Lord!" Alasdair shouted.

"Out of the passage!" Thorfast shouted from behind.

But Yngvar could hear nothing more, for the roar of the earth shattered his ears. The ground beneath him seemed to vanish.

And Yngvar fell into perfect darkness.

2

Yngvar fell into darkness. The cold earth battered him as he tumbled. He did not fall far but landed hard on his feet, which broke his fall and sent him sprawling onto a smooth, hard surface.

Something slammed over him. The blast of air pressure flattened him and filled his nose with metallic dust. He heard coins clinking against stone like rain. The horrific grinding slam of earth stopped and the abrupt rocking ceased with the sound. Yngvar was beneath a large rock, one that fortunately sheltered him from more rocks and dirt falling with him. Coins rolled or bounced into him beneath the rock.

He lay motionless on his side. Hot blood dribbled down his forehead and into his mouth. He tasted grit and copper. But he flexed his toes and gently moved his legs. He was not pinned, and he could feel his limbs. His knees ached and he thought of Gyna and her injured knee. The memory was nothing to him. Just something broken free, like all the rocks clapping to the surrounding ground.

When the noises died to nothing more than scattered pings of coins sliding down and chiming against the ground, he called out.

"Alasdair? Thorfast? Anyone hear me?"

To his shock, his voice echoed. Though he could not see his hand before his face, he sensed he was in a wide space. He waited for someone to call down to him, but heard nothing.

He heard the hiss of sand sliding free and the clatter of pebbles and debris following.

But no one answered, no matter how many times he called up into the darkness.

This must have been what the Byzantines had warned him about. They had spoken of earthquakes. They were horrible catastrophes that God visited upon wicked societies. The earth could shake with horrible violence for either an instant or for what seemed hours. Nor was God content to shake the world once, but would often do so many times after the first.

During Yngvar's time among the Byzantines, he experienced tremors underfoot. Such an experience had unnerved him, but his fellows laughed at him and blamed the rumbling on the distant volcano, Etna. He never expected an earthquake could generate such sudden force. Perhaps it had been a mere jolt, but it caused a collapse.

"Is this your curse, King Agamemnon?" He spoke to himself, loud enough to test the echoes. He dragged his hand across the floor—it was a floor, for it was smooth and hard stone—and gathered a coin into his fist. The world was utterly black, as if he had lost both his eyes. But he threw the coin with all his strength. It clinked against something hard, but it was distant. Yngvar now better understood the space he was in. He threw a second coin in another direction, but this toss struck nothing hard. He heard the coin bounce to the ground, then roll.

Gathering himself carefully, he sat up until his head bumped a hard rock. He felt along its edge until he found an open space, then tried to stand. He unfolded until he reached his full height. He prayed nothing more would fall and stood motionless until he was sure nothing else would collapse. He reached his hand up, and it stretched into the cold, clammy air.

Yngvar carefully explored the dimensions of his space until he determined he was in a clearing at least as tall as he was and wider than he could estimate.

The air was foul and smelled of mold and dirt. His breathing already felt labored, and he wondered how long he could survive. Would the others dig him out? Had the collapse killed or likewise trapped them?

He shouted for Alasdair and Thorfast.

His answer was a crash of more stone falling from above. The sound of shattering pottery met him and the scrape of iron on rock followed. Along with that scrape, to Yngvar's left, came a line of sparks that lit the absolute darkness with a dazzling silver light.

The flash was too brief for him to mark anything other than the location of the sound. But he realized something iron had been dislodged and scrapped across rock.

If he could strike another spark, he would scan the area for a way out now hidden in darkness. The sun would set soon. So even if a path up to the surface remained, in one short hour he might not locate it. If the gods favored him, he might feel air moving. But he could not count on that.

"I'm not dying here, King Agamemnon. I'll carry your name to the world to be remembered. But if you slay me now, you will be forever lost."

Dropping to hands and knees, he crawled toward where he had seen the spark. He feared striking his head or else stumbling. Even a slight injury in these circumstances would be fatal. If he were to have any hope of escape, he had to do his utmost to preserve himself. That meant moving with deliberation, even when he wanted to rush.

Chunks of debris and coins covered the floor. But as he traversed the hard stone he realized that the cave-in above might only be a small opening in the ceiling to this new chamber. Once he left the area where he had fallen, he found less rough debris. Instead, his hands crawled over older things he could only guess at. Things that fell apart beneath his hands or else split beneath his knees as he crawled. As his hands swept the darkness ahead, he felt what must be bones.

Cold terror ran through his body, tingling from his scalp to his feet. Ghosts and dwarves and other evil things of the deep earth could not concern him or else he would never escape. The bones under his hand made him imagine a draugr, the dead come to life once more, rising to choke him for trespassing in its grave. But Yngvar froze and nothing else stirred. Neither draugr nor dwarf moved through his blackness.

Only despair and a lingering death in the damp earth remained for him here.

He reached the point where he had seen the sparks. Despite his careful approach, he still had bumped his head twice, caught his pants on something pointed, and scored his forearm on a rock. But now he felt a wall, rough but worked by human hands. He patted around until he found the cold iron under his palm. He smiled as he gathered it close. A sharp edge bit into his fingers and he handled it more delicately. It must be an ancient spearhead. Feeling down, he found old wood attached to it and making it as long as his forearm.

Taking a long arcing strike, Yngvar sprayed sparks in a white shower. It was enough to confirm he held a spearhead and the remains of its shaft. He continued scraping, easily drawing sparks to glimpse the room.

It was beyond the feeble sparks to light anything but a small circle. Yngvar sought useful items in the flashing illumination. Not until he had struck sparks so that his shoulder grew sore did he discover his hope.

A puddle of thick oil had flowed onto the floor. Shards of broken pottery stuck up from it. The ancient oil might burn and afford Yngvar light to explore.

Fire could also spell his death. It might catch too violently, or else spread to the old and rotted things here. More insidiously smoke might choke Yngvar to death before the light could avail him any benefit.

But if he remained blind, he would surely die unless rescued. He doubted the others would reach him in time.

If they had survived themselves.

He banished all other worries. He needed light. A spark and oil might provide it to him, or may deliver a swift end to his days. He had to risk it.

Crawling until he touched the oil with his fingers, Yngvar considered what to do. To spark the oil puddle might be explosive, or it might be too much for a simple spark to ignite. A length of dry wood could serve, but he would never find it without light. He stripped away his torn pant leg. It had already been ripped in the fall. A long strip broke free.

He dabbed the strip into the edge of the oil, then crawled away from it. Then he took the dull iron spearhead and dragged it across the stone floor.

The sparks did nothing at first. But he smelled the sour stench of the smoldering cloth. He had nothing more to do than repeat his process until at last the spark created a red glow. He blew carefully at it. At first it seemed to resist, but then he realized the cloth had caught flame where there was no oil.

It burned up suddenly. Flashing with heat and light that dazzled Yngvar. But no sooner had it flamed to life it had vanished, leaving red glowing ashes to melt into the dark.

Cursing his luck, he tried again with a thicker ball of his pant-leg cloth. This time he wrapped it to the broken spear shaft, anchoring it to a splinter, then dipped only the tip into the oil. This time the spark caught more readily and soon he held up a burning torch.

He shouted with victory, holding the sudden blaze up from his face. The heat was strong on his hand, for the shaft was not long, but the light seemed incredible in the darkness.

The globe of light revealed a chamber three times as large as the one he had fallen through. The rectangular room had two walls barely within the range of his torchlight. Two walls were closer and showed more paintings of ancient battles and strange creatures.

Yngvar did not linger on this, but looked upward.

The ceiling had split and the contents from above had fallen into this chamber. The black coffin had fallen with it and shattered. It stood on its end, jumbled with other sections of stone and forming a triangular space beneath it.

"You saved me," Yngvar said in astonishment. For the black stone coffin had shielded him from everything else.

The contents of the coffin, however, had not fallen out toward him. Perhaps old King Agamemnon was now nothing more than shattered bone fragments scattered on the floor. Gold and riches sprayed intermingled with dirt and debris out everywhere beneath the hole.

He stood, now confident to move with the light. He moved toward the distant walls to throw torchlight onto what was obscured there.

Then froze in horror.

A dozen armored warriors stood at attention.

Draugr! The terror of these undead warriors staggered him.

They wore rotted leather harnesses and helmets that hid their faces. Huge round shields of bronze were painted with monsters, snakes, or octopuses. Their spears were ready in their hands.

Yngvar had no weapon beyond his torch. But reflexes sent him into a fighting crouch.

Yet the draugr did not move. They remained staring at him.

They were dead guards, not draugr, he decided.

Yet unlike the warriors of the chamber above, these stood as if at attention. Their spear tips were sharp as razors. Their helmets, though coated in dust and a patina of antiquity, were heavy and battle-ready. Their shields rested against their legs, but were mighty pieces of war gear. Had these guards been more than gray, withered flesh they would be formidable foes.

He approached, finding ropes fastened them to a kind of rack. They must have either died standing or else been first killed then set in place. Yngvar could not look at their rotted faces, for the shadows of his torch made it seem as if their eyes were alive. Despite a thousand years of death, these men still seemed haughty and mighty, as if they would not deign to look at him even if they hadn't seen a living man in a hundred centuries.

He touched one with his finger. The corpse had fused with his armor and the rack holding him erect. Yngvar nodded out of respect. These men would stand guard until the end of days. But what did they guard? Wasn't the king in the chamber above this one?

He picked a way back through the debris, stepping over the bones he had felt earlier. There were three hounds set out in a row, and Yngvar had crawled through their remains. In fact, they seemed to surround another black coffin, which had been crushed beneath the collapsed ceiling. The hounds were set beside this.

Rounding to the original coffin, he found it had indeed been shattered and opened. But nothing had been inside. He gasped. Why had so many riches been laid out for this coffin when it had been emptied. Or else during the jolt the corpse had been dislodged. That seemed unlikely.

If there was no king here, then how could there be a king's curse?

He looked to the other coffin. Its lid had been shattered, though it was now pinned beneath a slab of rock. Though it would be of no use to his escape, he stalked through the debris to draw up to the coffin and put his torch over the hole.

Something glinted within. He set the torch down, then pushed the shattered portion of the lid aside. It crashed to the ground. The shattering echoes dislodged a curtain of dust and dirt from above and spiraled a stench of rot into the air.

But here was the king. Whatever had been above must have been a distraction for tomb robbers, or else the tomb of a different king altogether. He would never know.

An ancient skull still with paper-thin flesh and wisps of long, gray hair looked up at him. His eyes were thin holes over two slits for the remains of his nose. A golden circlet sat on his head.

He tried to angle the torch to see deeper into the coffin, but feared setting the old corpse ablaze.

His hand hovered over the king's crown.

"You have no use for gold now," Yngvar said. "And I will treasure this as my most valuable prize. I will not melt it or hack it into bits. I will make it an armband and wear it in your memory."

He lifted the circlet from the skull. The skin tore and hair fell away. But Yngvar claimed his prize. The crown of an ancient king. He held it in his hand, staring at it in amazement. It was plain gold, etched with intricate scroll work designs. Time had filled the engraving with gray dust.

"Let your wisdom guide me, King Agamemnon. Theodoros said you were a fearsome warrior. So am I. If I wear this upon my sword arm, then every one of my strikes will be true. No man will ever best me."

The light from his torch guttered, and he realized time was running out. He needed to search this chamber or else he would lose his light source. Picking over the smashed and shattered remains, he tore free items of gold, silver, and bronze. Here were cups inlaid with jewels. Rings and necklaces of valuable stones. Shells of great beauty, mostly smashed, but others seemed to have only been picked from the sea this morning. Decorative weapons were lined in reach of the coffin. More lay crushed beneath rocks, but still the treasures here made the coins above seem worthless.

Those coins were meant to be a distraction. Their volume would stun the naïve, as it had Yngvar. No one would dig deeper to find the real treasures.

Now wearing jeweled daggers, rings, and necklaces, he was as a king himself. But he still had found nothing useful to dig out. He did find torches, ancient and dry, but once steeped in the oil burned brighter than his makeshift brand had.

But his throat was raw and his breath felt heavy. Smoke escaped up into the crack above. It seemed Yngvar's only choice. But to scrabble into that darkness would surely invite another collapse.

He sat against the coffin, laden with jewels, staring at the ten draugr tied to their stakes.

"It is noble for you to guard your kind," Yngvar said, just to relieve the silence with his own voice. "But you do so from too far away. Guards should never stray from their lord. Look. I have taken his crown. Though I mean him no dishonor, still I have lifted it from his skull while you stand too far to stop me."

He laughed. There was no humor in his voice. For it seemed he was again being mocked. The distant draugr did not need to move. He was already slain. He would die holding a king's crown amid inestimable wealth as bitter tears leaked from his eyes.

"I hear to die by smoke is a terrible death," Yngvar said. "I could set the room ablaze. I would choke and writhe like a speared snake.

The mighty Yngvar Hakonsson, killer of Danes, enemy of Erik Bloodaxe, bearer of King Agamemnon's crown, would die in the dark. But better to die swiftly than of thirst. Who will mark my passing?"

He set his torch between stones and watched its smoke twist along the ceiling to vanish up into the crack. Perhaps he should try to climb into it. He could clamber up the rocks and search for purchase above. The smoke had not backed up yet, suggesting a wider space to fill above. Maybe it might even escape out the top of the hill through cracks he knew were there from before. But no one would see it at night, not even under a full moon.

Deciding that he needed no more light, he would extinguish the torch. He kept the old spearpoint and more torches at hand. Now he was polluting the air and depleting whatever remained. He wondered if he would first suffocate or starve.

The torch flame was weak but steady. He stared at its glow then closed his eyes, still seeing an orange impression of it against his lids.

Who would mark his death? He had lived and struggled so long, but he had done nothing with his life. His father and grandfather at least had created a community where their memories would remain. Even his great-grandfather, Orm the Bellower, was still known in Norway. But Yngvar Hakonsson? He had squandered his life chasing gold. Now he would die buried with more gold than any man could imagine.

Yet be remembered by none.

No wife or son to mourn him. No stones raised to his memory. No hirdmen to sing songs of his glories around winter hearth fires. He had been gone so long that even his enemies must have forgotten his name by now. He smiled, remembering King Erik Bloodaxe once had a bounty on his life. It would remain unpaid, and King Erik would likely forget he had offered one.

Yngvar had chased gold and glory. He had found it.

And nothing more.

He shifted to the draugr again. Why were they so distant?

With nothing more to do than wait for death, he studied their corpses again.

Careful that his torch not ignite their dried flesh, he searched around their feet and the bindings around their waists.

His torch flame guttered and spun, making the shadows swim around them.

Yngvar looked to the torch.

It was guttering. There was air flow.

He stood up now and felt the wall behind him.

Cool air rushed through his fingers.

"You canny bastards," Yngvar said, pressing his palm into the cracks on the wall behind the dead guards. "You're guarding the entrance to your lord's hall. That's it, isn't it?"

He set the torch down and pulled the rack. Once ten men would have made it too heavy to slide. Now, once he unmoored the rack from the grime and rot that had fused it to the stone, it slid aside easily. Bronze shields rang on the floor, sending more dirt falling from above.

But Yngvar was heedless of danger now.

The wall behind them was cracked, and a strong current blew through the stone. He thought of the door he originally found to this tomb, how he had to bash an opening through a false wall.

He retrieved a heavy rock and began smashing against the wall. Each strike echoed beyond. Each strike brought more sand down on him and the room.

Yet soon he broke open a hole.

Fresh air flooded in, smelling of the sea.

"The way out!"

He pulled aside the remains of the wall, now easily falling away. He laughed, this time full of true mirth. For he would live. Once he had created a hole, he retrieved a torch and searched beyond.

A narrow passage led away into darkness. But human hands had carved it. A strong sea wind gusted into his face. Nothing had ever smelled sweeter or felt more refreshing.

"Farewell for now, King Agamemnon," he said, raising the stolen crown like a drinking horn toward the black stone coffin. "I will return for the rest. I will not forget your generosity, I swear it."

He proceeded down the long and narrow hall, torch ahead, into the whistling wind.

His heart was light as was his step.

Then the world rocked once more and the roar of the earth filled his ears.

3

Yngvar pitched forward. The floor beneath him shuddered and rocked. He heard ocean waves smashing against unseen cliffs. Dirt and rock thumped his head. He dropped his torch to cover his skull with both hands.

The lurching ground was like a ship in a storm. Attempting to flee ahead, he staggered and fell. Behind him, the passage collapsed.

The slam of the rocks was louder than anything else. The blast of dirt the collapse created shot him forward. He scrabbled to his feet and let the force carry him away from the danger.

Running with all this strength, he prayed to the gods for safety. The collapse continued, but it was distant now. He fled down the passage in the dark. His foot caught on the floor and he crashed to his face, breaking the fall with his arms. He lay flat, hands over his head, face in the dirt-strewn stone. He smelled the mineral tang of the earth. Tasted again more blood in his mouth. Waves roared and crashed with an unnatural rhythm.

When the rocking and smashing ceased, he was not sure. But he listened to the crazed smash of waves on stone, feeling vibrations through the ground into his cheeks and chest. It seemed the world was at peace once more. Though he dared not rise. His mind filled with irrational thoughts, as if his standing again would renew the quake.

He lay still until the violence of the sea subsided. The waves became a distant beat. The wind gusted down the tunnel, still whistling. A rock fell somewhere in the darkness behind. He had dropped his torch. But in his left hand he still held the golden circlet.

"A man must know what is important," he said, snorting dust from his nostrils as he collected himself.

The passage was dark, but now he could see a much lighter gray a short distance away. It was a jagged scar at the end of this passage. He approached it like sneaking up on a sentry. He could not dismiss the feeling that his steps alone would resume the quake. Yet he continued toward the light. Though it was shaped like a crack, from inside the passage he could see it was an archway. He paused just inside of it, letting the wind pull his hair back as he studied the area.

Stones and debris both ancient and new littered the floor. A fresh crack showed at the top of what must have also been a hidden entrance similar to the one he had found at the top of the hill. He slid to the edge of the crack, watchful of a collapse from above.

He clung to the cold, rough stone edge as he leaned out into the sea wind.

A slight ledge protruded beyond the exit. But it sheared off into nothing. Yngvar was no stonemason, but this ledge seemed man-made to him. Whether it would support him after all this quaking was another question. He did not want to risk a collapse, and so remained in the passage. He craned he is neck around to see what was beyond this ledge.

The sun had set and brought woolen clouds with it. A faint stain of rose blushed the western horizon. But soon all light would extinguish. The sea rolled in fat waves that broke beneath the ledge. He was near to the water's surface here, perhaps only thirty feet above it. It seemed a stone step led down from the ledge, but from his vantage it seemed these were broken away long ago. Maybe three stairs remained and led to nothing.

Still clinging to the side of the stone entrance, he twisted to face the sky. He was at the bottom of a massive cliff. this side of the island was unknown to him, as it faced away from the approach he had taken. He determined he was far down from the peak of the hill where he had entered the tomb. Enormous rocks and jagged hills filled the paths to this side of the island. He and Alasdair had hunted for eggs here during their first stay on the island. But neither had dared to go this far into the rugged terrain for fear of injury. Bad footing could have led to sprains and broken bones, which would have hastened the end of their lives. So this side of the island had remained a mystery.

With night upon him and a cool sea wind in his face, Yngvar smiled. He would not suffocate, though he might starve. Fate would decide for him, and his only task was to fight as hard as he could for survival. If the weave of his life ended now, all his struggle would avail nothing.

But the gods would not have shown him this exit unless they meant to taunt him with hope. It would have been a crueler jest to smother him in the grave with his treasure, to have crushed his body to juice that flowed over the gold he had coveted. Had he been a god himself, that would have been his decision.

So he believed the gods willed him to escape this trap.

He could not fear for anyone else yet. He had no way to know their fates. If the gods were still at play with their lives, then perhaps they survived. If they tired of Yngvar's companions, then they would be dead.

The gods were cruel and cared only for men who gave them glory and sacrifice. Yngvar had done little of either for a long time. So he wondered what torments they planned for him. For his Wolves, he hoped they had done more to please the gods than he had.

He curled up in the passage's mouth, just inside the door. If the quake struck again, he would rather drown himself than be crushed. It seemed more fitting to send his soul to the goddess Ran at the bottom of the ocean rather than leave his bones for worms to gnaw.

Sleep came easily, for he was exhausted. Rest was another matter.

He awakened screaming every hour of the night. The earth had again rocked or at least he dreamed it. Sometimes the waves would roll harder and the sounds of crumbling would echo from the passage. Most times, the world was bland and dark. The fear had been a mere dream.

When dawn again lit the sky, Yngvar roused from the hard earth. His joints were stiff and sore from the night breeze that had scoured him. His back and shoulders were tender from being struck by falling rocks. His knees were locked and hard to bend, the result of his fall through the ceiling. But no bones were broken and no cuts infected. He offered thanks to the gods for that much.

Every motion brought a new snap of pain. But he worked out much of it.

"You are not a hundred years old," he said, just to hear a voice even if it was his own. "But you are acting like it. Come on, boy. You've got a mighty feat ahead of you today. Got to make the gods lean forward from their benches and notice you."

Light still evaded the passage, for Yngvar determined it faced the south. The light slanted past it for now. By noon it might penetrate deeper, but never to the end of the passage. So he picked his way back until he could proceed no more.

He found his lost torch and the iron spearhead. The spearhead was bent now. Yngvar imagined whatever bent it might have split his skull had it struck him. He whistled at the thought of it, then tucked the spear underarm. The torch would be helpful, but of limited value. He could try to signal for help during the night, but who would come? Ships did not ply these waters regularly, and those that did ignored this island either out of superstition or ignorance of what lay buried here.

"But what will you drink or eat? Never mind about signaling a ship, you fool."

Yngvar folded his arms and studied the way ahead. Despite the crashing sounds he had heard throughout the night, the passage itself was not impassable. He stared at the pile of rocks that now covered the opening into King Agamemnon's grave. He scaled to the top of the pile of fresh debris and found an opening large enough for his head at the top. The air carried a nauseating stench of rot. How had he endured it before, he wondered? The tomb remained black.

Not even the scattered light that sketched the passage in faint gray penetrated here.

He could clear the debris enough to enter the chamber. He might find something helpful there. For the time, however, he returned to the ledge and cleansed his nose of the stench from the grave. The waves struck the cliffs gently. The wild rocking of the night before was a vague memory now. Fears were best forgotten, he thought, and prayed he would never experience an earthquake again.

After debating the wisdom of it, Yngvar moved onto the ledge. He had tried to test it with his foot, but could never exert the force of his full weight. In the end, he tightened his stomach and stepped onto the ledge. It held him.

He looked up at the cliff wall. It was rough and seemed to offer enough handholds. With ropes and spikes he could climb it. But he had neither, and anything from the grave would be too aged to be of use. If he tried to scale it with no aid, he might succeed. But he was no skilled climber. He spent his youth in the forests and grasslands of Frankia, and his adult life on the sea road. Some Norsemen of the deep north braved mountain passes as part of their daily lives. Perhaps they might climb this cliff with ease. He was no such man. He was more likely to plummet to his death, or become stranded halfway up.

"But it may be your only choice," he said. The roaring waves swallowed his voice and he remained staring up into a sky of white clouds.

The morning passed with him sitting in the passage entrance. He did not trust the ledge to hold him. While time was key, he did not want to rush to exert himself toward a fruitless end. With no food or water, he needed to conserve strength. He had to consider his best chances for saving himself.

Scaling the cliff would be the last resort. He realized if he waited until he was weak from lack of sustenance then it guaranteed a fall. The ideal solution would be a ship setting just beneath the ledge. For it seemed the ancient builders intended this as a sea-side entrance to the grave. Yngvar imagined ancient ships anchored by the stairs that led up here. All the treasures along with their king's body and his guards would have been carried up those steps into this very hall.

But the stairs were broken high above the sea level. No ship would anchor there again.

The day passed at a tedious pace. Yngvar's belly growled and his mouth grew parched. Yet no plan seemed viable. He slept most of the day, then into the night. He waited, but could not say what he waited for.

In the predawn of the following day, he awakened with a plan. While his companions might have been trapped or killed in the same collapse that had sent him through the floor of the tomb, One-Eye Petronius and his crew would have been aboard their ship. At worst, they would have endured rocking. Their ship was high-sided and unlikely to capsize or swamp with such brief jolts. Some men might have fallen overboard, but they should still be in the area.

By now Petronius would wonder if the curse had killed all of them. He said no man of his would set foot on that cursed island, even if it held more gold than the emperor's treasure vaults. Yngvar doubted the claim even when they dropped anchor offshore to await his return. By now they would expect a signal from Yngvar that would not have come. Would they leave the area, believing the curse had destroyed him?

Again, he knew greed when he saw it. Petronius and his men were as eager for the treasure as his own men. They just were not willing to accept the risk of claiming it themselves.

If they thought the treasure had been carried from the tomb and stacked on the shores, they would be drawn to it. They were only men, and the temptation of such a fortune would overcome all fears.

So before the sun crawled into the sky, Yngvar felt his way back down the passage and began excavating the stones that blocked the way into Agamemnon's grave.

The work carried on into the morning. It was slow and painstaking. He could not see but for the faintest of outlines. Searching out the easy and loose stones consumed hours. But he carried these off the pile and set them along the passage. He was not intent on completely clearing the stones. For one, most were too large and too embedded to remove alone and with no tools. Yet he did not know if he would bring the passage down by weakening the pile of rubble.

By the end of the day, he could squeeze his shoulders through an opening. That was all he needed.

His fingers were cut and bloodied. His nails were ragged and splintered. All of his muscles protested the effort he had spent. Yet he smiled.

The interior of the tomb was as dark as ever. He did not want to risk an open flame in here. For he did not understand where the oil had spread or what else he had knocked free in the subsequent collapses. His hands served as his eyes, finding what he sought still by the entrance.

"Come, my friend. I will give you a Norse burial. You have served your lord well. Now rest."

The desiccated corpse was light under his hands. The rack of dead guards, what he had thought were draugr, had escaped the worst of the collapse. They had fallen forward on their shields. Some of their bodies had broken into pieces. He carried away one such husk now.

Its stench was light, or else Yngvar had accustomed himself to it. He knew living men who smelled worse. Bjorn could smell bad, particularly after a battle when he refused to wash off the gore of enemies he had killed. That was a disgusting ritual of his. Where had he acquired such a foul habit, Yngvar wondered? He would ask once they were reunited.

Yngvar was certain Bjorn survived. He had not entered the tomb because of his size. The gods loved him most of all, for he was a berserk and a champion. They preserved him through scores of battles. They would not drop a stone on his head to slay him now. Whether Gyna had escaped was another matter. He feared what his cousin would do if she had not.

When Yngvar returned to the seaside ledge, he found the gods had both foiled his plans and aided him.

Rain started to fall. The stone ledge drank the first droplets. But the rain was steadying. Black clouds ushered in nightfall earlier. Yngvar set down the corpse and rushed back into the tomb. He found an old bronze helmet which he used to collect water. He dared the ledge to stand in the rain and let it wash him.

The rain delayed him another day. But it had satisfied his thirst and washed away the dirt and stench that clung to him.

Rainfall stopped after sunset. Yngvar listened to the dripping water from the edge of the passage. He set the corpse of the ancient guard down the hall and out of sight. He did not want to look at that dead face before sleep, which found him soon enough.

At last, on the morning of the third day, Yngvar set out the corpse on the damp stone ledge. He had a now-rusted and bent iron spearhead. But it still generated sparks that caught the dry cloth and flesh of the dead guard. His corpse had snapped at the waist, so hip and leg bones were still lost in the grave's darkness. The dried bones and skin that remained rolled into the flame that crawled along the corpse.

The stench was more horrible than Yngvar had expected. He thought it might smell like burning dust. Instead, a vileness more akin to burning dung struck him. The smoke rolled up from the body and, without a powerful wind to break it up, held together as it rose above the top of the cliff.

"Thank you, my friend." Yngvar nodded to the dead body. "If I knew your name, I would sing your praises to the living. But it must satisfy you that I will not forget your aid."

The fire burned fitfully but generated enough smoke to be seen on the other side of the island. He passed time gathering more flammable materials to feed the fire into the night if needed.

By the end of the day, Yngvar lounged by the heat of the low flames. It had become a pile of ash, filled with shattered wood and charred bones. The sour smell no longer bothered him. The long hours of boredom, the droning waves, the rolling sea, all combined to lull him into a dream. He did not understand he was hearing a voice until after it had stopped.

His heart leapt.

He rushed out to the ledge, skirting the fire and feeling its low flames hot against his legs. He turned to a sky of red and orange clouds. The edge of the cliff was empty, but he was certain he had heard a voice.

"Hey! Who is there? Do you hear me?"

Heat rose to his face when he realized he was waving his arms at nothing. He instead cupped his hands to his mouth and shouted with all the strength of his lungs.

After a brief pause the shadow of a head appeared over the ledge.

"Lord? Is that you? You are alive?"

"By the gods, I am alive, Alasdair. And so are you!"

Tears rose to his eyes and he was glad Alasdair would be too distant to see them. For the joy of not only surviving but knowing his dearest friend had escaped as well overwhelmed him. He lowered his head and wiped the tears with the back of his wrist.

"I saw the smoke and knew it was you." Alasdair's voice was small against the purring waves and across the distance. Backlit against the sky, he seemed like a black dot.

"Who else has survived?"

"Nearly everyone, lord. Though Thorfast and I were trapped for a day. We heard you calling out. Did you hear us?"

"I heard nothing. But this is glorious. We have all survived. And I have—"

He was about to reveal the actual tomb and treasure he had discovered. But some instinct warned him against shouting this aloud. Alasdair, however, did not seem to notice.

"I cannot reach you, lord. But I can bring food and wine until I can find a way to get you."

"Just bring the ship beneath this ledge," Yngvar said. "I can drop to the deck, or into the sea and swim a short way."

He laughed, feeling warmth spreading in his chest. His stomach growled, anticipating food. Even the mention of it set his mouth watering.

"That's not possible, lord. There is trouble. I will return with food for you. Do not fear."

Alasdair vanished over the edge of the cliff. Yngvar stared up at the space he vacated, waiting for him to return with an explanation. He waited until his neck grew sore, then spoke in a whisper.

"How can I not fear, Alasdair?"

4

Night felt like a cold hand wrapping Yngvar's body. Though back in the North, nights would still be cold in early spring, he did not expect a chill while in the Midgard Sea. Yet he had grown accustomed to the heat and now understood why many natives shivered at night. His fingers pruned with cold and he blew into them as he stared out at the moonless sky.

More than weather chilled him. Alasdair's cryptic warning filled him with dread. If everyone survived, yet they could not sail the ship to this point, what did it mean? Too many horrible answers sped across his mind. All of them concerned the treasure and the curse.

He feared his own arrogance in deciding how to lift the curse. He had fooled himself along with all the others into believing his plan would succeed. The thin gold circlet sat on his lap. The ancient gold was still warm from his clutching hands. He lifted it again, testing its pleasing weight.

"If I survive, great king, then I will honor my promise to you. Do not cling to wealth that serves you nothing now. Let me bring it back to the world. I will raise a hall, gather men, create a community and defend it, all with the gold you hoard here. I will share it with worthy, honorable men. It will be no kingdom as great as you once ruled. But once again your generosity will aid people who will praise your name."

But his words were small against the cold breeze whistling over the edge of the passage. The scent of the sea filled him with strength, even though his belly growled and his mouth again grew tacky with thirst. He would survive this. The cost of survival was yet unknown to him.

With nothing more to do than wait and think upon Alasdair's appearance, he nodded. As he did, strange thoughts crowded his mind as they often do before sleep. One shocked him awake.

What if he had not actually seen Alasdair?

What if he were imagining it? An idle and isolated mind was wont to play such tricks. His father had told him of castaways rescued from the sea and how their minds shattered even when their bodies survived. Long days floating alone in a ship had caused them to see companions who no longer lived.

He scrubbed his face. He had not been alone so long.

Yet he was desperate. There seemed no escape other than to risk scaling the cliff. While he knew the basics of swimming, the waves would crush him to the cliff face. Even Alasdair could not swim away. Besides, where would he swim to? This entire side of the island was a cliff wall with no beach.

He settled back again. To worry was madness. He would surely be speaking to ghosts if he continued with those thoughts.

Troubled sleep passed him along to dawn. When he again awakened, hungrier and thirstier, he rushed to the ledge then looked skyward. Alasdair was not there. The clouds that lingered over the area had left behind a thin scattering, indicating good sailing weather for the upcoming day.

"If I had a ship, I'd be far away from this place with a fair wind in my sail."

After waiting until noon, he decided he had imagined his exchange with Alasdair. Their conversation had been a strange conversation, and his sudden disappearance was equally weird.

"You've got to climb it," he said. "No one's coming for you and your mind is breaking apart like an iceberg in warm water. Now you're even talking to yourself like you're another person. Come on, Yngvar. You can't go mad after a few days."

Relentless silence and isolation was something he did not suffer well. Even when imprisoned in a wretched cell in utter blackness beneath Prince Kalim's palace, he still had his companions. Not knowing what had happened to the others drove him mad. Was he the only one to survive the collapse?

Nothing from the tomb would help him scale the cliff. Looking straight up its length, he felt a strange pull in his gut that fell to his crotch. He moaned at the height he faced.

"You will kill yourself up there," he said. "But better than starving to death."

He placed King Agamemnon's circlet upon his head. He had no better place to hold it. Its weight pressed into his temples, but it fit as if crafted for his head. He debated removing his boots, thinking his toes might hold better on the thin ledges. Yet his soles were not tough enough to endure the climb over rock, and so he left them on. He rubbed grit from the hall into his palms, then started up the side.

The first steps up encouraged him. He found easy purchase up the sides, both with fingers and feet. If the cliff offered this much the entire way up, then he would mount the top with ease.

Only this fortune did not last.

He was now three body lengths above the ledge. The wind had not fought him, but now it pushed against his back. He was glad the sea breeze shoved him to the wall. If hit from the side, he might blow away like a leaf. Though he would not land as lightly as one. The toeholds and ledges grew narrower as he climbed.

He made the critical mistake of looking down between his body and the cliff wall.

Though not far above the small ledge, he was high above the water. His head swirled, and that horrid fear tugged straight to his crotch. He closed his eyes and pressed to the wall again. The wind rushed across his back, billowing his shirt.

"Odin All-Father, send an eagle to carry me to the top. I was a fool to think I could do this."

Retreating down the cliff might be cowardly, but he discovered it was not even possible. He could not find the previous ridges he had used to ascend to this point.

He swallowed hard, then searched ahead for another ridge or crack.

This took careful study. He was approaching a bulge that protruded over him, casting the cliff face into shadow. How was he going to cross it with his bare hands? Go around it, he thought. That would lead him directly over the water and away from the illusory safety of the ledge beneath him.

But he decided he had no choice. He was finding a way up one step at a time. He sidled to the left, following natural cracks and ledges of the gray rock that brushed against his face. His arms and legs trembled. His shoulders burned. Worst were his fingers, already ravaged by excavating the collapsed hall.

Yet he skirted the bulge.

He clung to the side of the cliff. He imagined gulls flying through the sky would see him as a white bug resting on the cliff face. Peering up into the brilliant blue sky, he found the top of the cliff seemed impossibly far.

Having avoided the bulge, he discovered the cliff was smoother here. His strength was burning up just holding still. He could not afford to linger, especially as the wind gusted harder. Yet he could not see a way up.

At last he spotted a long vertical crack. It was just out of his reach. If he could get to it, he could fit his hands inside and use it to continue the climb.

He got as close to it as the ridges allowed. But it was not close enough. Even with a stretch, the vertical crack was still two hand lengths away.

Fear took over now. For he would have to make a leap and hope to grab firmly enough to prevent a fall. He closed his eyes, body trembling both with exhaustion and the terror of falling hundreds of feet to the sea below. The water would not spare him. From this height, it would be as good as falling on stone.

He rocked on his feet as best as he could while pressed to a ledge no wider than two fingers. The motion was more to pump up courage than momentum. This might be the last leap of his life. But he had no other place to go.

The moment in the air felt as if it would never end. The comfort of the cliff face fell away. Wind rushed between him and the rocks. His hands flailed out for the crack.

Fingers clamping down into the crack, he pulled hard to drag himself back to the cliff. He jammed his other hand right behind the first, so he had stacked both hands one above the other. His feet came to rest on the cliff face, and he held.

He laughed. The jump had been short, but having never attempted such a feat he had feared failure. Now he felt more secure than ever with both hands buried deep in the crack and his feet anchored to each side against the cliff wall.

"I did it!"

His voice echoed into the vast sea. Somewhere a gull called as if celebrating with him.

"I'll take that as a good omen," he said, still smiling.

But the smile faded as he needed to continue making progress. He debated how to climb using the crack. For to remove even one hand might cost him his grip. At last he determined he could climb with his feet as high as possible, then extract one hand at a time to reanchor them higher. Following this awkward procedure, he made swift progress high up the cliff face. The pressure on his wrists was enormous. One twist might break both of them. But with care and luck, he was now nearly to the top.

The gold circlet had slid down to his brows. He could not fix it easily, frowning and twisting to keep it out of his eyes. The temptation to look down struck him once more. Fear was below and hope lay above. Instead, he considered that the top of the cliff was now a body length distant from the extent of his reach.

The vertical crack had been as good as a rope. Yet it grew too narrow to fit his hands before reaching the top. His arms trembled, and his legs threatened to buckle. His knees burned and pinched. But he could not fail now, not with the top of the cliff at hand. He squeezed his eyes shut to clear his mind, then studied the cliff face again for handholds.

Fear of death was a harsh but capable teacher. For he now had an intuitive sense of what could hold him and what might lead to the next step higher. Sweat dripped from his brow where the circlet held his hair flat against his temples. The weight of it was like a stone on his head. What had felt so perfect now seemed enough excess weight to knock him loose.

Yngvar growled against the stone, willing himself to cling tighter. His strength had never been a question. But this climb required strength different from what sailing and swordsmanship demanded. He wondered if his fingers could grip a knife, much less a sword, once he was done.

The final steps led him as high as he could go. He would have to jump to grasp the ledge at the top of the cliff. From there, he could lever himself over the top.

"You did it, you fool," he whispered. "The gods are laughing. But so am I. Let's go."

He steadied himself, took aim for the rock he hoped to grasp, and mumbled a prayer that it would not snap free. Then he leapt.

The wind gusted at the same moment. It swept between him and the wall like an invisible hand slapping him away.

He blew back from the ledge.

His heart slammed into his throat, and his gut fell to his crotch. He flailed, one hand scratching stone.

One hand gripping the ledge.

Hanging by his left arm, he turned like a fish on a line. The temptation to look down overtook him. The foamy green water breaking at the base of the cliff seemed to beckon him.

His hand, slick with sweat from effort and fear, began to slip.

His feet scraped along the wall, seeking purchase, finding it the moment he thought his grip would fail. He pulled back to the cliff, pressing to the stone and easing the strain on his left arm. Wind blew across his back, as if patting him in congratulations.

But he was still only holding by one arm. He reached up with his right arm and pushed off with his feet. Hand slamming into hard rock, he grabbed it with a sharp yell of triumph.

Now he had to pull up.

He paused to breathe, blowing sweat from his face. The gold crown slid against the bridge of his nose.

One more pull and he would mount the cliff.

His groan echoed off the stone wall, but he heaved up with desperate violence. He sprang up to the top of the cliff. He saw jagged rocks pushing aside scrubby bushes and realized he had mounted the cliff. He laughed.

Then his golden circlet slipped from his head.

It clinked to the stone before him.

Then bounded back out over the cliff.

"No!"

He snatched for it out of instinct. The gold sparkled with the afternoon light as the circlet flipped into the air.

Stretching back over the edge, he realized too late he had consigned himself to falling the full height of the cliff. He had overextended.

His fingers grabbed the circlet.

He slipped off the edge and fell.

Hands grabbed him.

"Lord! Hold!"

Alasdair had seized him by the shoulders of his shirt. He threw himself backward, slamming Yngvar to the safety of the ledge once more.

With the gold circlet in hand, he slapped his free hand back to the ground. He gathered himself up. With Alasdair holding him by his shirt, he slid up onto the top of the cliff. He flopped to his side, gasping, eyes wide, mouth agape. He stared at the circlet in his hand.

He had nearly killed himself for this.

"Lord!"

Alasdair flipped him onto his back.

Yngvar looked up to the worry-creased face of his most loyal friend. His coppery hair hung down, matted with sweat. He grabbed Yngvar by the jaw and shook his head.

"Lord! Are you mad? I said I would return with food and drink."

Yngvar stared at him. Alasdair's wooden cross hung down, touching Yngvar's chest. He blinked at his young friend.

"I didn't think you were real."

Alasdair sat back on his knees. The lines of concern shifted to confusion.

"I am real, lord. Why would you think otherwise?"

"Well, last I heard, you were screaming for your life as a thousand pounds of rock fell on us. Maybe you were a ghost or my imagination."

Alasdair blinked. He pointed to a wicker basket set back in the grass.

"There is dried goat meat and a skin of sour wine there. And rope enough to lower it down to you."

"Thank you," he said. "But I don't think I can move just yet. My heart is racing. Please, I need to rest."

He lay heaving while Alasdair fetched the basket. A large coil of rope had been hidden behind it. Yngvar wondered if it came from the ship. Where else could it have come from?

"That rope," he said while Alasdair sorted through the basket. "That'd have been a help just now."

"I did not expect you to climb the cliff alone. The angels were surely with you, lord."

"Angels, you say? I thought to meet a Valkyrie before the sun set. I was a fool to make that climb."

Yngvar sat up now, rubbing his trembling arms. Alasdair offered him the wineskin which he accepted. He set the gold circlet in the rocky dirt. Alasdair nodded to it.

"A golden crown?"

"Ah, the wine is sour but my thirst is mightier than my taste. Yes, a golden crown. It's all I could carry away."

Alasdair's bright face darkened, but he said nothing more. He set out the hard, stringy meat. Yngvar remembered buying these provisions just days ago. He and all his crew had a rich share of Prince Kalim's treasures. They bought new weapons and shields, repaired helmets and straps, got new boots, and their fill of food and wine. They not only repaired the ship but replaced the rigging with fresh, strong rope with some stored for the future. Rope that now sat in a coil in the scrubby grass.

"If I had known you would be here, I'd have brought your sword," Alasdair said.

"Am I going to need it?" Yngvar, as eager as he was to learn what had happened during his absence, considered little else than the strips of dried goat meat. He tore into a strip, pulling hard to break off a piece. The salt was overwhelming, but local tastes of peppers and hot spices still stung his lips. He didn't allow the flavors time to permeate his mouth, but gulped down the meat.

"You might," Alasdair said. "There is no one to lead the crew with you gone, and this gold and this curse has the men at each other's necks."

Yngvar chased the hard meat with a mouthful of wine that tasted more like vinegar. He grimaced, but met Alasdair's eyes.

"Well, that's enough rest for me. Lead me back, and I'll set the men straight on who they serve."

Alasdair gave him a dubious smile, then gathered the rope and basket.

5

Yngvar's legs trembled as he eased down the steep scree-filled slope. The sun had crossed to the west, and only a handful of hours remained in the day. The high rocks cast long, indigo shadows across his path. Alasdair walked beside him, rationing the strips of goat meat.

"I meant them to last a few days, lord."

"I am eating for a few days of starvation," Yngvar said. "You didn't bring more wine?"

"There was rain, lord. I expected you gathered some of it. Besides, I cannot carry as much as you could drink."

Descending the high hills into the scrub and stunted trees covering the island, Yngvar spent his strength at the rate he replenished it with food. Yet if he would need to reappear as a strong and confident leader to his crew.

During the descent, sliding down slopes and lowering themselves from high rocks, Alasdair had described what he understood.

"You vanished from sight, lord," he had said of Yngvar's fall. "Then rocks caved in everywhere and I was in darkness. Thorfast was with me, both of us preserved by God's grace beneath stones that had fallen over us."

"It was more likely Odin to spare you," Yngvar said. "But I take your meaning. No matter how, I am glad you both survived."

"We huddled together. Neither of us dared to breathe, much less speak. It felt like any vibration could bring the stones down on us. Poor Theodoros was not so fortunate. At the time I had no idea of his fate, but rocks had crushed him from head to waist when we finally dug out. We heard you calling after a time. I called back, as did Thorfast. But it seemed you had become so distant, like you were in another place."

"I fell into another chamber. I was lucky to find a crack in the earth that led to where you discovered me. It was all cold darkness down there." He turned away as he spoke. He had not lied to Alasdair. But he could not tell him of the riches he had found. It seemed that should remain a secret to be revealed at a later time. One day he could return to excavate those treasures, but not today. He had tucked Agamemnon's crown into his shirt. It brushed against his flesh as he followed Alasdair.

"How did you and others escape? Once again, the gods have preserved us, though for what end I cannot yet say. It must be a great purpose, or else why pluck us from sinking ships and collapsing tombs?"

"God is mysterious, lord. Thorfast and I were trapped for a day. Bjorn had enough help from the Franks and the freemen."

Yngvar had insisted they stop referring to the mix of men who were once fellow slave-soldiers as such. Under the guidance of Lucas the Byzantine, they had followed Yngvar and were now his crew. So they were freemen, like everyone else. Their only hindrance was the language barrier between Franks and themselves.

"Gyna escaped, I suppose, or else by now I would hear Bjorn's wailing," Yngvar said as they continued down from the steep hills. Ahead he could see the highest hill that was the entrance to the tomb. From this approach, the entrance was masked from view.

"Her knee no longer bothers her, it would seem. She must have darted out of that passage like a frightened bat from a cave. From what I saw, she was unhurt. Unlike Nordbert and the other Franks that followed us in."

"They were injured?"

Alasdair shook his head.

"They were killed, lord. All we could find of Nordbert was his arm. The rest was under rock. It also crushed the other Franks. Petronius is saying it's too much effort to dig them out and we'll just leave them buried in place. But that is not sitting well with the others."

"Wait? Petronius? One-Eye? What is he doing here?"

"I'll get to it, lord. You should know that the Franks are unhappy about everything with Nordbert dead. For one, they blame Gyna for it. They were in the rear, and should've exited ahead of her. But yet she escaped. They're claiming she pushed Nordbert and the others aside on her way out, and so hindered their escape. Some are demanding justice."

"Justice?" Yngvar stopped. "For surviving? That is madness."

"I said it is madness, lord. Bjorn and Ewald have not helped, either. Bjorn started thumping men on their heads and screaming down anyone who argued with him. Ewald hardly knows his Frankish, and so his clumsy words have insulted the others."

"And Gyna herself can't be helping." Yngvar shook his head, imagining the three worst-tempered of his companions attempting to restore order.

"Actually, she has taken to hiding. She doesn't want to see anyone. I do not understand her, lord."

"Strange, I agree. What of Thorfast?"

"Like me, lord. Just trying to bring peace. But he has his own group now, with Ragnar and Lucas the Byzantine. It sets him apart from the rest. Some freemen like him. Others seem to hate him. But once we were rescued, Ragnar took it upon himself to see to Thorfast's care. It's like our relationship, lord. Only Ragnar is a dull-witted fool."

Yngvar burst out with a laugh. "Well, I will not claim Ragnar is anything more than a respectable warrior. I'm glad for his friendship with Thorfast, but now is not the time to form groups. Has Valgerd survived without injury?"

Alasdair smiled at her name.

"God preserved her, lord. She has suffered enough already. She took to the ship when the waves struck. She was the first through the rubble to find me and Thorfast."

"Waves?" Yngvar remembered how the sea had crashed against the cliff wall. "I suppose high waves fell upon the beaches."

"From what I was told the waves dragged a few men out to sea and washed away some supplies. Valgerd was at the beach when she saw the waves. She, Hamar, and a few others got aboard our ship and steered it back to shore after the waves carried it out. Without their foresight, our ship might be adrift and carried to the rocks."

They continued walking in silence. The ground had leveled out and spilled toward a path between two huge boulders. Yngvar considered all he had been told, then at last asked the question he feared the most.

"So, what of Petronius?"

"He was already on the island when Thorfast and I were rescued. He brought many of his crew, claiming that the earthquake happened because of the curse. Now that it is done, he is telling his men they've nothing to fear. Not all believe him, but enough of them have come ashore. More of them than our own men. Beyond those crushed in the passage or washed out to sea, falling rocks killed others. I understand one of the Franks died from fright. Just collapsed during the earthquake and never rose again."

"So Petronius now has the advantage of numbers, and they've conveniently overcome their superstitions to join us on the island."

"Many of his crew remain on their ship."

"But Petronius helped rescue you and Thorfast?"

Alasdair shook his head. "Bjorn and our crew dug us out. Petronius and the others are helping themselves to the gold."

Yngvar stopped. "The gold is buried. What do you mean?"

"The earthquake opened up what looked like cracks in the earth. But these were rooms and passages exposed from the earthquake. You would not even recognize the entrance we used. It has all collapsed. Petronius has followed one of these passages back to the room you found. I guess there either was another hidden entrance or else a crack opened to it. I've not been in it myself. But Petronius and his men are carrying out gold back to their ship while our men mourn for the dead. They have paid the price, and Petronius is claiming the spoils. A fight is coming, lord."

Yngvar put both hands to his head and stared at Alasdair.

"You're right. A fight is coming. That is my treasure! The others are just standing by?"

"The Franks want Nordbert and the others dug out and laid to rest in a Christian grave. They can't stand to let their souls become prisoners of the pagan demons that haunt this island. Thorfast is not seriously injured, but he is weak. Bjorn and Ewald worry about Gyna. Bjorn has tried to threaten Petronius, but he swears he is simply collecting it for all of us to divide up in a safer place. And until just yesterday everyone wondered if you were still alive, lord. I told you it is all madness."

"And you would leave me on that ledge while Petronius steals our gold?"

"Lord, I thought you would need more help to escape that ledge."

Alasdair's face turned red, and Yngvar wiped his hands over his face.

"Ah, sorry for that. You did your best for me, more than anyone else. I am grateful for everything. But we have to stop Petronius from stealing everything."

"Now that you are here, lord, I'm certain we can recover."

The news invigorated Yngvar's flagging strength. His stride increased, and his vision sharpened. His palms itched for his sword, but he had no weapon to grip. He had treated fairly with One-Eye Petronius and was stung with a betrayal. Soon he was leading Alasdair back toward their camp on the beach.

At the top of the final slope that led out of the steep and rocky hills, Yngvar saw a complete change in the landscape.

Fallen tents were not reset. It seemed a giant had scattered rocks across the campsite, but these had tumbled off the high jumble of stones that provided a windbreak. He had never considered these capable of falling atop his men. Fresh graves were dug to the side of the camp, and groups of his crew worked among these.

Bjorn was easy to spot, even from this distance. He was like a boulder among pebbles. His shouting was thin and weak over the long rock-strewn distance. But a line of Byzantine crewmen were passing heedlessly in front of him. They shouldered heavy burdens, and Yngvar thought of the treasures being carried off.

"Lord, look to the west." Alasdair tugged his sleeve and pointed. "There are the passages."

A series of regular trenches led from the beach toward the hill where Yngvar had first entered the tomb. Along the lengths were small rectangular spaces which must have been rooms that had collapsed in the quake. The Byzantines and others crawled through these like ants in their tunnels, passing back and forth.

"Some of our men are carrying away their own gold," Yngvar said.

"That is good, lord."

"No," Yngvar said. "That is how men loot and steal. There will be no fair division of spoils, for they will hide coins for themselves."

While doubting his own men, he felt Agamemnon's crown shift beneath his shirt. He clamped it still with his hand.

"Lord, there is plenty for all. But Petronius will take most."

"Let's hurry. We need to divide this up fairly before those Byzantine dogs leave us with only stones."

Yngvar's arrival did not generate any excitement beyond the stares of the Franks digging graves for their dead companions. Bjorn's shouts were clear now.

"Half of every sack you carry out goes to my ship or I'll leave you with half a head. Understand?"

The Byzantines nodded as they passed, but none met his eyes. They were stopping aboard Yngvar's ship, which sat on the beach, and shaking out coins from their sacks. Their own larger ship sat at anchor in deeper water. But they had beached their rowboat near Yngvar's ship.

"Using that rowboat slows them down at least," Yngvar said. Yet Alasdair had already gone ahead of him. Yngvar stood alone.

At last Bjorn noticed him. His single eye widened and he stopped shouting. He rushed to Yngvar, smiling, with arms held wide.

They embraced, Bjorn nearly crushing him.

"Cousin," Bjorn said. "Alasdair said you were trapped on a cliff face. I'm glad you are here."

Bjorn smelled like dust and sweat. His massive arms clamped Yngvar tight.

"Hey, what is this?" Bjorn pulled back and patted the crown hidden in Yngvar's shirt.

"I will show you later," he said, pushing Bjorn's thick hands aside. "What is happening here? Where is Thorfast? Petronius?"

Bjorn growled and shook his head. "Everything went to shit. Nordbert is dead and his crew have all lost their fucking wits. They keep saying they will never see home again, that we're cursed, God has left them. Christian nonsense about holy ground for their dead. I just don't fucking care. Gyna won't talk to anyone but says she's fine. Thorfast got his head knocked around."

"Wait, Alasdair said he was fine?"

"Well, his head is still on his shoulders. But I can't say where his fucking mind is. Says his ears are ringing all the time and he feels like heaving his guts out. So he's got his people hovering over him."

Bjorn waved dismissively toward the large rocks where one of the few standing tents remained rippling in the warm breeze.

"Petronius is carrying off our treasure," Yngvar said, drawing closer. "What are we doing about that?"

Bjorn's single eye blinked. The ruin of his other eye twitched.

"I got him to agree to split with us. Half and half, and he's putting half of what his men dig up on our ship before they take the rest off the island."

Yngvar smiled, gently patting Bjorn's chest as he drew close to whisper.

"Who is measuring that half? How do you know they're not carrying more to their ship, where we will never get to see it for ourselves?"

Bjorn looked up as if in thought. "Well, Hamar is on the ship and Valgerd too. So they must make sure we get our share."

"But you don't know if they are? Shouldn't you be up there instead? You're scarier than either of them."

Bjorn's face darkened and he looked away. His voice was a low growl. "It's a fucking mess. Now that you're here, things'll get better."

Yngvar slapped his cousin's shoulder.

"You did fine. But let's put your terrifying face to better use. Fetch me Petronius, and if he resists, then crack his head and drag him here."

Bjorn's face turned from red to a golden glow of pleasure. Without another word, he ran toward the collapsed tunnels where men hefted treasure-filled sacks out of the rubble.

Yngvar found Thorfast's tent and ducked inside. He was laid out with a gray cloth around his head and a dirty sheet covering his body. Ragnar knelt beside him, sharpening a dagger. The metallic scrape filled the tent.

"How is that shrill sound good for his head? No wonder his ears are ringing."

Yngvar sat beside Ragnar, who smiled brightly but otherwise did not move.

"We heard Alasdair had found you. I'm glad you're back. It's time our own takes command again."

"I had hoped this one would've done so." Yngvar snapped his fingers against Thorfast's thigh. His white hair hung limp by his head as he strained to look up. He scowled at Yngvar.

"Can't you see I'm dying? Go back to your ledge. It'll be more peaceful there."

"Heard you knocked your head," Yngvar stripped away Thorfast's sheet, revealing torn and dusty clothes from the collapse. "You can whine like a grandmother another day. Now you need to stand up and look strong."

Ragnar dropped his dagger and whetstone, then barred Thorfast from rising.

"He can't stand up. He'll puke his guts out."

"Get up," Yngvar said while pushing Ragnar back. "I don't know when you both became old women, but I need strong warriors now."

Thorfast groaned and held the bandage to his head. Yet he did not resist. "The Franks won't listen to us now that Nordbert is dead. They're blaming you for everything."

"I heard they blame Gyna."

"Her too, but they blame you for making them hungry for gold. They're saying it's not Christian to be so greedy."

"Their god and his priests are plenty greedy for gold. I'll remind them, but first I need you standing with me. So up you go."

He heaved Thorfast to his feet. For an instant he seemed ready to vomit but steadied himself. Yngvar searched his pale eyes. His pupils seemed strange, but it could have been due to the low light.

"He hasn't been well," Ragnar said. "If it comes to a fight—"

"We're not fighting with anyone. We just need to remind Petronius of our bargain "

That bargain had not been for a full half of the treasure, Yngvar thought. Men killed each other for far less than the gold here. Still, he would attempt to appeal to honor. Petronius had been honorable thus far.

He exited the tent while Thorfast groaned behind him. Alasdair waited outside, the dazzling sunlight shining on his coppery hair. He carried Yngvar's longsword in both arms. A green stone shined from its pommel.

"It is best if you are armed, lord. It will make you look more like your old self."

He accepted the sword with both hands and nodded to Alasdair. The blade was perfectly balanced and light in his grip. He wished he knew who had forged such a magnificent weapon. Even Prince Kalim, who could not have cared for a Northman's sword, had valued it enough to place it among his treasures.

"Have you seen Gyna yet?" he asked Alasdair, who slowly shook his head. "Gods, the men admire her more than me, I think. She needs to stand with me before I address them. Go fetch her. After Bjorn, she likes you best of all."

"I'll take Valgerd with me. She might help persuade her."

Yngvar stood at the edge of the camp, adjusting the baldric of his longsword so it hung easily at his hip. He set his palm on it as Ragnar and Thorfast joined him.

"No one seems to have noticed I was missing," he said, watching the Franks and the freemen mill around the campsite. "Not one greeted me, much less looked at me."

"None of them have ever lived through something like this," Thorfast said, his voice tired and weak. "The world swallowed their leader and their brothers, but spit out gold in equal measure. Do you laugh or cry? Do you help the injured or make sure you have the most gold for yourself?"

They waited and watched. At last, Alasdair and Valgerd were leading Gyna between them. Ewald, her Saxon nephew and self-proclaimed future king of the Saxons, trotted behind more like a pup than a future monarch. From the opposite side, Bjorn led Petronius. The two walked like old friends. Bjorn was actually missing an eye, carved out of his head by King Erik Bloodaxe. Yet Petronius, who had both eyes, was oddly called One-Eye. When angered, excited, or exhausted, one of his eyes would drift out of focus, earning him the name.

Both Yngvar's and Petronius's crews paused in their tasks as they realized their leaders were gathering at the edge of camp.

"Looks like you'll have your meeting," Thorfast said. "Will it serve for me to just stand here and look angry? I think I will fall over otherwise."

Yngvar nodded.

"Just support me and all will be fine. We'll have this gold divided up fairly and it will satisfy everyone."

Thorfast snorted. "Fucking Byzantines are about as trustworthy as the Arabs. It's your head that took the harder blow if you believe otherwise."

"All will be fine."

Yngvar patted the pommel of his sword and felt the warm gold of Agamemnon's crown hidden in his shirt.

6

Yngvar greeted Gyna with a nod. She looked stricken with grief, surrounded by Alasdair, Valgerd, and her nephew Ewald. Though she had no visible wounds, she seemed bent with pain. Ewald lightly held her by her shoulders.

She stared at him, then slowly returned the nod. The others guided her next to Thorfast and Ragnar.

"She's been like this since they accused her of killing Nordbert," Thorfast whispered from behind. "Not even Bjorn can cheer her, though he's not been much of a joy to be near either."

Yngvar turned to find Gyna glaring at Thorfast. He raised his brow to him and nodded toward Gyna.

"So, you've got your sword back." Thorfast spoke brightly, changing the topic. He patted the sheath of Yngvar's sword. "Why haven't you named it yet? Such a fine blade so suited to you needs a name."

"I'll name it later." Yngvar watched Bjorn crossing the rock-strewn camp with its collapsed tents and fresh graves. He had Petronius with him, though he seemed a mere child next to Bjorn's height.

"You always say that," Thorfast continued. "Ever since Ireland. You should give it a name like Head-Taker or Bone-Biter."

Bjorn and Petronius were gathering followers as they neared.

Yngvar twisted his palm on the pommel of his sword as he watched.

"It's more impressive to say 'Bring me Blood-Drinker' than to just ask for your sword," Thorfast said. "It needs a name."

"I'll name it when we return home."

Thorfast clicked his tongue. "Make it a good name. Prince-Killer or Corpse-Maker, those are good names. Or something that sounds like a sword being drawn. Serpent-Breath! Wait, I think I've heard that name once. How about Gold-Gather?"

Yngvar turned again and frowned. "That's a stupid name for a sword."

"Well, you're not coming up with many of your own."

"Be silent or I'll wrap that bandage on your head around your mouth instead. Weren't you barely able to stand a moment ago?"

"Fresh air has done me good. Maybe I shouldn't have been lying on my back all this time."

Yngvar now tapped Ragnar's shoulder. "Go fetch Lucas the Byzantine. The two of you climb into those rocks up there. Bring something to lever them free when I give you the signal."

Ragnar blinked and the others stared. He smiled patiently.

"Do as I ask. You will thank me later."

He studied the ridge near the edge of the camp. The large rocks there seemed loose. Bjorn and Petronius were about to pass beneath them. Yngvar strode forward to intercept them at that point.

"Let's go speak to your ally."

The others followed behind, though Gyna required some prodding from Valgerd and Ewald. Alasdair and Thorfast stayed close at his side. He kept a long stride, for he did not want Petronius and the men following him out of the shadows of the rocks. He stopped them in place.

"Well, they have rescued you," Petronius said. "God be praised."

He was not especially large, though a lifetime of sea-faring had hardened his muscles. His face was lined both from sun and scar, but he had the affable look of a capable friend. Two sea-green eyes sparkled from beneath bushy brows. Yngvar had liked Petronius from the day they first met, when Yngvar had commandeered his ship to attack the Arabs pursuing his Wolves.

Yngvar just did not trust him.

He could trust no one with so much wealth.

"God or gods, I will praise any that have spared me death." Yngvar smiled, but realized his words sat ill with the Franks who had also followed Bjorn and Petronius.

"Not all have been so fortunate," Petronius said, speaking a barely understandable Frankish he had learned from Yngvar and his men. He looked meaningfully to the Franks, who had joined Yngvar's side. "I will pray for their souls."

The breeze rushing between the high rocks filled the silence. A few of the Franks spoke their magic word, amen, or else crossed themselves. Yngvar watched Ragnar and Lucas climbing onto the rocks above Petronius. His men had predictably lined up on his side, ensuring they stood where Yngvar desired.

"You'll pray for them, but you can't be bothered to dig them out and give them a proper burial." Yngvar crossed his arms, meeting Petronius's eyes.

"It's too dangerous to dig deeper," he said. "It was enough to rescue Thorfast and Alasdair."

"Not that you had much to do with their rescue," Yngvar said. "You were helping yourself to gold."

Petronius gave a wide smile.

"It's what we are here for. It's why these men died. If we do not unearth it then their deaths become meaningless."

Yngvar counted the heads of Petronius's crew as they ceased their excavations to join the gathering. The rest of the Franks and freemen joined. None noticed Ragnar and Lucas moving into position on the rocks, each with a long spear in hand. The thin shafts would probably snap before shifting those rocks. But he just needed to create the idea of a collapse.

"I'll agree to that much," Yngvar said. He turned to the Franks. "Nordbert was a good man. All the men who perished were good men. Their names will not be forgotten, not while I live."

"They're dead because of her."

One of the Franks, a thin man with dark bags under dark eyes, pointed at Gyna. She flinched as if prodded with a knife.

"You don't know fucking shit!" Bjorn stepped from Petronius toward the Frank. "Don't talk about what you ain't seen yourself."

"Bjorn! These men are grieving for their master and brothers. Show them understanding." Yngvar spoke louder, addressing the Franks and freemen. He spoke Frankish, ignoring Petronius and his Byzantines for the moment.

"I am not a Christian. You know I keep the old ways. No matter our beliefs, fate and death touches every man, from the greatest king to the least of beggars. Norbert and all the others who died have been called by their god. My gods will call for me one day. There can be no doubt."

He let his eyes linger over Gyna, who had wrapped her arms around her torso. Ewald held her as if protecting her from a winter gale.

"Those who died were brave and loyal. They had traveled far from home at the request of their lord, never offering a complaint and honoring their duty. I am humbled to have sailed with them. We have come upon a dark time, and it is easy to be fearful. But we must not let fear rule our words and actions. For then we will have dishonored their great memories. When they left this world to go to their god in his palace of clouds, they left believing their brothers would continue to honor their duty as they had to the moment of their deaths. We shall not turn upon ourselves. We shall not accuse each other without proof. We will do what Nordbert and his fellows expected of us. We will bury them with the respect they deserve and bring their shares back to their families in Frankia."

The Franks looked to their feet. Some nodded. Others frowned. But none offered any retort. Gyna seemed on the verge of speaking. Yngvar hoped she would remain silent, for even an apology might turn the Franks back to anger.

She shook her head, as if she had decided against speech, and let Bjorn take her from Ewald. She shrank into his side, head down.

Yngvar turned back to Petronius, once more speaking his thickly accented Greek.

"Do not provoke my men," he said, smiling. "Or else I would think you are deliberately trying to stir trouble for me. Only half of your crew are on this island, might I remind you. The others are on your ship."

Petronius inclined his head. "I did not mean to cause you hardship. It is curious that you counted my crew. I might think you planned trouble for me."

"Counting is unnecessary for what is plain to see. What helped you to overcome your fear of this island? Last we spoke—when we made a very specific agreement with witnesses—you were certain that to touch the sands of this beach would mean death. How is it now half your crew no longer has such a fear?"

"The earthquake," Petronius said. "Clearly, it resulted from the curse which you and your crew have accepted for opening the king's tomb. We have no more to fear."

"But not all of your crew believe that," Yngvar said. "Or else they'd have joined you by now. No one wants to miss a chance to pocket a few jewels for himself unless their fear of the consequence is greater."

Petronius shrugged. "But you will lift the curse. You learned the name of the king buried here? Alasdair said your enslaved scribe named the king before he was crushed to death. Probably killed for speaking that name aloud, if I had to guess."

"I learned the name," Yngvar said. He raised his voice and looked past Petronius to his crew. They had dark, impassive faces. They were pale with dust from digging through the collapsed halls and rooms.

"Now that I know the name of the king buried here," he said. "I will raise a stone to his memory and bring him back to the world of men. Once I restore the long-lost spirit of the king to glory, in exchange he shall lift his curse. I am certain of this. Every king craves glory and to be remembered by history."

"Then what is his name?" one of the Byzantine sailors shouted back to Yngvar. His companions grumbled with him.

Yngvar reached into his shirt and pulled forward the circlet of gold. He held it up in triumph.

Perhaps because the Byzantines had seen so much wealth recently, they did not react. They stared at it as sunlight ran along its edge. Through the circle of the crown, Yngvar saw Lucas and Ragnar leaning on their spears above the others.

"I show you now the crown of King Agamemnon!"

Petronius blinked. His crew looked in astonishment to each other. They murmured as Yngvar smiled with triumph. Petronius also smiled, but it was dark and sly.

"King Agamemnon, you say?"

Yngvar nodded, lowering the golden circlet. He looked to Thorfast and Alasdair, then the Franks. Alasdair translated into Norse for Yngvar, and soon his men were smiling with him.

Petronius began to laugh and clap his hands.

"You are more overjoyed than I am," Yngvar quipped.

"Either your slave lied, or we have indeed found Agamemnon's tomb. But you will not lift the curse from yourselves by returning him to memory. Agamemnon is a hero known to every child in the civilized world. One stone raised to his memory would do nothing to further his fame. In fact, nothing you can do would bring him more glory. He will be remembered long after our bones have turned to dust."

Yngvar glared at Petronius, who raised both his palms and stepped back.

"I would not lie to you, my friend. Go into the world, and speak his name. Where civilized men gather, they will know his legend better than you. He is one of the greatest heroes of the Greeks."

"Then you too are cursed," Yngvar said. "And if not by Agamemnon, then by all the gods of the North! I will assure it."

Yngvar raised the gold crown in his fist, forgetting he gripped it between white knuckles.

Petronius stepped back in surprise, but he also flared with anger.

"You would curse me? And what have I done to you? I aided you all this time, brought you trade from the mainland. Been your companion and ally, and you curse me in your gods' names."

"Half of the gold?" Yngvar pointed with the circlet back toward the collapsed halls. "You took no risk. You left my friends buried in rubble or else let them die unaided. Then you helped yourselves to my treasure."

"Your treasure?" Petronius drew closer.

Bjorn, who couldn't understand the words, understood the threat and he growled from behind. The Byzantine sailors also understood, and they reached for the hilts of their daggers. No one carried swords except for Yngvar, as all had been too encumbered looting the tomb for heavy weapons.

"My treasure," Yngvar said. He shoved the circlet into his shirt. "I found the island. I read the map—"

"With my help," Petronius said, slashing his hand as if physically cutting off Yngvar's words. "You didn't know what you were looking at."

"The gods promised this treasure to me. They led me here, twice, and I swore to this King Agamemnon that I will raise a stone to his name in the North. Not a man knows him there, I can assure you. But I will expand his glory and avoid his curse. He has already aided me once. He will do so as long as I carry his crown and keep my promise. For if I do not, then I know the king will slay me. No, it is my treasure. You agreed to help me with it for a third share to split among your crew. Now you grab half."

"I came to new terms with Bjorn."

"Bjorn is not the leader here," Yngvar stepped back, holding his arms out to either side to keep Bjorn or anyone else away from the Byzantines. Petronius saw this and gave what seemed an unconscious nod.

Yngvar glanced to Lucas and Ragnar, who were watching so intently it seemed they had forgotten their purpose.

"A one-third share," Yngvar said, easing his voice. "That is all. I cannot calculate such a share when you have rushed your so-called half onto your ship. I will never know how much you stole, but I demand you return what you have carried away. Pile it on the beach where all can see, and we will make a fair reckoning according to the bargain we set before arriving here. There is no new bargain."

"I disagree," Petronius said, smiling sadly. "Bjorn was eager for my help, and so we reached a new agreement. You may watch us divide the treasure as we dig it out. But I will not have what we've already divided brought back to the island."

"You will." Yngvar reached for his sword. Petronius, who armed himself only with a long dagger, stepped back with his sea-green eyes wide with shock. The Byzantines drew daggers. The Franks and freemen shouted in confusion.

"You've gone mad," Petronius said, his own hand touching but not drawing his dagger. "None of us will profit from bloodshed. We are all armed, even if only with daggers. Would you have a battle here?"

"I would not," Yngvar said, smiling. He looked up to the rocks and shouted. "Lucas, Ragnar, be ready to shove those rocks when I give the word."

Lucas and Ragnar snapped up and returned to their spears, where they motioned as if preparing to topple the boulders poised above Petronius and his crew.

Everyone gasped when they saw the two men. Ragnar steadily worked his boulder, and dust hissed down the stony wall. Yngvar hoped it would not dislodge.

"Hold!" he shouted. "Not just yet. But Petronius and the rest, you stay right there. You see, one stone is ready to fall. How many more will follow? You'll all be crushed before you can reach me."

"You damn fool." Petronius whirled back to Yngvar. "That whole wall might collapse. You'll kill yourself too."

"I won't," Yngvar said. "All of you throw your daggers to the ground out here. You will get them back once I account for all the gold. Petronius, you will be my hostage. Your men will remain under those stones. If anyone moves, Ragnar and Lucas will crush them and I will kill you. Bjorn and Alasdair, plus whoever they take, will go to your ship to return with the gold. If that ship leaves while you're with me, you'll suffer and your crew die. So pick one of your men to go with them and warn your men to cooperate."

Petronius's eye drifted out of focus and he gritted his teeth.

"So much for friendship," he said.

"You will still be a very rich man," Yngvar said. "I intend to be fair, unlike you. These threats are just precautions. Your crew on the ship might decide that gold is enough for them and abandon you."

"Half a crew couldn't get far in that ship," Petronius mumbled. He let his shoulders slump, threw down his dagger. "The rest of you do the same. Let's be done with this and get our gold."

"That is wisdom," Yngvar said. "We have scales and will divide the gold with perfect fairness. You will have an exact share to parcel out to your men as you will. I am grateful for the shelter and aid you offered us after we killed Prince Kalim. We would never have recovered without you, and so you have earned your share. Simply sit here and wait for your gold. Then we will part ways, each of us richer than we ever dreamed. It is not such a bad fate."

Petronius's eye did not return to focus, and he said nothing. He lowered himself down and folded his arms. His crew followed.

Yngvar remained with his sword drawn, then explained his plans to the others.

Bjorn and Alasdair discussed who they would take. Yngvar wanted the treasure on the shore before sunset, and to have divided it before dark. Thorfast returned to lie down in his tent, and Gyna left with Valgerd. Yngvar kept the rest of the Franks and freemen with him to watch the Byzantines. Though they first went to fetch spears and swords.

After most of the afternoon had passed with the rowboat making three trips between shore and ship, the gold was all piled on the beach. Hamar along with two other men had dumped the gold from Yngvar's ship with the rest. Yngvar understood men on both sides would have stashed coins and other small riches for themselves. A gold ring would hide easily. He could do nothing for it. But after a tedious afternoon of waiting and swatting at flies, a vast treasure hoard glittered on the beach.

It seemed much smaller beneath the open skies than it had in the cramped space of the tomb. Still, he could fill his decks with sacks and chests of coins. Even the richest kings of the north would be hard pressed to match the gold spread out here.

Then there was the additional treasure below the false tomb. That would be worth a future trip, when he could bring miners and skilled men to properly extract everything. He was uncertain of his plans for that treasure. But he assumed once others realized he had plundered the island, no one would venture out to seek more. That deeper treasure was for his future.

The sun was low in the west, gold and red clouds drifting along the horizon there. The tide lapped the shore. Yngvar's ship rested proudly on the beach, casting a long shadow where Hamar and his assistants rested from hauling gold.

"Come," Yngvar said to Petronius. "Get your weapons. There is gold to divide."

Petronius said nothing, nor did his men. They picked through the rough pile of daggers, each man seeking his own weapon. Yngvar waved Lucas and Ragnar off the high rocks. Both disappeared from sight as they climbed down.

Yngvar still maintained the advantage, as he and all the others now armed themselves with war gear, whereas Petronius and crew had none. They had either set swords aside, now out of reach, or had left them aboard their ship. While Yngvar would not openly threaten his allies, he was glad for the advantage.

The crowd circling the treasure pile stared down in reverent silence.

"It's like viewing a holy relic," Alasdair said in a whisper.

"A pile of gold as long and fat as three dolphins," Thorfast said.

"Like dolphins in a coat of jewels," Bjorn added.

Gyna stared over Yngvar's shoulders, saying nothing. But the gold light reflecting on her face showed her eyes bright with anticipation.

"We will build a hall for our family," Valgerd said to Alasdair, grabbing his arm as they both gazed down at the incredible wealth.

"I will build a hall for my people," Yngvar said. "And I will gather hirdmen to it. They will wear coats of mail and iron helmets. The master smiths of Frankia will forge their swords. I will give them gold for loyal service, and we shall keep the land safe for all."

"I think I'll buy a new whore every night of the year for ten years," Thorfast said.

"Ever full of noble thoughts," Yngvar said. Some of the Franks laughed and agreed.

"It will be no easy thing to divide this evenly," Petronius said. "We must first know the weight of what we have, then divide it into thirds. With your small scale, we will be here all night."

"We fill the gold and silver coins in separate chests of equal size and set jewelry and small things aside to be divided. We will do the measurement and division before sunset. You Byzantines are not as skilled at dividing spoils as Norsemen. We do this all the time."

By the time the night had arrived, and a bonfire built to cast a bright light over sparkling gold now filled in sea chests, the treasure had been counted and divided. Yngvar had two-thirds for himself and his men. Petronius had a third of the wealth.

"There might be more within the ruins," Petronius said. "But we have carried off as much as we dare. When Bjorn fetched me, I was already considering ending the dig. The tomb seemed it might continue its collapse. We are better leaving scraps behind than risking our lives for them."

"I agree. The gods will not be so merciful as to spare our lives twice. We shall leave with the dawn," Yngvar said. They stood together by the shore with bonfire light painting half of their faces yellow. The early night sky was deep blue and scattered stars blinked like the pile of jewels they had laid in the sand earlier that the evening.

"It has been a great adventure since meeting you," Petronius said. "We killed many Arabs. Raided a prince's treasure room and unearthed a king's fortune. I dare say, I should follow you rather than return home."

"You've no need to rejoin the Byzantine navy now, not with this much gold. You can buy yourself ships and crews, then kill Arabs for the rest of your days if that is your desire."

Petronius shrugged. "I'm not sure I will want to fight any more. This gold is enough for a comfortable life. But I will not be living as a king like you will."

They embraced forearms, then saluted each other as two soldiers of the Byzantine military. Yngvar would never again make such a salute, and he felt a sense of regret. They both paused, smiling warmly at each other while men from both of their crews looked on.

Then Yngvar returned to camp to rest before the betrayal he knew would come.

7

The sun had not yet risen, though a thin white light shined on the eastern horizon. Yngvar stood by his ship and watched the waves rumbling onto the beach. High tide was just beginning and so he could launch to sea with first light as long as the waves did not strengthen. Looking farther, he saw the outline of Petronius's ship. It was bigger than Yngvar's and stouter. They built Byzantine naval ships to ram and could easily shatter a longship's hull. But it would have to catch Yngvar's ship first. He believed his ship faster than anything in the Midgard Sea. With Hamar steering, pursuers would never catch the ship unless a treacherous wind favored them.

Yngvar's eyes were heavy still, for he had slept fitfully. He awakened every hour panicking that all his gold had been stolen. He had slept under the open sky by the embers of the bonfire, keeping only a blanket and his sword near. Whenever he awakened, he would stare into the dark night and listen. But he heard only snoring and the purr of waves striking the beach. The guards he posted remained alert and looked toward him whenever he lifted his head.

He relieved the last guards, since he could not sleep. Alasdair roused to keep him company, but Yngvar sent him back to Valgerd's side. "Both of us shouldn't be unrested," he said. "We are not yet off this island. We may need our wits come the dawn."

So he had sat on a rock and stared at his ship, where he stored the treasure and guards slept in shifts on the deck. Lucas the Byzantine's freemen comprised the bulk of them. The Franks preferred to sleep on land.

Petronius and his crew had taken their shares to their ship and would remain at anchor for the night. It relieved Yngvar to hear it.

But he also suspected Petronius might lead men ashore in the darkness. With only a single rowboat, he could never land enough men at once to make an attack. But Yngvar did not worry for an attack as much as for theft. A few skillful men might carry away his treasure. Yet nothing had happened all the long night. Now, as the sun crawled into the sky, he wondered if he was seeing threats where there were none.

He heard the crunch of steps on the sand behind him and turned on his rock. Gyna approached, swathed in her gray cloak. With the breeze catching her hair and cloak, she seemed like a shadowed ghost emerging from the night. When the embers of the bonfire threw light onto her face, she seemed gaunt and haggard. Of all of them, Yngvar guessed she had suffered the worst. This long journey so filled with pain and defeat had worn her down.

She said nothing, but Yngvar shifted on the rock to make space for her. She stared at it a moment, then slipped beside him. Despite the balmy air, she pulled her cloak tighter. They both stared into the sea, where the foam of waves showed gray in the dawn twilight.

"He saved my life," she said, her voice small and hesitant. Yngvar had to turn to hear her better.

"Who did? Ewald?"

Gyna shook her head. "No, I forever save that boy's life from his own pride. Nordbert did."

Mention of Nordbert made Yngvar's shoulders slump. Of all the noble Franks, Nordbert was his favorite. The man knew how to lead a crew and a ship and was as loyal and brave as any lord could hope. His Uncle Aren had done well to entrust him to aid Bjorn. Now he was dead.

"They accused me of killing him," Gyna said, staring ahead. "But that's not what happened. Everything was collapsing. I saw Thorfast swallowed into the dark, like dwarves from the deep snatching him away. I couldn't move from fear. The ceiling and walls fell in. Norbert pulled me out just when the passage would have crushed me. He thrust me ahead to another man, who pushed me ahead of himself. I heard screaming, but when I turned there was nothing but rock behind me. I just kept going. What was I supposed to do?"

"There was nothing you could do," Yngvar said.

"The shaking was so violent and quick. It ended before I got to the exit again. But the walls were still coming down, and earth piled at my feet. Bjorn had come in after me, but he couldn't get far. He's too big. He yanked me out and carried me down the path before everything fell in."

The sun continued to rise. Gyna pulled her cloak around her neck as if she were in a winter storm.

He slipped his arm around her shoulder and pulled her close.

"The Franks are just in shock to have lost their brothers. They know you did not kill Nordbert or the others. Do not take it to heart."

"I thought them to be like brothers," Gyna said. "We have traveled so far together. Fought side by side. But they turned on me. Blamed me for Nordbert's death. Who can support what I have said? I haven't witnesses."

"The gods have witnessed it," Yngvar said. "They have seen Nordbert's bravery and marked it. You will carry his story forward so it will never be forgotten. Such is the gods' plan for you. The Franks will realize it soon enough. It is better that they remember Nordbert's death as heroic rather than a senseless accident. They will realize it soon enough."

"Bjorn made it worse," Gyna said. "As soon as someone mentioned the idea I might've passed Nordbert and caused him to become trapped, Bjorn flew into a rage. Now everyone thinks that is a sign of my guilt. What do I do?"

Yngvar sighed. "I cannot say what is best. Bjorn's temper makes him ill-suited to lead others. But it seemed he was the only one left willing to lead. I will work with the crew, get them to understand. By the time we are home again, they will forget all of this."

Gyna smiled, but not with humor. "Home? Where is that? I have been running around with you for so long, I had forgotten my home. But when I returned to where I grew up and found Ewald—found my sister and her husband dead—I remembered where home really is for me."

The wind rustled the grass and the waves crashed on the beach. His ship would soon catch the water and be ready to sail. The men would soon rise with the dawn.

Yngvar withdrew his arm.

"What about Bjorn? He would not fit in with the Saxons."

"He might surprise you," she said. "They love fighting and have plenty of it to do between Danes, Franks, and their own tribes.

Bjorn would never set aside his ax. And if you will truly give up the sea road to become a barley farmer, what would Bjorn do?"

"Nothing is settled yet," he said. "Now, gather yourself. Your long face makes you look guilty, and you are not. You are a proud warrior who stands with me in the shield wall. Enemies cannot beat you with a sword or spear. Yet will you let feeble lies defeat you? If you are grateful to Nordbert, then you will not let his death be remembered as a murder. You will fight for his reputation."

She smiled again, but this time with gratitude.

"I am glad you are back," she said, standing from the rock. "You give Thorfast too much credit for his speech. You are better at it than him."

The first light of the day brightened the sky. Gyna returned along the path she had taken to him. Yngvar listened to her receding steps as he watched other men rousing from their sleep. His eyes moved instinctively to Petronius's ship. He saw motion there.

"Lord," Alasdair said through a yawn. "We have spent another night on a cursed island yet I feel more refreshed than ever. How is that possible?"

"It is because we are not cursed, not so long as I am sincere in bringing Agamemnon's name north."

Alasdair joined him by the rock and stretched. More men were rising from their blankets. Others stubbornly clung to sleep.

"If he is so well known to the Greeks, then learned men in Frankia and elsewhere will know him." Alasdair stepped ahead of Yngvar to stare harder at Petronius's ship.

"Learned men in their city homes or noble castles, maybe," Yngvar agreed. "But not to the farmer or herdsman. I shall spread his name among the common men and raise a stone to his greatness so they will remember him long after I am gone to sing his praises. And for that the spirit of King Agamemnon is with me and aids me."

Yngvar withdrew the gold circlet from his shirt. It was warm from sitting against his skin. He considered how to make it an arm band. He could cut away a small section and bend the gold to fit his arm. It was not so pure that it would be too soft to hold.

"Lord, I think Petronius is ready to sail."

Yngvar stood beside Alasdair. "The question is which direction. If he turns toward us, we must make a shield wall."

"A shield wall?" Alasdair stepped back in surprise. "Do you think he will attack us?"

"I am not sure what he will do. He tried to claim half of our gold, but I believe he took more than half and left only enough to fool us. Why wouldn't he want all of it?"

"Because we were allies," Alasdair said. "We had an agreement."

Yngvar stared at Alasdair. His smooth, bright face turned red as he realized how naïve he had been.

"Help me get the rest of the men ready. We cannot be asleep if he tries to land here."

Yet as Yngvar walked among Frank and freeman, prodding the sleeping man awake, he saw that Petronius's ship was turning out to sea. Once they were all awakened, the three-masted ship was already growing smaller on the horizon.

All the Wolves had gathered together as equals now, for the first time since the earthquake had separated them. The others who were close but not yet part of Yngvar's closest companions—Valgerd, Ewald, Hamar, Ragnar, and Lucas the Byzantine—stayed at their edge. The other Franks and Freemen gathered by the ship, many climbing aboard to gaze at the enormous wealth they had claimed.

"We will divide the treasure once we have arrived safely in Frankia," Yngvar said.

"Frankia?" Bjorn's single eye widened in surprise. "I thought we were done with it? We should go back to Brandr in Norway, no?"

Their eldest cousin's name had not been mentioned since leaving Norway. They had not been long apart, yet to Yngvar it seemed a lifetime. Would he have to divide a share with Brandr? At one time he would have without hesitation. Now, after so much suffering, he reconsidered. What had Brandr done to deserve a share?

"Frankia," Yngvar confirmed. "Or have you forgotten half of our crew have families there? Or that your father was dying but may still live and wish to make peace with you?"

Bjorn frowned and shifted on his feet, looking aside. Yngvar continued.

"Where we go from that point will be for us to decide. We could return to Norway, but we defied King Hakon to come here."

"The lad will be happy enough when we bring him gold," Bjorn said, laughing. Yet no one else joined him.

Now Yngvar frowned and looked aside. "After all, we have bled for this gold, I will not share it with a boy who names himself king of Norway."

"Well, he did not name himself, but a meeting of all the jarls confirmed him," Thorfast said. "And we have sworn to serve him, which we must do if—"

"I am an oath-breaker," Yngvar said. "Let me state it plainly. I have sworn as I must to preserve myself and those sworn to me. I know it is wrong to demand loyalty for oaths when I have not been as loyal as I should have to my own lord. But I do not make greedy and ridiculous demands of those sworn to me. I do not ask them to share gold that I have no right to. So forget oaths to King Hakon. After all I did for him, he gave my reward to Brandr."

Yngvar had known King Hakon awarded a portion of his ancestral lands to Brandr when that award should have been his own. He had tried to convince himself that Hakon's choice was reasonable, given

Brandr being the oldest of them. But he knew it for the insult it was intended to be for not obeying King Hakon to the letter of his command.

"I thought you were fine with it?" Thorfast asked. "We have a duty to the king."

"Enough!" Yngvar held up his hand. "If you want to return to Hakon and put your share of the gold into his hands, you'll not find me in your way."

Thorfast made no reply. But he folded his arms and glared at Yngvar's outburst.

"Now, we have made our preparations. The tide is coming in. We should launch soon and make a full day of sailing. Petronius has gone. We should do the same before anything else befalls us here."

They parted, and Yngvar stood watching after them. Each of his companions went to their own groups. Alasdair joined Valgerd in collecting their belongings. Gyna and Bjorn left with Ewald for the ship. Ragnar and Lucas the Byzantine joined with Thorfast. Even Hamar had gone to find the crew and prepare to sail.

He suddenly felt bitterly alone.

The weight of King Agamemnon's circlet of gold weighed against his side. He pulled it out, examining it once more. He then decided to make an armband of it while waiting for the rest prepare to sail.

When he finished cutting the circlet and fitting the band, he held a small bit of gold in his palm. He stared at it, thinking of his morning and of what lay ahead.

"Some things can never be put together again once broken apart." He weighed the gold bit in his palm, then stuck it back into his shirt.

They missed the high tide. Yngvar owed Nordbert a better burial than what he had gotten. He led the Franks to where they had found him last. But a rock had fallen and caused more dirt to slide over the place. They spent the morning and part of the afternoon digging through the rocks. The heavy scent of rot plagued them and flies assailed them as they carried away rubble. Yet once they unearthed white, bloodless flesh, more earth broke free from the surrounding walls and buried them again. Agamemnon had claimed their bodies and would not release them. The Franks conceded this and instead said prayers over the collapsed tomb and raised a cross of wood where they had found the bodies.

Gyna had stood with the Franks while they prayed. Most eyed her with suspicion. Others ignored her. Some nodded. Yngvar hoped their irrational anger would subside now that they settled Nordbert's rest. If they continued to make Gyna feel guilty, she would have more reason to return to the Saxons.

Though the afternoon brought low tide, they launched to sea without issue. If there was any tension with the Wolves, it was from Yngvar's brooding on their future together. It seemed despite everything they had endured and how hard they had fought to reunite, they would go their own ways. He had never expected this voyage to the south would end like this. He had never expected an end to the Wolves.

Yet the farther they sailed from the island, the more his mood improved. The rocking of the ship on the open sea and the spray of salt water on his face refreshed him. He left sour feelings in the foamy wake of the ship. Wind filled the sails and the crew relaxed. They were going home rich as lords. No one could remain unhappy for long in such circumstances.

They sailed through the afternoon without reaching for an oar. The treasure was piled up around the mast, kept in sea chests and leather bags. A seal-skin tarp covered these, weighted down with stones. To anyone glancing at the deck, it would seem nothing more than their belongings or perhaps some meager spoils. Yet every man glanced at the pile, and Yngvar was no less guilty of it. Any who paid attention would know the entire crew concealed something in the chests beneath the tarp.

By early evening, Alasdair called for land ahead. Yngvar was uncertain of their exact location, having relied on Petronius to read the maps taken from the fortress at Pozzallo. He knew they were somewhere between Sicily and Greece. That enemies were to the north and south was all he needed to know. Land ahead could mean trouble.

But with the end of the day coming, and the land seemingly

nothing more than a scattering of small islands, he ordered Hamar to set the course for them.

"We travelled far today," Yngvar said. "And we will be on open sea for weeks. So we should value a rest on land where we can find it."

The surrounding crew voiced agreement. Hamar leaned on the tiller, and the ship shifted toward the edge of the northernmost island.

"We'll scout a place to land," Yngvar said. "Loop around the chain then settle for the night. Better to be certain we are alone than to find pirates hiding there."

Hamar steered a careful approach, nosing toward the northern island on the clumped islands that were little better than rocks and scattered palm trees jutting from the sea. A strange current and the threat of rocks just beneath the waves funneled them naturally around the northern tip.

Yngvar's gut tightened as they approached.

"I don't like it when we are herded," he said. He leaned on the rails, straining to see across the water to the black islands ahead. The sun was behind it, creating a harsh orange glare.

"Maybe we should've approached from the south?" Thorfast now leaned with him by the rails, cupping his eyes against the sun. "But I see nothing but waves and rocks. Not much of a beach here."

"We could at least anchor in calm water to rest the crew," Yngvar said. "Or else we sail through the night. There'll be plenty of that ahead of us, though. We should at least scout these islands. Still, something is bothering me."

The ship glided closer. Its shallow draft let it glide like a leaf over waves. The men seated themselves with short oars. Others worked the sails to control their approach.

Yngvar's unease only grew as the ship rounded the northern island. Hamar had maintained a distance from the coast which was all rock and drop-offs where scrubby bushes clung. The ship was about to cross the middle and present its side. Yngvar could not help but imagine being rammed.

"Alasdair," he called. "I need your sharp eyes. What is that I see? Look just behind that spar of rock."

Alasdair brought Valgerd with him and the two stared hard into the intense glare. Both shielded their eyes.

"I can't be sure, lord," he said. "The sun makes it impossible to tell."

"Exactly my fear," Yngvar said. "Does it look like the tip of a mast to you?"

"Mast?" Alasdair leaned forward with Valgerd. Now both were half over the rails. Alasdair gasped, then Valgerd.

"Hamar, take us out to sea! Men, get the long oars down and row!"

Thorfast leaned forward, his white hair burning orange in the evening light. "What did you see?"

Yngvar had already started walking the rows, shouting at men to exchange short oars for long. He ignored Thorfast's question, intent on regaining their edge in open waters.

Bjorn, who had been sitting on the deck in a circle with Gyna and Ewald, shot to his feet and grabbed an oar from the rack.

"You hear him! Row!"

"I still don't see it," Thorfast shouted back. But Yngvar did. He pointed from the opposite end of the ship where Hamar leaned on the tiller.

A black ship slipped from behind the far side of the island. The vessel was big and sturdy, but still only a patrol ship by Byzantine standards.

And it was a Byzantine ship. The wind was not with it, but the long oars were down and beating the water.

"Petronius, if I'm not mistaken," Yngvar shouted back. "And I think he wants our gold."

8

The glare of the setting sun had kept the telltale mast of Petronius's ship hidden from Yngvar's sight. But now they were clear black lines against the ruby horizon. The Byzantine ship slipped confidently from behind high rocks. The sails were still catching the wind. They were long triangular shapes that billowed into fullness as the oarsmen worked the ship from the rocky coast.

"Bastard sailed ahead and waited there half the day," Yngvar said. Hamar was at his side, pulling on the tiller. "You know what to do. I'll get shields off the racks for the crew."

Hamar stared in disbelief. "Petronius? I'd not have expected treachery from him."

Yngvar wasted no time in debating what temptations a pile of gold and jewels could do to a man. Petronius had been a convenient ally, but never a genuine friend. Yngvar had liked him well enough. But that did not mean he trusted him.

He retrieved his own shield, then pulled others from the racks to set by his oarsmen. Thorfast and the rest did the same. Yngvar wished for his mail shirt, but waited to have a new one made for him in Frankia. The weight of it on his shoulders would be a comfort now.

"Lord, it really is Petronius. I recognize the ship." Alasdair stood with both hands on his hips. "He planned an ambush."

"That he did," Yngvar said, lacing his arm through his shield, then drawing his sword. "I saw it in his eyes. We carry too much gold for him to let us sail away. But we are faster and have every advantage. With the gods on our side, we will prevail."

Petronius had a good angle on them. Had Yngvar not ordered the turn when he did, they might have drifted in front of Petronius, offering the chance to ram then board his ship. It would have risked all the gold, but as Petronius had only a third share, it would be an acceptable risk for him.

So the two ships converged, but Yngvar was ahead. He went to the stern and stepped up to the neck. His longship could reverse as easily as moving the steering board from one end to the other. Whereas their headings fixed and trapped Byzantine ships.

He cupped his hand to his mouth and shouted across the spreading wake trailing his ship. The sails snapped and the mast creaked as the ship pulled ahead.

"If you had wanted a race, we could've done it any time."

Petronius seemed to struggle to understand, then shouted back through cupped hands.

"Give us the gold. I have more men. A bigger ship. We need not fight."

"I agree," Yngvar shouted back. "No need to fight. Because you'll never catch us."

Now the oarsmen exchanged the short oars they expected to use near the shore for long oars to propel them to sea. When they hit their first stroke, Yngvar grabbed the ship's neck to keep from falling as it lurched ahead.

"You will have to land sometime," Petronius shouted back. "I will be behind you. The gold is mine!"

Yngvar waved him off, stepping down to the deck where Alasdair waited. The oarsmen, mostly freemen, kept a steady pace. The Franks worked sails and rigging or else awaited their turn to relieve the freemen. The sea stretched ahead of them, and the wind kept their sails full.

"Lord, why is he attacking now?"

"While we were on the island, he could never get all his men to bear on us all at once. He'd need to come up with some excuse to land them, which I'd never have fallen for. That's why I insisted he take his gold to the ship. He'd have no reason to remain on land with us. But if he boards us, he could swarm our decks and overwhelm us. Not to mention he could break our ship and force us to surrender. You've seen him do it to the Arabs. Our ship would snap like a branch. He might not even get the gold before we sank."

Alasdair stared behind Yngvar. "We are already pulling ahead. He'll never catch us."

"Our men will run out of strength," Yngvar said. "But he has more men to rotate through his oars. If the wind betrays us, then he could close the gap. If he caught us while we're exhausted, we won't offer much of a fight. I'm glad he does not have archers and regret not having my own."

Night was approaching and the sun burned bright on the western horizon. The wind, however, did not blow west. It forced them to sail northwest, which was back toward Sicily. Yngvar wanted every stroke of the oars to lead him west to where the Midgard Sea spilled into the great northern sea. He wanted to be gone from these lands and never return.

Petronius and his ship had faded behind them. But they had not given up.

Alasdair and Valgerd kept watch on the Byzantines, having the sharpest sight of the crew. The wind blew Valgerd's golden hair over her shoulders. She seemed to grow tired of her watch and instead joined Yngvar by the tiller.

"It seems they have lost heart. They no longer follow so closely."

"They are resting all their oarsmen," Yngvar said, studying them. "We should keep our pace and continue putting distance between us. We cannot trust fate to let us escape him so easily."

The crew had slowed but not ceased rowing. The sky had darkened and clouds moved in to block the stars. Yet they only needed to sail in a western direction. Their only disadvantage was Yngvar fearing to sail too close to shorelines. He wanted as little attention as possible while he slipped out of the Midgard Sea with an ancient treasure hidden under a seal-skin tarp.

All of his wolves had now gathered together by the steering board. Bjorn's face glistened with sweat from rowing. He blew through his beard and rubbed his single eye.

"We should turn on Petronius during the night and clear his decks, the fucking traitorous bastard. Sail around and hit him from behind while he's looking ahead. Take the rest of the treasure. He didn't fucking deserve a third of it."

"But you were willing to grant him half," Thorfast said. His head was still wrapped in a bandage, which Yngvar doubted was necessary.

"You weren't no fucking help," he said.

"I was injured!"

"Enough," Yngvar said. He scanned all their faces, from Gyna, to Alasdair, then to Bjorn and Thorfast. "Bjorn's idea is one choice. I doubt we will shake this pest easily. Petronius is right that we will eventually have to make landfall. If he stays close to us, we will have to fight."

"So let's fight," Bjorn said. "Not like we ain't stood up to tougher enemies."

"They are trained Byzantine sailors," Yngvar said. "Even if they're not the army, look at us. We're not a strong shield wall. The freemen have trained to fight as skirmishers."

"We just need them to hold the flanks for us," Bjorn said. "Ain't it true, woman?"

He elbowed Gyna. But rather than her expected bloodthirsty snarl, she winced and said nothing. Yngvar stared at her as did Alasdair.

"Let's focus on escape," Yngvar said. "We'll row a fair bit longer, then let the wind take us. The men will need a rest. I will not feel safe until we gain the sea roads back to the north. Here we are locked into a sea with only one exit."

"It's not like he will leap ahead to block us," Thorfast said. "We will leave him behind and never worry for him again. Yngvar is right. Let him have his share and let's not risk more bloodshed than we've had already. There is too much blood on this gold right now."

"And there's the curse," Gyna said.

She lowered her eyes and seemed to shrink under the stares she received in answer.

"I'm not worried for a curse," Yngvar said. "I swear to you, that king saved me from being crushed when the earthquake happened. If he wanted me dead, then that would've seen to it then. No Gyna, fear no curse. I wear this armband now, which once was a king's crown. While I wear it, King Agamemnon guides me. I am sure."

"Well, the Franks aren't sure about the curse. They've been muttering about it," Gyna folded her arms, and looked tentatively toward the men resting on the deck.

"When you hear mumbling, remind them we've all got more gold than any low-born man deserves and we're alive to enjoy it. They just have to row hard, and we will be back in Frankia. Gold will buy us spearmen then, and we will have no worries after that. I will break the curse."

Gyna nodded.

Yngvar wondered at the change in her spirit. Perhaps she only needed a taste of enemy blood to renew her old fighting spirit. It seemed the only thing that united her to Bjorn. But he had more to worry for than her attitude. They had all reached a decision and so followed it.

They sailed through the night. The crew rested. Yngvar and Hamar traded shifts at the tiller. By dawn, the clouds from the day before remained, though they were high and thin. Yngvar did not fear rain.

The winds had shifted during the night. Hamar had done well to keep them as close to a western heading as possible, but now the wind blew east. The crew groaned as the dawn awakened them, knowing from the gathered sail they would have to row.

Alasdair was already searching behind them.

"There is a ship on the horizon, but I am uncertain it is Petronius."

"It's him," Yngvar said without looking. "He won't give up until he knows we are truly beyond reach."

"And that's Sicily ahead," Hamar said.

Yngvar groaned. "I wanted to avoid that place."

He scanned across the rails toward the long blue strip on the horizon. How Hamar knew this was Sicily, Yngvar was unsure. It could be the mainland. He knew their rough heading, but a cloudy night had hid the stars from him. Perhaps he had unwittingly steered them closer to the very place he hoped to avoid.

"Well, here's something else you'll want to avoid."

Thorfast stood in the prow with Gyna and Ewald. More of the crew were gathering to them, each straining to look into murky western dawn. Yngvar left Hamar to steer and joined them.

Stretched into a line spanning the horizon were scores of ships.

Arab ships.

"A whole fleet," Yngvar said, touching his neck where he once wore Thor's hammer.

The crew groaned alongside him.

"We've got to turn back," Thorfast whispered. "We'll either be driven to Sicily or else we'll be caught in their lines."

"I can't fucking see so far," Bjorn said, banging his heavy fist on the rails. "How many ships is a fleet? That word makes no sense to me."

"Every Arab ship you can imagine," Yngvar said. "Smallest to largest, all lined up and sailing this way. They've got to be reinforcing their victory in Sicily. That's all I can think of for the Arabs to send this many ships."

They were dark shapes still. But the largest ships showed points of lamplight. Thousands of men must be loaded onto the ships, along with their gear and livestock. The might of the Arab empire was not lost on Yngvar. Between them and the Byzantines, Yngvar understood how low even the grandest king of the north stood in comparison. The Arab fleet sailed in a wide arc, with smaller ships on the wings to scout and chase away other ships.

A ship like his would be marked, caught, and destroyed without the main fleet ever pausing. A death trap lay ahead.

"Reverse," Yngvar shouted to the crew. "Hamar, reset the steering board here. We go straight back into the east."

"But that'll take us to Petronius," he shouted back across the deck.

"One ship or one hundred ships, which would you rather face?"

Hamar growled in frustration. Yet he and another crewman disassembled the steering board and tiller. Yngvar ordered the sails struck to catch the eastern wind and outrun the Arab fleet.

Turning any other ship would be an arduous task. But Yngvar's ship, like all Norse ships, had dual prows. Before the Arab fleet closed any distance, they were already shooting away from it.

Yet they had not gone unnoticed. A group of five smaller ships on the nearest wing to Yngvar broke away.

"They will chase us off or try to capture us," Yngvar said as he watched the ships veer from the main body.

"It's the square sail," Ragnar said, stepping between Yngvar and Thorfast. "Probably think we're Norse mercenaries for the Byzantines. They'll mop us up if they can."

Their sails caught the wind and the crew pulled the long oars. For now, the Franks had their turn at rowing. Lucas the Byzantine and his freemen, all former slave-soldier companions of Yngvar's, waited their turn.

"If we had javelins," Lucas the Byzantine said. "We could pick off those damned Arabs one by one. You remember how we practiced with those? I could put a javelin through a fly's asshole."

"The empire's war is not yours to fight anymore," Yngvar said. "You're free to make all sorts of enemies."

Lucas laughed. While he, Ragnar, and Thorfast had formed a close bond, he and Yngvar had been squad mates at the Byzantine garrison at Pozzallo. Even when Yngvar became a bodyguard of the fort commander, he never forgot his ties to Lucas and the other slaves. He and Alasdair had both used their new freedom to aid Lucas and the other slaves. The small act of kindness had repaid Yngvar fourfold by now.

They kept a good pace ahead of the Arab ships. Yngvar's chest warmed with pride, believing his ship was truly the fastest in the Midgard Sea. Perhaps only another longship from the north might challenge it. But Yngvar doubted even that much. His ship was lighter and more flexible than any other he knew.

Yet despite his pride, the Arab ships had proved to be faster than he had expected. In truth, he had never raced against the Arab vessels. They had once pursued this very ship to shore, but Yngvar thought it due to the exhausted state of the crew rather than the Arab ships' native speed.

He rethought that assumption.

"They're closing on us," he shouted. "We've got the wind. We just need your backs. Give us some fresh men on the oars."

So the Franks and freemen switched out their duties. Sweat blew off their dark-bearded faces as they surrendered their oars. The ship slowed while the exchange took place, and Yngvar watched tensely as five ships leaned forward with the wind on their sails.

"Lord, that is Petronius ahead." Alasdair stood in the prow atop a cask of wine. He clung to the neck as the ship jumped and cut through the waves. "He's not turning."

Yngvar whirled back. "Has he not seen the Arabs?"

"Only if he's blind," Hamar said, straining with the tiller. "I'd say he's steering straight for us."

Now everyone not busy with another task looked past the prow to the triangular sails marking the ship headed for them.

"That's madness," Thorfast said. The wind caught his pale hair, fluttering like a banner behind him. He had at last abandoned his head bandage. "We'll both be caught if he tries to board us."

Yngvar's stomach lurched when he realized Petronius's intentions.

"He will not board us," he said in a small voice. Thorfast squinted at him as if unable to hear. "He will ram us."

"Ram us?" Thorfast's face twisted into doubt and confusion. "He'd sink us along with all the treasure."

"Exactly," Yngvar said. "Petronius hates the Arabs. If he can't have the treasure himself, he won't let the Arabs have it. He'd rather it all go to the sea bottom."

"Surely he's better letting us escape," Thorfast said. "He should cover our retreat, then try for the gold later."

Yngvar grimaced. "He might do that. But Petronius seems to have no sense when it comes to Arabs. They're his bitterest enemies. Hamar, takes us around him."

"That will let the Arabs gain on us," Hamar said. His square face was red both from strain and frustration. But he understood Yngvar's frown and leaned on the tiller to adjust their course.

Unlike a battle on land, one at sea unfolded too slowly for Yngvar's nerves. Movements were all in the open. Enemies were too distant to read. The result of his decisions took too long to learn. In battle, he relied on harassing and infuriating his foes into rash decisions that he could exploit. At sea, there was too much time for an enemy to regain his head. Now, he watched Petronius angling his ship to match his own heading.

"That fool bastard will cut us off," he growled through his teeth. "What is he thinking?"

Enemies behind and to the front, Yngvar could only walk the decks exhorting his men.

As Hamar had predicted, the angle to avoid Petronius had allowed the Arab ships to gain on them. They were now close enough to see the dark shapes of men on the decks. Many were leaning across their own prows as if eager to reach out and snatch them.

"Don't let up the pace," Yngvar shouted. Yet the Franks were tiring. Some had already dropped off their oar to let a freeman replace him. Exhausted men would never win a fight. Yngvar called for a rotation. It was not a good time, but this would be his last chance to refresh his oarsmen.

"Row for your lives." Lucas the Byzantine sat at the front oar and shouted over his shoulder to his men. "Row for gold and freedom."

His exhortations lent strength to the flagging men, and the former slave-soldiers shouted as one.

Yet Petronius had drawn closer and was speeding with the wind.

"Give me my ax," Bjorn shouted. "I'll jump to his ship and take his fucking head!"

Ewald, Gyna's Saxon nephew, raised his sword in union. The two of them were serious, Yngvar knew, but he hoped Petronius would not reach them.

Yet he did.

Despite the speed and wind, the bad angle and high waves worked against him.

The Byzantine ship now drew parallel to his own.

Petronius stood at the side of his ship.

"You damn fool!" Yngvar shouted across the gap. Their oars were perhaps a single length apart as they beat the waves. Sea spray flew over the rails and the hull shuddered as it crashed through waves. "Do you see what is behind us?"

Petronius leaned forward, cupping a hand to his ear as if to hear better. Then he laughed.

"I have eyes only for my treasure," he shouted back. "Give it to me."

"You must be blind," Yngvar shouted. "The Arabs are gaining."

So they were. The five ships sliced over the waves without effort. Yet Yngvar felt as if the sea were forcing him back toward them. The oarsmen pulled, groaning and swearing, but the ship seemed to never gain speed.

"I will guide you to shore," Petronius shouted back, glancing toward the closing Arabs as if they were not even worth his notice.

"Die, you pig-fucking traitor!"

Bjorn shouted the curse, and he raised his ax overhead.

Yet it was Gyna, standing beside him, who made the stronger statement.

Wordless and resolute, she lifted onto the rails with Ewald's help. She held the rigging for balance. Her other hand lifted a long throwing spear over her shoulder.

It flew gracefully across the gap. It seemed to wobble and bend in a time all its own. The air cradled it like a delicate gift. It arced down toward Petronius.

His eyes widened with shock, and he leapt aside.

The spear sunk into the chest of the man behind him. He screamed and vanished from sight.

Petronius's crew howled with rage.

Yngvar and the others watched in astonishment at the perfect cast. Despite the rocking ship, the rush of wind, and the blast of sea water between them, Gyna had cast a spear and slain a man.

And so she had drawn a life and turned greed into a blood feud.

9

The ship shuddered as it crashed through another wave. Warm, salty water splashed across Yngvar, rousing him from the astonishment of Gyna's impossible cast. She remained poised on the rail, one hand on rigging and the other hanging free, Ewald bracing her legs. She seemed like a Valkyrie deciding whether to take the soul of the slain man to Valhalla. Yet it was a Byzantine she had killed.

Yngvar hoped the bastard went to the hell of his Christian god.

The Arab ships still followed, but no longer seemed to be gaining. Petronius's ship dogged them. But Yngvar felt as if Gyna had dispelled whatever force had been holding them back. They were already pulling ahead.

The early morning light raked the deck of Yngvar's ship, casting long shadows of the rowers laboring at the oars. The freemen were slowing. Lucas the Byzantine turned on them.

"Row till your shoulders tear," he shouted. "Don't stop!"

Petronius had reappeared, looking between his deck where his crewman had fallen and Yngvar's ship.

"You'll pay for that," he shouted back. "You killed my brother!"

"He has a brother?" Thorfast asked. He had retrieved his shield from the racks, as many of the Franks were doing now.

"I don't know," Yngvar said. "But he looks mad enough for it to be true."

Though Yngvar's ship nosed ahead, the two ships remained matched. The Byzantines, former friends and allies, now looked hatefully from their ship. Yngvar heard their curses and was glad that half his crew could not understand what they said.

"Ten of your men for one of mine," Petronius shouted while drawing his sword. His face had gone so dark with rage all Yngvar noted were the whites of his eyes and his clenched teeth.

"Take your loss and go," Yngvar shouted in reply. "You can't catch us."

Petronius raised his sword and shouted a curse.

Bjorn and Ewald both raised their weapons and returned it. Gyna had stepped down and was now placidly sitting on the deck against the gunwales.

"We're slipping," Hamar said. "But the Arabs are trailing off."

Yngvar could see the heads of Petronius's rowers rocking in unison. They had redoubled their effort to close the gap. A glance over the stern and Yngvar confirmed the Arabs were lagging. Though they had not surrendered pursuit.

Lucas the Byzantine stood from his oar and let another slip onto his sea chest to take up his spot. He walked down the line and cursed his freemen.

"Row, you bastards! Your lives depend on it. Freedom and riches! Row for it."

Yngvar appreciated Lucas's help. While the freemen respected Yngvar, they responded better to one of their own. Lucas was the oldest and most experienced, and being a former Byzantine citizen who had fallen into slavery seemed to earn him more credibility from the others.

The freemen roared back.

Petronius's ship once again lagged.

Then the boarding hooks and ropes flew across the gap.

Yngvar watched one splash uselessly into the water, the caster screaming in rage and hurriedly reeling it back.

"The bastards are serious," Thorfast said.

Petronius angled his ship closer. Yet Hamar shifted over, maintaining the gap.

Lucas the Byzantine screamed at the rowers.

Another cast of the boarding hooks flew from Petronius's ship.

One thumped into the rails, but snapped free with a hunk of rail attached.

Another landed squarely in Lucas's neck.

The sharp hook dug into his flesh. Yngvar saw a flash of bright red and Lucas jerk backward.

Then the rope snapped taut and Lucas the Byzantine flew off the deck into the sea.

Yngvar blinked. Lucas had been standing one moment, then vanished the next.

The oarsmen did not notice. Most of the crew had not noticed, intent as they were on Petronius and the pursuing Arabs. Only the man Lucas had been facing sat dumbfounded.

"Keep rowing," Yngvar shouted, taking up Lucas's place. "We're almost away."

Petronius's crew made one final cast before Yngvar's ship slipped ahead. The hooks never reached his deck.

The Arabs had again picked up speed. It seemed they had been hanging back to decide which of the two ships would lose the race, then pounce on the laggard. The five Arab ships now shifted toward Petronius.

Yngvar walked the rows of oarsmen, slapping their shoulders and offering them encouragement. The wind gusted stronger, straining the sail and mast. The ship responded with a lurch.

In the next instant, they were two ship lengths ahead of Petronius. As the rowers worked their oars, the gap only widened.

Soon, they were far enough ahead to relax their pace. Petronius had to cut away and evade the Arabs. The Byzantine ship cut hard to the northeast and the Arab ships responded in kind. Yet Petronius had a lead and the wind. He might yet escape, but he would not follow Yngvar.

"We've got enough of a lead," Yngvar said to the crew. "We'll rotate out now. But we've got to keep heading east, Hamar. We need to find a safe place to land, then rest and resupply."

Thorfast crouched where Lucas had been standing. The other freemen were only just learning what had happened, despite Lucas having been dragged to his death before their eyes.

"All that marks him is a drop of blood," Thorfast said. He stood from his crouch, holding up a reddened index finger.

"He was a good man," Ragnar said. "I liked him."

"Bad spot of luck," Bjorn said, leaning over the crowd of men now surrounding where Lucas the Byzantine had stood. "But did you see Gyna's cast? Was that not guided by the gods?"

Ragnar glared at Bjorn but said nothing.

"If the gods had guided it, they missed the target," Thorfast said. He wiped the blood on his pants. "Lucas was a good man. We didn't like each other at first, but he was a friend."

"He was a friend to us all," Yngvar was quick to add. He addressed the freemen in Greek. "Lucas wanted you to be free and rich. Do not forget this. I will not forget this. You will have your shares when we are in Frankia. From there, you can do as you want. Freed men all. I will make sure Lucas is remembered."

The freemen nodded. Most were too winded or exhausted to react. Yngvar hoped they would handle Lucas's loss better than the Franks had done for Nordbert.

"Lord, we have lost both Petronius and the Arabs," Alasdair reported from the stern. He stood on the wine cask so he could see across the neck. Hamar guided the ship beside him.

"That is well," Yngvar said. To the Franks on the oars, he waved them on. "Keep rowing for now. The more distance we create, the safer we are. We will all rest on a shore tonight."

While the crew either flopped to the deck or else silently mourned Lucas the Byzantine's sudden death, Yngvar went to Gyna. She remained seated with Valgerd at her left and Ewald at her right.

"A beauty throw?" Ewald said in his hesitant Frankish. "My auntie is strong."

"Your auntie is strong," Yngvar repeated. He stood over her. She looked up to him, and he extended his hand. "I'd ask you to walk with me, but the best we can do is to cross to the other rails."

She smiled weakly, accepted his hand, then stood. It was warm and rough in Yngvar's. When she stood, she held it a moment longer than needed, drawing a raised brow from Yngvar. She followed him to the rails, while Bjorn glanced over with his one eye hooded.

"Why did you throw?" Yngvar asked. He wanted to blame her for enraging Petronius and providing him with a hero to avenge. If the Byzantines had not lost a companion, they might have settled for the gold they already had. Now Petronius might fan their anger with a more noble cause than greed alone.

"It was the right thing to do," she said. "I saw it clear enough. Didn't you? If I had killed Petronius, they'd have fallen to fighting among themselves. They'd never organize enough to come after us. Someone would try to take command, claim Petronius's share, then they'd be at each other's necks. But I missed. Now I have made it worse."

Yngvar nodded and stroked the beard on his chin.

"Well, that's a lot more thinking than you usually do. I just expected you wanted to see someone's blood. I don't disagree with you. I just never expected you to think so deeply."

Gyna smiled. "I've learned a lot on this journey. I'm taking home a treasure richer than gold. My father would've called it wisdom. I've been thinking, which is new for me. Thinking about my sister and father, my family, Ewald. I have to think or else that boy will get us both killed."

"Well, it was a good plan," he said. "But for the time now, I need the bloody-minded Gyna to come back to me. I fear we've started a fight that will not end without one side destroyed."

"Will he find us again?" She faced into the wind, her dark hair blowing across her face. "There are no tracks in the sea."

"There are only so many places we can reach," Yngvar said. "The Midgard Sea is wide enough to lose one ship. But he knows it better than any of us. He knows where we must land and how far we can travel with the supplies we have. He helped us buy the supplies, after all."

Yngvar sighed and leaned on the rails.

"I have been a fool once more," he said. "My father and grandfather built strong halls to protect farms and families. They had wisdom and knew the right things to do, the right people to trust. But I have none of their skills. I just ran off with my friends to seek gold and glory. I've learned nothing. I should have known Petronius and his crew would be tempted. I should have kept him at sword's length, rather than welcome him as a brother."

Gyna's hand was light on his shoulder. He looked up from staring at foam breaking along the hull. She smiled, warm and genuine. He had so seldom seen anything like this from her. He stepped back in shock.

"You've been a great leader to us. You've taken us this far. You'll get us home and make us rich. Bjorn and Thorfast believe in you. I swear Alasdair worships you after his own god. Do not be hard on yourself. It was not wrong to trust, especially since Petronius had been trustworthy until today."

She squeezed his shoulder, then left him standing by the rails. Bjorn watched from across the deck as she went to him. He folded his arms, and his one eye fixed on her.

"Lord, you mentioned landfall?"

Alasdair appeared beside him. He pinned the wine cask underarm.

"If we sail south, we will find a shore. It will be in Arab territory. But I'd trust them more at this point than I do the Byzantines. They might try to force us to serve in their broken navy."

"The Arabs will do us no favors, lord."

"Right," Yngvar agreed. "They'll directly attack, making our choices simpler. Besides, if Petronius sails after us, every Arab on the water will mark him. He's sailing a Byzantine naval ship in their territory. That'd be too dangerous for him to risk seeking us. While the Arabs would just see us as adventurers or traders. We just need a place to rest and let Petronius become lost. He might even settle for the gold he has and forget about us. Time might bring him to reason."

"He seemed mad enough to keep after us," Alasdair said, "But you are probably right, lord."

So they sailed south, not knowing precisely where they would land but knowing full well land was near. This provided Yngvar a measure of comfort. Even a fool could follow the southern coast to the open sea. From there, the sea roads home were well traveled and clear. They were not without dangers, but a Norse ship in the north was something to fear.

Land showed as a purple stripe on the horizon by noon. Within hours they were sailing along rugged coastlines searching for a hidden place to land. Lone fishing boats spotted them but never drew near, nor did they bolt off to warn others. Their ship continued along the coast, letting the wind guide it. By evening, they took aim at a beach where rough slopes of orange sand and rock swept back towards low mountains dotted with sparse scrub.

"The hills will shield our fires from local people," Yngvar said. "We may camp here tonight and rest."

They beached their ship with the sunset. Alasdair and Ewald led separate scouting parties to ensure the area was safe and to retrieve firewood. Yngvar and the rest set up camp and established watches for the treasure. When the scouting parties returned with no reports of local people, he allowed the men to set campfires.

Their frantic morning at the oars had fatigued the crew, and they welcomed the rest. Yngvar estimated they could rest here another day before they would have to resume their journey. He hoped for a quick journey north to Greece where they would buy the supplies needed to finish the journey out of the Midgard Sea.

He slept that night in high spirits and awakened the next morning refreshed.

The horsemen swept down from the hills with the first light. The guards at the edge of camp sounded their horns, but the attackers charged with reckless speed.

"By the gods!" Yngvar shouted, tossing aside his blanket and snatching his sword from the sands. Alasdair awakened with a start, Valgerd popping up beside him. She shrieked when she saw the horsemen.

Yngvar kicked Bjorn in the backside, ending his snores. Thorfast and Ragnar were both sitting up and rubbing the sleep from their eyes.

"Horsemen!" Yngvar yelled as he roused the camp. Franks and freemen both scrambled up to grab shields and spears.

But they were too slow and the horsemen too swift.

Yngvar guessed at least twenty lean horses, mostly chestnuts but gray and black coats intermixed. Their riders wore long robes of pale blue with white head covers that were more akin to hooded cloaks than the Arab covers he was accustomed to seeing. They were dark-bearded, dark-faced men whose war cries bounced off the surrounding hills.

"Make a shield wall in a circle," Yngvar shouted. "On me! Ignore the ship!"

He did not want to communicate to these horsemen he had anything more valuable on the ship than its sail. The horsemen were now thundering around him, and his crew had barely thrown off their blankets and grabbed their shields.

One of the Franks skipped forward with a spear, but Yngvar roared at him.

"Shield wall! Don't throw away our weapons!"

The Frank turned and fell back into the circle of men forming around Yngvar just as the first horsemen galloped into their midst.

The first horse seemed as tall as a mountain and its rider a shadowy god of death wielding a spear. The Arab screamed a shrill, hooting cry. But he did not charge home. Instead, he drove his horse around them, keeping his spear lowered at them.

Yngvar felt Alasdair's shield touch his, and he touched Thorfast's shield. All around the others formed a circle, pulling in tightly. Yngvar glanced over Alasdair's head to see Valgerd standing beside him with a dagger and a round shield that exposed only her eyes to the enemy. He would have ordered her to the center of the circle, for the shield wall was only as strong as its weakest spot. But the other horsemen were quick to follow their earlier companion.

These Arabs galloped around them in a circle, each one screaming and holding a spear toward them. They were dark, shadowed faces in blue robes that snapped with the wind. The hooves of their horses sprayed sand into the wind. The ground vibrated beneath Yngvar's feet. The air smelled of horse sweat.

But the Arabs did not attack.

They were terrorizing them. They drove in a dizzying circle with such speed that Yngvar could not fix on any of them. Bjorn roared in frustration.

"I can't see them running like this. It's all a fucking blur."

"It's no better with two eyes," Thorfast said. "Each horse runs like Sleipnir."

Sleipnir was Odin's eight-legged horse, the finest and fastest horse in the world. Yngvar agreed these horsemen raced with speed and skill. But soon their dizzying circle slowed and they filed back toward the hills.

"Stay steady," Yngvar said. "Hold the circle."

"They will charge us," Ragnar said. "We're doomed."

"No," Yngvar said. "We've got spears. They won't want to kill their horses. They just herded us like sheep. Now, see, they're reorganizing to approach us again."

A rut of horse prints circled Yngvar and his ring of shields. He held a sword, as did many others, but enough spears protruded between the shields to make a charge certain death for some of their horses. The Arabs either recognized this or else would dismount to fight. In the north, men rode horses to battle, but hardly ever into one. The Franks were most famous for attempting horse charges, though it failed on a strong shield wall. Perhaps the Arabs knew this as well.

Yet they lined up, spears leveled, their horses' sides heaving. They mumbled to each other in their strange language. The air was full of dust and haze from their wild charge. Gnats clung to the sweat on Yngvar's cheeks. The morning sun was already firing the heat of the day.

At last the horsemen advanced, steady with their eyes narrowed and knuckles white on their spears. Sparks of light rolled from their white edges.

They stopped out of spear range. Yngvar beat his sword to his shield and roared defiance. The rest joined him so that iron and wood thudded together to fill the shore with the echoes of battle.

The Arabs smiled and laughed. At last, one rider stepped his horse ahead of the others. He was tall and straight on the black horse's back. He held the horse's mane in one hand and swept his spear along Yngvar's front as if it were seeking a target.

"Who are you to challenge us?" Yngvar shouted at the leader. He spoke Norse, hoping he would recognize it as the language of traders. Yet the man ignored him and continued to examine the group. He switched to Greek.

"Fool! Do you come seeking death?"

Though Yngvar's accent distorted his Greek, the Arab smiled and nodded. He swiveled his spear to point at Yngvar.

He spit at the threat. His men cheered this and growled challenges.

But another Arab pulled up his horse. He was shorter and fatter than the other. His beard hung to his chest like a blast of black night. His voice was deep and full of humor.

"You speak Greek, but you are not one of them," the Arab said, whose Greek sounded fluent to Yngvar's ears. "That ship. You are from a faraway place. I've never seen the like in these waters. Who are you?"

"I am your death," Yngvar said.

The Arab laughed, his belly quivering beneath his robe.

"I could name myself the same to you. But we have not drawn blood. Let us not declare ourselves enemies yet."

"You charged us with leveled spears." Yngvar waved his sword across the line of Arabs facing him. "What shall I call you if not enemies?"

The Arab's smile shifted, though Yngvar could not tell if it was impatience or arrogance. He did not like the smile either way.

"I shall introduce myself, then," the fat Arab said. "I am Rida al-Ghazi. I lead these men, and many more like them. You have made yourself a guest in my lands, it would seem. I would ask what your intention is here, but I see you are well armed. So will you surrender your weapons and become my guests? Or shall we be enemies?"

Yngvar looked from the man named Rida to his ship. He looked back to Rida. Behind him, on the ridge of the hills, at least another twenty horsemen appeared. They began picking their way down the slope.

He looked again toward the ship, then back to Rida.

"We will get aboard our ship and sail away. You will never see us again."

"Do not be in a hurry to leave," Rida said. "We have little news here, and I understand there is much news to be had of the Byzantines. But only rumors reach me. I would at least have you stay to learn what you have seen and heard."

"I can tell you now, and then we leave," Yngvar said. "We do not know much."

Rida shook his head as if Yngvar were a boy who could not understand a simple instruction.

"You can be a guest or an enemy," he said. "But you cannot leave yet. Now what shall you choose?"

10

Chapter-10

The sun rose at Yngvar's back, a good sign. The light would be in his enemies' eyes rather than his own. Alasdair's shield trembled against his, whose own shield clattered on Thorfast's to his left. The rest of his crew held a tight circle with round shields presented to the Arab horsemen that lined up before them. Spears and sword blades protruded, warding off any attempted charge by the horsemen. At such close range, Yngvar guessed they could not bring their mounts to speed for a proper attack. But they still fought from horseback, which gave them an enormous advantage.

The Arab horses clopped at the earth and side-stepped until their riders stilled them with quick yanks of their manes. The fat Arab called Rida al-Ghazi smiled from atop his horse and stroked his midnight black beard. His companion sat his horse next to Rida, gazing past Rida toward Yngvar's ship.

Yngvar shifted his gaze to the dozen or more horsemen letting their mounts pick paths down the from rocky, orange hills.

"Thirty-two," Alasdair whispered beside him.

Yngvar nodded. They were a close match in numbers. But horses in battle were unpredictable. One blow from their hooves would break a man's skull like a dropped egg. Yet they could also throw their riders. The way these men handled their mounts, however, led him to believe they would not be easily dismounted.

"What is your answer?" Rida al-Ghazi patted his horse's neck idly as he watched. He set his spear in a sling at the horse's side. He carried no sword, only a sheathed dagger tucked under the cloth belt of his light blue robe.

"You leave me little choice," Yngvar said. "But if you expect us to lay down our weapons, then I will gladly die first."

"You would sell your life for a sword?"

"A man dies when it is his time to die. If it is today, then what do I care? I can fight you and die gloriously. If I am to die, and surrender, then I die in shame. No matter. Today I die in any case. We do not fear death in battle. Rather, we seek to die in battle. It is a shameful man who dies in his bed. So, try to take our weapons. When I am in the hall of heroes in Valhalla, I will step outside to piss on your fat head for the rest of your days."

Rida's brows raised and he blinked. "I did not understand all of what you said. Your Greek is expressive. You talk like a Byzantine. A curious thing I must know more about."

The two sides glared at each other. The additional horsemen reached the bottom of the hill now and they kicked their mounts into a trot. Dust from the sandy ground billowed around them.

"We're running out of advantage, lord," Alasdair whispered.

"Did we ever have advantage?" Thorfast asked from the opposite side.

"I have a plan," Yngvar said.

"Of course you would," Thorfast said. "Does your plan include eagles lifting us to safety? Because I see no other way out of this. What is the fat one carping about, anyway?"

"I'll explain it to him," Ragnar said. He had served as a Byzantine scout and met Thorfast in his travels through Sicily. He spoke Greek with enough command to translate into Norse for the others to understand their situation.

"It will be a hot day. I want to get out of the sun," Rida said. "What is your decision?"

Yngvar did not move and made no answer.

Rida wiped his face and pushed his hand into the recesses of the white head cover he wore. He scratched at his neck and grimaced.

"Very well, keep your weapons. But in return, I must have hostages."

Yngvar smiled and whispered to Thorfast.

"And there's my plan."

"Not this again," Thorfast moaned.

"Why not? It works." Yngvar then spoke to Rida. "Very well, I will become your hostage."

The distaste was plain on Rida's face, as Yngvar had expected. He had seen how Rida's eyes continually flitted to Valgerd throughout their parley. She was a beautiful woman, slender with a strong chin and shining eyes. Her golden hair was like spun gold in the sunlight.

He stared at her now, and as she understood Greek, she lowered her shield. She spoke in Norse to Yngvar.

"He wants me," she said. "I will go."

"No," Alasdair said. "I won't allow it."

"I'll be fine," she said, pushing him back with her shield.

"Yes, she will be a good hostage," Rida said. His eyes flickered with delight, as did the man seated on the horse beside him. "She will ride with me. But first, she must put down her weapons."

"I have a dagger in my skirt," she said. "Gyna showed me how to hide it there."

"I know she did," Yngvar said, trying not to smile. "When the moment comes, put it to his neck and we will sail away from this mess. And drive it home if you must."

"Lord, you can't be serious." Alasdair looked between her and Yngvar. Rida laughed at his consternation.

"Tell your boy his sister will be safe with me." He then turned to snap something at the Arab beside him. He seemed disgusted at the order, but slipped off his horse and held out his hands to Valgerd. He lifted her up to the horse, and Valgerd made a show of her helplessness by squealing and acting as if she might fall.

"Gyna, you taught her to act too," Thorfast said.

"She knew that before I met her," Gyna said. She was positioned directly behind Yngvar, next to Bjorn. Yngvar glanced over his shoulder, speaking Norse.

"She'll take him hostage for us and we'll bargain our way back to the ship. The freemen don't know what's going on. Ragnar, try to explain it quietly."

Valgerd clung to him like a desperate maiden. She even whimpered, which seemed to please both Rida and his companion.

The other horsemen had now trotted up to their earlier companions. The line of horses and warriors in sky blue robes was intimidating. While he wouldn't mind taking a horse for food, as he had not eaten good horseflesh since leaving Norway, he did not want to face a wall of them in battle.

The Arabs shouted back and forth, with Rida shouting merrily to his riders. The Arab next to him shouted and pointed toward Yngvar's ship.

"What's that about? My ship is no concern of yours."

Rida shifted back around, Valgerd's slender white arm barely reaching around his fat waist.

"Of course your ship is my business. It's on my shore. I should make certain you have nothing hidden under that tarp."

"Like the Byzantine navy? Is this how you treat guests? Hostages and a search of my ship. I forbid it."

"Forbid!" The fat chieftain leaned forward on his horse. "You've reminded me of a word I've not heard in many years. For no one forbids Rida al-Ghazi anything on his own land. Least of all foreigners carrying weapons to my shores."

He now sat straighter in his saddle and pulled a thick hand through his shock of black beard. His eyes glowed with the power of a man accustomed to absolute obedience. Thirty-two mounted warriors must make a king in these lands, Yngvar guessed. It was a fair number of warriors, but he had battled far stronger enemies.

Rida barked orders and gestured toward the ship, punctuating each with an arrogant smirk to Yngvar. Three riders trotted toward it. Yngvar's crew let out low moans as they realized the riders' goal.

"Silence! Don't give away our treasure." The Franks silenced, but the mix of races among the freemen meant they only shared Greek as a common language. So he repeated the order for silence only.

But Rida was sharp-eyed. He nodded slowly, barked more orders, and the three men dismounted to climb aboard Yngvar's ship.

"You are making a mistake," Yngvar said in a low voice.

Rida glared at him. "What do you hide from me?"

As he held the Arab chieftain's eyes, he saw Valgerd's free hand creeping toward her waist.

"My ship is my home," he said, gritting his teeth. "And you invade it with your horse-loving bastards."

"Careful how you speak to me," Rida said, leaning forward. "Or you will know only sorrow."

Valgerd's hand stopped beneath the waist of her skirt, just behind the cord cinching it to her waist. She found the dagger.

The three riders had boarded the ship and now removed the stones holding down the seal-skin tarp. Their robes fluttered like blue flags as the wind strengthened.

"How quickly hospitality turns sour. Is that the custom of your people?"

Valgerd's clear blue eyes met his.

He nodded as imperceptibly as he could.

Valgerd's hand tore free from her skirt. The dagger flashed in her hand.

Then it fell to the sand with a thud that sounded as loud as storm waves crashing against a cliff.

Both Rida and the companion beside him looked at the dagger dropped in the sand between them.

Valgerd's already pale face turned the color of spoiled milk.

Rida exclaimed something in Arabic. His companion reached for his own long dagger.

Then the Arabs on Yngvar's ship screamed as if set afire.

Yngvar, Rida, all the riders, and all Yngvar's crew turned to face them.

They had opened one of the chests, revealing the blazing gold coins and gleaming jewels. The coins shimmered like the scales of a golden dragon. The Arabs staggered back in amazement.

Rida again exclaimed something in Arabic.

Valgerd yanked his head-cover over his face.

Yngvar sprung forward.

His sword lanced the neck of Rida's horse. It screamed and kicked back. Valgerd shoved Rida away, sending him flying forward while she fell off the back of the horse.

The spray of horse blood struck Yngvar in the face, blinding him with hot, salty gore. He spit it out, searching for Rida.

"Get the fat one," he shouted. "Don't kill him!"

The injured horse screamed and sprayed blood in an arc over Yngvar and his crew. Its lifeblood also drenched the horse beside it, causing that horse to rear in panic.

Two horses thrashed about the sand and Yngvar held his shield out to protect against flailing hooves. From below his shield he saw Rida piled face-first into the dirt, his butt sticking up to make him look like a heap of blue robes. He did not move.

The dying horse bowled Yngvar aside as it flailed directly into his shield wall.

The crew had barely any time to react. Alasdair and Thorfast fell aside. Yngvar saw that much. Then he had to scurry back as the horse reared up and kicked out.

Valgerd shrieked as she rolled away from the other horse, whose rider was cursing in his guttural language. He had dropped his spear and held the horse's mane with both hands. But that beast was slathered in blood, and the scent of it had sent it mad with fear.

His own crew shouted as the bleeding horse thrashed among them. They scattered, but it caught someone beneath its flailing hooves. Yngvar could not glimpse who it had been. The poor man had crumpled like dead wood beneath it.

He drew his dagger, then leaped on Rida's prone form. The chieftain had blood running from his nose, and his dark eyes were wide and dazed. But he seemed to recognize Yngvar, who shoved his dagger up to his throat.

The horse cried out behind him, followed by a heavy thud.

Farther away, he heard the other horse's panicked calls and the rider's cursing. But he did not turn from Rida.

"Now we see how much your men love you," he whispered. "Stand and call them off."

Rida blinked as if not understanding what had been said. Yngvar saw his defiance and expected resistance.

Then a spearpoint hovered over Yngvar's shoulder, killing that defiance. Hamar had brought his spear around in time to help Yngvar raise the fat chieftain.

Yngvar's men scattered. Rida's horsemen were now closer, their spears poised, but they wavered. In a half-dozen heartbeats their leader had been captured and his horse killed.

Yngvar looked to the ship. Rida's three men were loading gold into their robes.

"Someone stop them," Yngvar said. "Hurry!"

A group of crewmen ran for the ship. The horsemen seemed ready to bolt after them. But Yngvar, holding his dagger to Rida's throat, would not allow it.

"Tell your men to stand down and surrender their weapons."

Rida inhaled, and Yngvar pushed hard. The thick beard sheared away as he forced the sharp edge into Rida's throat. He squeezed his eyes shut, then called out in Arabic.

The riders, who seemed confused, pulled up their mounts but did not drop their weapons.

Yngvar looked behind once more. The horse had died among his crew, with one unfortunate victim trapped under its body. Thorfast and Gyna were working with others to lift the horse aside. Alasdair had gone to Valgerd, who was shooing away his attention.

"You will pay for this humiliation," Rida said. "They will hunt you down."

"Get in line with all the others hunting me," Yngvar said. "Had you been reasonable and let us leave, you'd not be going for an ocean journey with us."

"What?"

Hamar forced his spear into Rida's back. Though he did not

understand Greek, his timely action emphasized Yngvar's threat enough so Rida raised both hands.

"You'll come aboard with us and remain a hostage against your crew following."

"I'm no fool," he said. "You will kill me."

"I will not kill you," Yngvar said. "I want to leave in peace. Order your men to drop their weapons and we will leave right now."

The mention of weapons brought the sounds of combat. The three Arabs had decided to fight for the gold. The other horsemen looked to Rida for instruction, but he shouted something to them that made them pause. Though they looked on with tight mouths and flexing hands.

The Arabs were encumbered with the riches they sought to steal. Yngvar's crew hacked them down easily enough, though one seemed to have been slashed across the thigh. He now lay on deck holding his leg.

"I'm sorry," Valgerd said. She looked up at Rida with a scowl. "He turned back and knocked the dagger from my hand."

"You were brave," he said. "And we have what we want. Are you hurt?"

"My hip throbs. But I am not as hurt as that poor man."

Again he turned to the fallen horse and the crowd surrounding it. It seemed someone had heaved the horse aside and now half the crew crouched over whoever it had pinned beneath it. He noticed Gyna had turned to Bjorn and buried her face in his shoulder. Her nephew Ewald patted her back.

Thorfast's white hair was plain to see between the crowd. Who could it have been to cause Gyna to weep?

Rida struggled, but Hamar pushed his spear along with Yngvar pushing his dagger.

"Tell your men to drop their weapons. I will set you down on the shore once I'm certain your men do not follow."

"What was that treasure? Where did you steal it from?"

Yngvar ignored the question and pushed his dagger hard enough to draw blood. Rida gasped, then shouted to his men. They looked to each other, then to the rider who had finally mastered his blood-covered horse. The animal still preoccupied him, then he realized the others looked to him for direction. He angrily waved them forward.

The riders threw down their spears, cursing and spitting at Yngvar.

"Who is the other one?"

"My nephew," Rida said.

"Looks like your nephew might be happy to see you go. Maybe when you are set ashore again the great Rida al-Ghazi will just be a king without his kingdom."

Rida growled but said nothing more. The riders remained seated on their horses, glaring angrily at Yngvar and his crew.

"I can bind him," Hamar said. "Me and the lads will keep him prisoner. You go see about that one."

Hamar pointed with his chin at the crowd surrounding the fallen man. Two other Franks joined to take over Rida's capture. They looked saddened.

Yngvar along with Alasdair and Valgerd pushed to the front of the circle. Thorfast hovered over the body. He had just finished setting the man's hands upon a sword laid over his torso.

Ragnar's head had been staved in. Yngvar only recognized him from his clothes and the fact that both Gyna and Thorfast were grieving. For Ragnar had been a friend to them both, aiding in Gyna's escape from Prince Kalim as well as being a companion of Thorfast's during his time in Sicily.

"He survived so much to be killed by a horse," Thorfast said. "Poor bastard. He was a good man."

Yngvar shook his head. "A shame. He was a good man, and a good friend. Take his body aboard the ship. We can't linger here or these Arabs might decide our hostage is worth less than the gold they just glimpsed."

They had little to carry away from their camp, having slept beneath the stars. Hamar and other crew had bound Rida in rope. His stomach protruded like a sack of grain. Yngvar felt an urge to slice it open and let his guts spill out. For Ragnar had been a good man and had died senselessly, all for this arrogant pig. But without Rida, they risked becoming trapped or killed on this shore.

The Arab horsemen edged closer. Even without weapons, they could trample men on the ground. It would be a foolish and desperate ploy. But they had glimpsed the riches on the ship. Such gold made fools of even wise men.

Yet respect for Rida held, and the horsemen watched with expressions that shifted from anger to sorrow. Many made signs with their hands Yngvar did not understand. Rida shouted at them, his voice cracking with emotion. But as Hamar dragged him to the ship, he obediently fell into line.

They threw off the slain Arabs after stripping them naked. It was to ensure any stolen gold fell out of their robes. The crew made to heave the corpses into the surf, and a cry rose from the horsemen.

"Don't give them more reason to come after us," Yngvar shouted. "Set them on the shore and cover their bodies with their robes."

After they carried out his orders, Yngvar ordered the ship launched. A dozen crew pushed her onto the waves while the Arab horsemen stared on in silence.

"They should not have bargained with us," Gyna said. "It cost them their advantage." She and Ewald joined Yngvar at the rails to watch the shore recede. The Arabs only now advanced to gather their dead. She looked back to where Rida was tied to the mast.

"Auntie is right," Ewald said. "We are too strong."

He smiled and laughed, but Yngvar shook his head.

"We were fools who got caught. You let over thirty horsemen go unnoticed."

Ewald's smile fell and he held up both hands in protest.

"I saw nothing. They came from nowhere. I swear it."

"Ewald would've found them if they had been near," Gyna said. "Don't blame him."

"No matter, we have lost another brother today."

They all turned back to where Thorfast knelt beside Ragnar's corpse, draped in his blood-stained cloak. Bjorn stood behind him, hand on Thorfast's shoulder.

"He lost two friends in as many days," Gyna said. "He will blame it on the curse."

"He won't," Yngvar said with a laugh.

But what else could it be?

The golden armband he wore, Agamemnon's crown, felt as heavy as lead. He tightened it and went to join Hamar at the steering board. He had more to worry for than curses as they sailed back into the Midgard Sea.

11

Petronius cursed. Not a simple curse, but a long stream of invective. His exhausted crew lay on the deck, their naked torsos shining with sweat. He mopped his own brow, stemming the trickle of sweat into his eyes. His was not from physical exhaustion, but nerves.

He had barely escaped the Arabs.

In truth, they lost interest. They were escort ships intended to find enemies and either deflect them or signal back to the main fleet. They chased Petronius well beyond their remit and so turned back. One simple Byzantine escort was hardly worth chasing, especially since the destruction of the western navy.

"Captain, we need to do something."

Standing in the bow of his ship, he stared out at the distant strip of land he once called home. The late day sun turned the clouds red. It bought him a strange memory of his childhood home, sitting on a dock and watching gulls soar over the waves as the sun set behind them. His cousin Cyril sat with him. A year his junior but taller and stronger than Petronius, he stared up in simple fascination. Cyril had been strong and tall. All the women loved him. But he had never been smart. Petronius always looked out for him.

"Captain?"

He had protected Cyril all his life. Through countless battles. Through that affair with an officer's wife that should've seen both of them flogged to death. Through illness, poverty, famine. Petronius's eyes began to sting.

"Captain?"

Then he had ducked. A simple reaction. That crazy bitch had the eye of a hawk. And Cyril had been standing right behind him as always.

"Captain, the body."

The crewman touched his shoulder, and Petronius whirled on him.

"Don't I fucking know it? God, man, stop harping on me!"

The crewman backed away. Like the others, he was shirtless. His waist sash was dark with sweat from both the heat and rowing. His curly beard glistened with it. He inclined his head and stepped away.

Cyril lay on the deck, covered in a sheet that was now mostly blood red. The deck was slick with his blood. He had never seen a man bleed so much as Cyril. He was truly bigger than average in every way.

Despite all the madness, someone had the foresight to cut away the spear shaft that had embedded in his chest. A small knob protruded under the sheet covering him. Petronius wiped his eyes, then turned to the crewman who had tried to rouse him to action.

"He spent all his life on the sea," he said, his voice conciliatory. "So to the sea I'll return him."

The crewman seemed about to ask another question, but Petronius's eye was out of place. No one questioned him when he became One-Eye.

"Ah, and Isaac, you will be First Mate now that Cyril is dead."

The crewman, Isaac, blinked, then he saluted.

Petronius went to his cousin's body and knelt beside it. He stared at the shape of Cyril's face beneath the sheet. His high nose formed a bump beneath the cloth. Petronius smiled, thinking how often he teased him for the size of his nose. The ship rocked and creaked on the waves. Rose sunlight crawled across the deck, deepening the red of his cousin's blood. Petronius's eyes stung as he lifted the bloody shroud from Cyril's face.

He wished he hadn't. He expected a quiet, beatific expression on his cousin's face. Instead, it was frozen in a grimace of pain. Someone had closed his eyes, but this only enhanced the eerie sensation of witnessing his cousin's final moments of agony. Petronius snapped the sheet back over Cyril's face.

"They'll pay for this, brother," Petronius said. They may have been cousins, but Cyril had acted as his true brother for as long as he could remember. "I will avenge you."

The rest of his crew looked on, at least those with the strength to sit upright. Isaac knelt beside him.

"Once you have made your peace, we should pray for him and—"

Petronius held up his hand. Isaac did not have to describe dumping Cyril's weighted corpse into the sea to be eaten by fish until his bones settled to the muddy floor. The thought of such a strong and vibrant man—such a good man—rotting in the sea because some insane Norse bitch made a lucky cast set him trembling.

He moved through the next hours in a daze. Once the men recovered, they paid respects to Cyril. Petronius insisted on wrapping his cousin's body, helping Isaac and another crewman. But he could not finish. He surrendered the job to another crewman and returned to the bow, avoiding the looks of his men. He leaned on the rails and cupped his hands over his face.

Had Cyril died in a fair fight it would have been a different feeling altogether. But treachery had felled him. The damn Norsemen.

He had liked Yngvar and Alasdair well enough. Commander Staurakius had trusted them, and they had been keen to kill Arabs. So he accepted them, and even remained with them after Arabs obliterated the navy at Messina. They were good soldiers. But then the others joined and the Norsemen changed. They were developing civilized habits, and then their old friends returned, restoring their barbaric ways. Their old gods and strange habits. Their weird language and belligerent attitudes. Their arrogance repulsed him most of all. So they bested an Arab prince who was ninety percent fool and ten percent dandy. But to hear them brag of it, to carp endlessly about their exploits. To sing songs about it, blessedly in a language he did not understand. Well, you might believe they had destroyed the whole Caliphate on their own.

What fools. And then to renege on their bargain for the treasure. He thought Yngvar and the others were dead. The cyclops Bjorn had made a fair deal for an even split of the treasure in return for Petronius's aid. That share was more than the original bargain, but those bargain-makers were dead. Or so he thought. But Yngvar, changed from an Arab-hating and free-spirited man into an over-cautious miser, had threatened to crush him and his crew.

Crush him! Did that little Norse turd know he could have attacked at any time? How accurate and fast were boulders in a fight? No, he had willingly sat down and let Yngvar have his way. There was plenty of treasure for all. The Norsemen had risked the island's curse after all, something half his crew would not do. So he surrendered. Why kill needlessly?

Well, now he learned the answer to that question. Norsemen were barbarians, and their promises meant nothing.

They had killed Cyril.

Isaac summoned him to Cyril's funeral. The new cloth was still blotted with blood. How much did his cousin have? They said prayers, promised to see him again in heaven, then crossed themselves. Petronius kept his remarks brief. Cyril was a good and loyal servant of the emperor and God. He died bravely, facing the enemy. What else could he say? The crew were not family. They hadn't guided Cyril all his life. They hadn't sworn to keep him safe and then step aside to let him die.

He watched the corpse splash into the sea. The gentle waves lapped at him, then gathered him under. Tight wrappings bubbled and loosened in the dark green water. But the stones, folded into his wrap, sank him. Now he was a fluttering gray shadow beneath the waves, soon a smudge, and then vanished.

Bubbles broke on the surface to mark where Cyril sank to his rest. The ship rocked gently, waves slapping the hull. No one made a sound. The creaking deck and the distant call of gulls were all he heard. He searched for the gulls like he had done with Cyril so many years ago, before the navy and gold and Norsemen.

Facing his crew once more, two he found on their knees scrubbing the residue of Cyril's blood. But he had spilled so much the boards would forever be stained. Petronius nodded at the crewmen willing to meet his eyes, trying to keep his face tight and chin raised.

"Sir, your orders?" Isaac asked. He wore a gray shirt, though left it unbuttoned to the waist. He was a handsome man with a lean body ruined by acne and a white burn scar across his stomach.

"Orders," he repeated. "Orders are to make port tonight. We've got to resupply."

Isaac shared a nervous look with the man beside him.

"You have a problem with my orders?" Petronius asked.

"Sir, we have the gold."

Petronius tilted his head back. "Ah, yes, our treasure. You want to divide up shares now that there's one less share. Maybe if we wait longer, there'll be less of us left. Divide it up, then."

"No, sir, that is not what I'm saying." Isaac held up his hands for peace. "But if we make port, and we have treasure all in one place, well, inspectors might find it. Then we'd have trouble, sir."

"We have trouble now. What's a bit more? But I take your meaning. We've already counted out shares. So let's divide them up. Treasure for all, right? Come on, boys, let's count the gold."

The crew perked up at this. Cyril's passing meant little to them. Even though they had sailed with him as long as they had with Petronius, they dumped his memory overboard with his body. Would they do the same for him when the time came?

They were at anchor and the only sails nearby were headed to port and not to sea at this hour. Yet anchoring so close to shore would draw attention, particularly from anyone who recognized the cut of his sails. The navy had been destroyed, but not every navy ship. Many were still trying to regroup months after the disaster at Messina.

With the last light of day, they counted out shares. Isaac, who always enjoyed the trust of the crew, oversaw the divisions. Petronius, being captain, earned an extra share. During the division, men quibbled and some came to shouts and shoves. But despite the riches on the deck, no one tried to steal and no one drew blades. Perhaps it was their discipline that kept them from grasping for more.

More likely, it was because there was little to divide.

"We can't retire on this," Petronius said. The crew were all gathered around the central mast, each one now vastly richer than they had ever been.

"It is not as much as we could have had, sir," Isaac said. "But it will have to be enough."

"Right, it is not as much as we should have had. First the Norsemen broke their deal with us, and then they killed Cyril."

The crew looked to each other. Petronius saw it in their eyes. He awarded them enough gold to fear losing it. Dividing the treasure had made them cautious.

"Sir, we tried to catch them. The sea is full of Arab ships. We should return home."

"Return home?" Petronius stepped back in mock surprise. "You deserters will return home? If you wanted to go home, you should've gone right after Messina."

"Sir, there are still ships returning home even now," Isaac said. Much of the crew nodded to support him. "Every time we've gone to port we've heard the stories."

Petronius folded his arms, smiling. "So let's agree to go home. Now, what do you suppose happens? How long do you suppose before news of your gold gets out? Ah, you think it's yours by right? Naturally, we get to keep whatever we can claim from the enemy. But do you really believe that once some senior officer figures out how much gold we have that he'll let us keep it? Are you all so fucking daft? You'll be hung by your ankles until every coin falls out of your clothes. Every board on this ship will be pulled apart so that not a single jewel is missed. And we'll probably all be thrown in chains for hiding it."

He glared at the men, and none dared look back.

"We don't have a home anymore. And we don't have family, except ourselves. Some of you got women on shore, I know. Suspect a couple of you have kids too, though they probably don't know you're the father." A few of the men chuckled. "We can go fetch them when we've settled. But unless you want to be pirates for the rest of your days, you'll need more than this."

"Sir, it's still quite a lot of gold," Isaac said. But now Petronius noted he spoke with less conviction.

"It's got to last all your days. You planning on dying next week? Think about it. We can't go back to the empire. Eventually we'll get caught, and the emperor doesn't forgive deserters no matter how old they are."

Petronius paused on that statement to let the men recall executions of traitors and deserters. They had all witnessed that bloody spectacle at least once in their careers.

"So we've got to build a place of our own, fortify it, hire men to keep it safe, bring in traders. It all costs money. You want to throw in from your own shares? How much are you going to have left after that? Maybe you want to go out alone and see if old One-Eye Petronius is just full of shit? Go ahead. I'll stop by whatever city you settle in to visit your head that'll be hanging from the walls. Or maybe, being just one man with a lot of gold, I won't find you because you were robbed and your corpse left out for dogs to eat. For my part, I'll stick with my family."

No one, even Isaac, dared to meet his glare now. He suppressed a smile, for he knew he had convinced them. Now to bring it home.

"There's a ship full of treasure out there. No one knows about it but us. The Norsemen took the curse for themselves. You all saw that island swallow them. They're the marked ones."

Some crewmen flinched. Petronius was not certain he even believed himself. That curse had kept men away for ages, and if it was Agamemnon's tomb, then it would be a powerful curse. But he was Christian. A good priest could defeat a pagan curse.

"I know what you're thinking," he said. "I'm thinking it too. But what does a curse matter now? It doesn't get worse because we take more of the gold for ourselves. So forget about it."

Isaac cleared his throat, and men looked to him. He tilted his head back.

"I fear no curse," he said. "God protects me and God wills me to have these riches."

Isaac looked from man to man, and they raised their eyes to meet his and nod. Petronius felt his stomach unknot. This was why he made Isaac First Mate. He needed Isaac on his side to persuade the men.

"That's right," Petronius said. "I agree with Isaac."

The crew shifted and mumbled a rough agreement. Some still rubbed the backs of their necks, but they would soon come around.

"God will guide us to what should have been ours from the start."

The agreement grew louder and Petronius's smile widened. More than gold, Petronius owed Cyril vengeance. That bitch, Gyna, would have to die along with her cyclops lover and her Saxon nephew. Then the others, Alasdair and the traitor Valgerd, along with the white-haired Thorfast. In the end, Yngvar will be left alone. That would be his punishment for his betrayal and Cyril's death.

"Sir, we don't know where the Norsemen went," Isaac said. "How will we find them?"

"They are clever enough to know where to escape us. They went south toward Caliphate lands. They think we won't follow them there, at least not in this ship. So already we can guess their general position. Better than that, we know where they want to go. There is only one way home for them, and we can be there ahead of their arrival."

"At the Strait," Isaac said, nodding. "But we would have to pass through Arab lines to do that."

"So will the Norsemen," Petronius said. "But we won't need to thread that needle. We know roughly where they went. They will be short on supplies by the end of tomorrow. Without rain, they will need water. If we hurry, we can spot them at sea. A Norse ship with a single square sail coming out of the Caliphate territories could only be them."

Isaac nodded, as did some others. Still others frowned while considering the plans.

"And here's another advantage we have," Petronius said. "We can get news. We're still the Byzantine navy to the average fisherman. Strange sails will be noted and remembered. We will know where the

Norsemen are and where they are headed. And we know this sea like we know the moles on our lovers' necks. We'll find them."

One of his crew spoke up. "Find them but not catch them. Their ship flies like a dolphin over the waves."

"We don't have to catch them," Petronius said. "I've got a plan for that."

He let the crew search each other's faces while he enjoyed the suspense. At last, they looked to him to explain.

"Again, we're the Byzantine navy. We've been buying supplies for the Norsemen because they can't risk coming to port. So we go to port and resupply. Boys, we buy ourselves bows and sheaves of arrows. Stack the deck with a mountain of arrows. The Norsemen don't have bows. But if we do, then we only need to draw close enough. Then we'll shoot out their crew. We'll set fire to their decks. We'll tie them off, board them, kill who remains, and take what God has set before us."

The crew voiced approval and clapped their hands.

Petronius clapped with them, smiling.

"Let's get us to port. We've weapons to buy."

The crew cheered. Petronius looked back over the rails and thought of Cyril.

Your revenge, he thought, and my riches all in one sweep. The Norsemen will die, I swear it.

12

The Midgard Sea enveloped Ragnar's body in ghostly green hands. Bubbles escaped from between the cloth bindings as his corpse sank into the water. Blood flowed out from beneath the stained wrapping over his head, appearing like wisps of hair. As Yngvar watched from the rail with the crew lined up to either side, he hoped the wrapping would not come loose before he vanished into the darkness.

Rida's dying horse staved in Ragnar's skull. Yngvar had not seen it himself, but according to Thorfast the horse struck him from behind as he tried to escape. Then it stomped on him before finally collapsing atop him. Most of Ragnar's brains emptied from his skull and his bones crushed under the weight of the horse. Wrapping him for burial had been like wrapping slush.

"You had better stay away from me," Thorfast said. "Anyone too close dies."

As Ragnar sank into the water, the crew turned from the rails. Only Yngvar and the other Wolves remained with Thorfast.

"It was fate," Yngvar said. "Today was Ragnar's day. But he died facing an enemy. He will wait for us in Valhalla."

"At this rate, he won't wait for us long."

The midday sun shined through a break in gray clouds. Sweat

prickled on Yngvar's forehead. At least while at sea there were no flies or gnats to torment him. He could not endure another summer in these lands and looked forward to the cool north, even if everyone else seemed to doubt they would survive the journey.

"We have faced our last battle," Yngvar said. "Now that we are on the sea, we will make a straight line home."

"Before Petronius became our enemy," Thorfast said as he stared at the spot where Ragnar had gone to rest. "He warned us the weather could be a threat this time of year. Between winter and summer, then summer and winter, he said, the sea could betray you. We're not home yet and there's a curse to be settled."

Bjorn, who had been standing quietly beside Thorfast, growled.

"Don't start being gloomy. We ain't going to listen to what that traitor had to say. He was probably just trying to get us to stay close so he could rob us."

"It's not just him who said it," Yngvar said. "I've heard the same from the freemen. All we can do is pray to Thor."

"I've got a better idea than praying," Thorfast said. He turned around against the rail and nodded toward Rida, who was tied to the mast. "A sacrifice. Gut that fat bastard and hang him from the spar."

"Human sacrifice?" Alasdair put his hand to his chest where his wooden cross would have been. He had lost it during the collapse. "That is too much."

Thorfast shook his head. "It wasn't too much for our grandfathers. The gods were stronger in those days. They listened to us then. Now they let us flounder and die like fish left out on a hot stone. Maybe it's because they don't get enough blood from us."

Alasdair frowned and Valgerd grabbed his hand as if the suggestion alone frightened her.

"He's a prisoner," Thorfast continued, staring hard at Rida. "And he owes us a life for Ragnar's. What harm is there in sacrificing him? Not like we will make him part of the crew and grant him a share of the gold."

Thorfast laughed and looked to Yngvar. But his smile faded.

"We can't sacrifice him," Yngvar said. "The crew are all Christians.

We'd have them at our throats if they thought we'd be dragging them into a bargain with their devil."

"Well, don't tell them what it is," Thorfast said angrily. "But I will not stare at that black walrus breathing the clean air while my friend is rotting at the sea bottom because of him."

"He'll face justice," Yngvar said. "But I'll not sacrifice him. Besides, I've done nothing like it. I will not begin now."

"It can't be hard," Thorfast said. He glared at Rida, who watched them with his head tilted back. Thorfast ran his finger across his neck. "You just cut open his throat and bleed him into the sea while praising Thor. Then we sail home on water made smooth with his blood. Sounds fine to me."

"Lord, you can't be seriously thinking of this," Alasdair said. "Animals are one thing, but not a helpless man."

"Are you going to offer the Arab a reward now?" Thorfast rounded on Alasdair. "Spare me your Christian ways. This whole fucking land is full of Christians and they have no worries about killing people they don't like. And what good is your god, anyway? All these Christians are in the same ship as me, facing the same curse. What good is a god who let himself get killed?"

Alasdair's pale face flushed red and his brows knitted together. He tore his hand from Valgerd's, both his fists balled.

"I have never mocked your gods."

"Because my gods are not weaklings."

"Enough!"

The shout came not from Yngvar, who remained transfixed by the sudden hostility between two brothers. Instead, Gyna put herself between them.

"Alasdair, now's the time for a bit of that Christian patience you talk about. Thorfast and I have both lost a friend who helped save our lives. And looking at the cause of his death isn't easy."

Alasdair blinked at Gyna, but he let his hands relax.

"Thorfast, we're not sacrificing prisoners to the gods. Yngvar has given good reasons. Do you really think sacrificing the Arab solves anything? It'll just enrage everyone else and we'll lose their loyalty.

And that will end poorly for us since it's five swords to twenty-five. Use that smart head of yours and think about it."

Thorfast stared at her, then frowned in disgust.

"Where the fuck did you come from? Bjorn, who's this woman hanging around with you?"

But he nodded to Gyna's logic and he looked to Alasdair.

"Your god's still a weakling, but I'm sorry for what I said to you. You deserve better."

Alasdair shook his head. "We'll all relax when we've left this place. I didn't mean to make you feel bad."

"Well, you two gonna kiss?" Bjorn put his big hands on both of their shoulders. "I say we take all those bad feelings and work it out on that fat bastard tied to the mast."

Yngvar looked to Gyna. The corner of her mouth turned up and she shifted her eyes from him. As the others went to Rida, he held her back.

"Thank you for that."

"You weren't leading. Someone had to or else poor Thorfast would've found out how quick Alasdair could tear off his balls."

"They're both fast," Yngvar said. "I'm not sure who'd come out on top, and I hope to never find out. Anyway, I'm glad you stepped in."

"Do you still want bloody-minded Gyna? Seems you've got enough bloody-minded friends."

He stared at her. Her smile faded, and her eyes shifted toward Rida, where the rest gathered. Bjorn had his back to them. She looked at him, then glanced to Yngvar.

"We've got to keep them from killing the prisoner before I find out if he's any use." Yngvar pushed past her, but she remained in place by the rails.

Rida was surrounded yet he held his head up with a fierce pride that only defeated men seemed capable of summoning. Yngvar knew the feeling well, ice cold terror in your heart but the heat of rage on your face. Ewald, Gyna's nephew, had been standing guard beside him. It seemed unnecessary, but Yngvar was not letting a loose rope bring him disaster. Despite his earlier criticisms, he knew Ewald to be a vigilant man.

Thorfast had slapped Rida's thick face so that the redness showed even on his dark skin. Bjorn laughed like he used to laugh when tormenting captured rats when he was a boy. Though Bjorn was a fierce berserk, he had never been a cruel man. So only Thorfast had drawn a dagger that he teased across Rida's protruding belly.

"Before you ruin my deck with Arab guts," Yngvar said. "I want to learn what I can from him."

"What's to learn?" Thorfast asked. "We know which way to sail. You think he knows a faster way?"

"I want to learn what we don't know," Yngvar said. "Like why is there a whole Arab fleet between us and the strait out of the Midgard Sea. Who knows what else he can tell us."

Yngvar guided Thorfast's dagger back to his side. Rida frowned at him, sweat trickling from his thin hair. He had lost his head cover during the struggle to take him captive. His hair was thin and shaved close to his head. His beard was so black and thick it looked fake, like goat fur hanging from his neck. But up close Rida showed he was not a young man. There were spots around his eyes along with deep lines. Fat had puffed out his wrinkles so he had seemed younger.

Thorfast obliged Yngvar and the others stepped back. Ewald remained with his spear and now readied it in two hands.

"Stick him if he tries anything," Yngvar said. "But I think he's tied."

"Stick him," Ewald repeated, as if learning a new phrase, which was likely. He gave a sharp nod.

He and Rida eyed each other. Despite being bound to a mast, surrounded by enemies and empty ocean, he seemed proud and confident. Of course it was a show. Yet Yngvar admired the attempt. He spoke deliberately in Greek, being slow enough so his accent would not overwhelm his meaning.

"Well, now you are on my ship and in my home," he swept his hand across the horizon. "The sea. So if I paid you the same hospitality in my home as you paid me in yours, well, I wonder how you'd enjoy that?"

Rida's nostrils flared and he glared at Yngvar. But he soon turned aside.

"You attacked me first," he said. "You killed my favorite horse."

"And you wanted to take my favorite sword and run about my ship as if it were your own." Yngvar grabbed Rida's chin and forced him to meet his eyes. "You should have let us leave in peace. Your sorrows are all of your own making."

He offered a bitter sneer. "It is ironic that I am held captive amid the greatest treasure I've ever seen. Where did you get it? Who is chasing you for it?"

"That is not your concern," Yngvar said. "You will not live long enough to find out, anyway."

"So you will not set me free." Rida's voice was low and rough. "You will let your white-haired dog chew me up before you drop me in the ocean. You are a barbarian."

"I lost a good man because you tried to take us captive. There must be justice for it."

"The horse that killed him is dead. How does that concern me? If you hadn't cut the horse's neck, your friend would've been fine. Blame yourself."

Yngvar backhanded his knuckles across Rida's face. The Arab yelped with surprise. Thorfast, Bjorn, and Ewald all laughed. He knew Rida spoke the truth, but was loath to hear it. He wondered if Thorfast would agree with the Arab.

"There is a huge Arab fleet headed to Sicily. It blocks our way out of the Mediterranean Sea. What do you know of this? I may let you live if you are useful."

"Ah, so you think the Caliphate shares all its plans with Rida al-Ghazi? You flatter me, barbarian. In truth, there was a time when the powerful and noble walked beside my family. But poor Rida has fallen to shame and ruin. He and his family dwell in the desert with his band of horsemen. We are shit stuck to the bottom of the Caliphate's sandals. Long have they tried to scrape us away, but somehow we remain. Yet a huge Caliphate fleet? It can only mean war with the Byzantines. They forever vie for Sicily. The Caliphate will claim it, but the Byzantines cling to their memories of glory long lost. They call themselves Romans still. Such foolishness."

Yngvar shook his head. "You are worthless. You've told me nothing. Sicily is already fallen, and the Byzantines are in retreat. They will not return, at least not anytime soon."

"So, that is what I have heard. But only rumors. Yet enough of the same rumors make me believe it must be true. That is very good news for Rida's family but bad news for Rida himself."

Yngvar studied the Arab, wondering if the Rida he mentioned was himself or another person of the same name. The old Arab might have struck his head when Valgerd threw him from his horse.

"You speak nonsense," Yngvar said. "If you cannot be plainer, then we will judge you for your crime and decide your punishment. It will not take long."

Rida shrugged his shoulders. "My half-brother serves the emir of Sicily. He must enjoy the conquest of that island. But he is why I had to flee so far and live on a barren coast with Berbers and others I'd rather not associate with. So you see, with his power growing I will never return to the life I had as a young man."

Rida's dark eyes unfocused and he looked at something no one else he could see.

"But I have been gone so long, that dream died years ago. My wife and daughter would not recognize me now. And soon my name will be forgotten by even the fools who followed me into ruin. I will rot at the bottom of the sea."

"That is likely your fate, Rida al-Ghazi."

Yngvar turned his back on the Arab. Ewald remained poised with his spear, brows raised as if asking permission to impale Rida.

"I didn't get all that," Thorfast said. "But your expression tells me he had nothing interesting to say. Not surprising. Just a grubby Arab who thought himself a king because he owned some horses. Let's have done with him."

"His family served the emir of Sicily," Yngvar said. It seemed a significant point, but he could not connect it to anything that mattered now.

"Well, that's cause enough to kill him," Bjorn said. He grabbed his ax that leaned against the gunwales. "Hold him over the side and I'll crack open his head. Don't want his brains staining the deck."

But a formless thought worked at Yngvar's mind. The golden

armband, King Agamemnon's crown, itched his arm. He rubbed it as he thought. Was the king trying to warn him?

"He may be a valuable hostage," Yngvar said. "Our way passes through the Arab fleet, if they're still arrayed against us."

"I'm sure the whole Arab fleet will stop to chat with us and ask if we have a friend of the emir aboard," Thorfast said, mocking Yngvar's thoughtful tone. "After all, he looks like royalty with that torn, dust-stained robe of his. And if I'm not wrong, I think our friend has pissed himself. The Arabs will welcome us and probably pay a reward worth more than all the gold we have aboard right now."

Bjorn roared with laughter. Yngvar looked back to Rida, whose defiance seemed to have ebbed away. He did have a dark stain on his light blue robe by his crotch.

"Lord, do you think what he said is true?" Alasdair stood with Valgerd, both holding hands, and studied Rida.

"He has no reason to lie," Yngvar said. "He thinks his life is at an end. He's pissed himself with fear of torture and death."

"Then he might really be a useful hostage," Alasdair said. "You are not wrong, lord."

"We are just full of disagreements today," Thorfast said. "The Arab has no use to us. We are not going to Sicily. We're going home."

"Well, it would not make much difference to keep him alive until we are away from here," Alasdair said.

"He's a drain on food and water," Thorfast said. "And then he'll need to shit and piss, and we can't even get a bucket under him while he's tied up there. I don't want to smell his shit for the next week. I don't want to look at him for the next week."

"I will ensure justice," Yngvar said. "But it needn't be swift. I have chosen vengeance so often, and it has not always repaid my choice. I believe the Arab may yet serve a purpose. The gods placed him with us for a reason we cannot yet see."

"Well, I'm done playing games for the gods," Thorfast shouted. His face flushed red. "We have no business in Sicily. He has no value. He's a drain on us. I say he should face justice for Ragnar's death."

"Thorfast," Yngvar said, trying to instill patience into his voice. "I have decided to keep him alive a while longer. I did not forgive him for Ragnar's death."

The red on Thorfast's face deepened to purple.

"I don't give a fuck what you have decided! Keeping the Arab alive affects all of us. We vote on this as a crew. You'll not be making all the decisions."

Yngvar stepped back. Thorfast's eyes nearly glowed with rage. Even Bjorn set his ax down and raised his callused hand for peace.

"Come on, now. Ain't no reason to get so mad."

"I'm fucking mad! I've been through the shit for this pile of fucking gold. Everyone is dying. We're all fucking cursed. And we're fanning that Arab's fat ass! He killed my friend. I want a vote."

For the second time this day, Gyna appeared as the voice of calm. She put her hand on Thorfast's shoulder.

"We'll have that vote," she said. "And you'll live with the outcome even if you don't like it."

Thorfast blinked at her, then narrowed his eyes at Yngvar.

"Explain it to the freemen. I didn't have all the free time you did to learn to speak fucking Greek."

Yngvar's arm itched beneath the gold band. He looked from Gyna, to Bjorn, to Alasdair and Valgerd. Ewald had lowered his spear. No one spoke.

He swallowed and slowly nodded to Thorfast.

"We'll hold a vote."

The sun disappeared behind dark clouds, and the wind blew hard against the hull to drive them off course.

13

The ship drifted with the strong wind. The deck rocked and an oar that had fallen from the rack now scraped across the boards to clatter against the treasure chests set by the mast. Yngvar held the rails with one hand for balance. Hamar stood with him, struggling with the tiller. He had to follow the course set by the wind. This was the greatest weakness of all Norse longships. Yngvar knew Petronius did not need to fear capsizing in a strong wind. But the lightness and shallow draught of the Norse longship meant it could easily flip.

So they headed directly north rather than east.

The crew assembled before him, all seated on sea chests, casks, or boxes. Alasdair stood beside Yngvar, but he smiled at Valgerd who made a seat out of a large coil of rope attached to the anchor stone. Gyna, Bjorn, and Ewald stood at the opposite end, wrapped in cloaks even though the wind was warm. A light cloak warded against wind burn, and Yngvar wished he had worn his. But explaining the vote to the crew in two different languages preoccupied him.

Thorfast stood at the far end, but opposite Gyna and the others. It pained Yngvar to see him standing there alone, arms folded, scowling at their fat prisoner tied to the mast.

Rida remained bound, his dark beard flipping with the wind. He tilted his head to catch Yngvar's attention.

"I am flattered, barbarian. I have generated so much discussion."

"You are being judged for the death your horse caused," Yngvar said. "This is your last chance to speak in your defense. Some men speak Greek. They'll witness your defense."

Rida laughed as if he were not tied to a mast and awaiting death.

"You should judge my horse or you your girl. If she had not pushed me from the saddle, I might have prevented your friend's death."

"What were your plans for the girl?" Yngvar nodded to Valgerd. She sat sunk into the coiled rope, her clear eyes narrowed at Rida. She spoke Greek better than anyone, but Rida did not know this.

"She was a hostage," Rida said. He seemed offended but also could have been mocking Yngvar. "I could not trust you with weapons in my home. As you have shown me, I was right."

"You wanted more than a hostage," Yngvar said, stepping closer. "I saw how you looked at her."

"You will judge me for what you believe were my thoughts?" Rida snorted. "Go on with your mock trial. I know the outcome as well as you do."

The ship rocked with the violent waves and the wind pushing it north. Hamar tied the tiller in place to ease his work, but leaned on it as he waited. The rest of the crew looked expectantly. Thorfast smiled bitterly, arms folded and leaning on the rails.

"You know what to do," Yngvar said in Frankish. Valgerd translated to Greek for the freemen. "There are thirty-two of us. You all have a vote on the Arab's life. I say he should live a while longer, for he may have a purpose to our future. We would judge him once we know that purpose. Others believe he should face swift justice for Ragnar's death."

Yngvar looked to Thorfast, who nodded sharply to this last statement.

"So raise your hands if you want him dead now."

Twenty-nine hands rose above the crew's heads.

Rida roared with laughter.

Only Gyna, Alasdair, and Yngvar stayed their hands.

Gyna clucked her tongue at Ewald, who might not have understood what he voted for. She then slapped Bjorn's arm, which he raised high overhead.

"It's my vote, woman. Why do we got to feed an Arab who wanted to kill us?"

"Because he might have some worth alive. We could kill him later, you fool."

Alasdair paled, staring at Valgerd's raised arm. He blinked repeatedly, his hand reaching for the wooden cross that he no longer wore.

Yngvar felt heat on his face. The arms remained wavering overhead, and he motioned them down. Thorfast clapped his hands in triumph.

"It is a fair vote," he said. "And no one wants this worthless sack of flesh hanging around. He earned his death."

"We promised to set him ashore," Yngvar said. It was a weak and meaningless statement.

"None of the Arabs expected us to really do that," Thorfast said. "You saw it in their faces. They made peace with his loss and let him go. They just didn't want to cause his death. But they were happy to be rid of him."

Yngvar scratched the back of his head and looked to Rida. His eyes were bright with sarcasm.

"So you kill me now, just as I knew you would. My arms are cold and numb. It will be good to be free of the ropes for a moment, even if it is to die. So go on. I am ready to find paradise."

Yngvar looked back to his crew. They appeared saddened, even though they claimed victory. Each must have their own reasons for their vote. Yet Yngvar was stricken by how little he understood his own men. They had been willing to do as he asked, even when they did not believe in it. It was a strange sense, one that blended disappointment with pride.

"Thorfast, you'll do the bloody work," Yngvar said. "But you'll clean up any mess you leave on the deck."

"I'm not interested in messes," Thorfast said. He drew a long dagger, ironically a Byzantine blade that tapered to a point. "I just want to gut him and throw him in the sea. Ragnar's ghost will find him down there and make him pay. That's all I want."

"It's the will of the crew," Yngvar said. "You were right, and I was wrong. I am sorry."

Thorfast turned to him, his face tight with anger. But when their eyes met, it seemed to recede. "Never mind it. I just want to get out of this place. It is not just an island that is cursed. It's this whole fucking sea."

Alasdair and Valgerd now huddled together, and it seemed they fiercely disagreed with their choices. Yngvar could not hear the words, but the frowns, Alasdair's gesticulations, and Valgerd's crossed arms revealed more than words alone.

Gyna was chastising Bjorn and Ewald. Her nephew smiled happily, leading Yngvar to wonder if the boy was simple. Bjorn imitated Valgerd's crossed arms and turned his one good eye aside.

"Of course he should pay," Gyna said as Yngvar walked up to them. "But he also might have a use to us. We'll never know now."

"Auntie, he's a killer. A bad man," Ewald said. "We kill bad men, yes?"

"You will one day be king of all the Saxons?" Yngvar asked. Ewald beamed at him and nodded. "Well, remember this lesson. Men, even bad men, have their uses. Do not throw a life away so readily."

Both Gyna and Bjorn looked at him with raised brows. He rubbed his face and groaned.

"I'm not a friend of the Arabs. I just have a feeling the gods wanted him to be with us. The gods do not talk to me. But I have guessed at their whispers, and I have seldom been wrong. Now, are we throwing a boon from the gods back into their faces?"

"We'll know soon enough," Gyna said, nodding toward the mast.

Thorfast stood with his dagger ready as others untied Rida. The crew was ready for vengeance, Frank and freeman both cried out for blood. Ragnar had straddled both of their worlds, being a Greek-speaking Norseman. His death meant more to everyone than either Lucas the Byzantine's or Nordbert's.

Rida shouted something in his own language, looking toward the sky. But Thorfast tore him free of the entangling ropes and ended his cries. The wind blew stronger now, pressing Rida's blue robe to his body. Thorfast's white hair blew across his face causing him to twist his head about to better see.

Hamar looked to the sky as well.

"Something's not right," he said. "The weather's changing for the worse and it's changing fast. I feel it in my joints."

"You need not feel it there," Yngvar said. "The sky is growing darker by the moment."

He had heard tales of violent storms that came from nowhere and ravaged ships and shorelines. Humidity increased. Yngvar smelled it and felt it on his face.

"Thor is angry with us."

Thorfast and Bjorn dragged Rida forward. The fat man struggled, but more to recover his dignity than to resist. The strong wind flipped Thorfast's cloak over his head. Bjorn laughed and helped untangle him.

"Lord, maybe you should stop this?" Alasdair left Valgerd with her arms folded. His face was still red.

"Wait, you can't believe we've angered Thor?"

"No, lord, but a storm is coming the moment we chose to kill the Arab. It must be a sign."

As if to emphasize Alasdair's words, a gust of wind shoved against the ship. The hull rocked to one side, and water broke across the rails. A blast of warm water struck Yngvar and salt ran into his mouth. He stumbled forward but grabbed the rail to keep upright. His eyes shut against the sting, but he blinked it away.

When he opened his eyes, it had knocked half the crew flat. Thorfast and Bjorn were on their hands and knees, while Rida sat like a fat bear cub beside them.

Thorfast's dagger had fallen from his grip.

"The dagger!" Yngvar shouted.

Another wave struck the ship as the wind refused to relent.

"Tie off," Hamar shouted. "To the rails. The storm will hit us hard."

The dagger skidded across the deck, carried by flowing water. It bumped into Rida's leg.

"Thorfast!" Yngvar shouted. He could not wait another moment and lunged forward.

But a third wave smashed into the ship, and now scoured the deck. Yngvar felt as if he had stepped on ice. He crashed hard on his back, and warm sea water sloshed over his face. He rolled helplessly with the force of the breaking wave, blinded.

All the crew cried out in panic. The sky had gone black with clouds that ambushed them while they voted on Rida's fate. Their ship was fast and flexible, but easily swamped. The force of the oncoming storm already threatened to sink them.

"Tie off!"

"Unstep the mast!"

"The gold!"

These shouts rang through Yngvar's head as he shook away the sea water. He was facing the gunwales. With a curse, he flipped around and castled up to his feet.

Rida had seized Thorfast's dagger.

In the rolling chaos, he had seized Valgerd as well.

The two were drenched. Rida rested with his back to the gunwales. His perfectly black beard had plastered to his chest. His dark skin showed through patches of his soaked robe. Thorfast's dagger was at Valgerd's pale neck. The scar from the last time she had been in the same position was still fresh. Her golden hair was flat against her head. She held her head back from the dagger point.

"Now if you had just kept your word," Rida shouted over the roaring wind. "Then this would never have happened. Set me ashore or she dies."

Alasdair sprang. His sword was already free from its sheath.

A wave buffeted the ship.

A blast of green water exploded behind Alasdair, engulfing him. Rida and Valgerd disappeared from sight. Yngvar continued to leap forward, reaching to where he expected to find Rida.

Only he was gone.

And Valgerd with him.

Alasdair landed against the rails at the same moment. His sword shined with water. His eyes were bright with hatred.

He shouted, but in the next moment the storm's full force struck them.

The ship spun with the wind. One of the freemen flew overboard by Yngvar's side.

"Tie off!" Hamar yelled again. He had done as much, Yngvar could see. But the world had become darkness, wind, and sea foam. Bodies lay flat in terror on the deck. Yngvar held the rails, but his wet hands would never hold against the violence.

The ship tipped the other way. A heavy chest of gold slid to the other side. Yngvar lost his grip but grabbed Alasdair in time to pull him back. He was leaning over the rails calling Valgerd's name.

They both rolled back, tumbling through saltwater as debris washed over them. Yngvar crashed headfirst into the gunwales. White flashes exploded across his vision from the intense pain. But he still held Alasdair's shirt in his hand.

"We need to tie off," he said.

Alasdair looked at him through coppery hair clinging flat to his face. His eyes were wide with shock and he did not seem to see anything.

The ship continued to rock and spin. Rain sheeted across the deck now, slashing like a cloud of cold needles across Yngvar's exposed skin. But he found the rope ties and bound one to Alasdair's leg. The water had soaked the rope, making a strong tie difficult. But when he had finished tying it to Alasdair's leg, he ran the other end through the rails. It wasn't the securest spot, but in the rocking waves and blinding winds it was all he could do.

"Pull it tight," he yelled into Alasdair's ears. "I'll see to the others."

He stood. The ship lurched and he crashed to his side. A man, he could see more than a dark smudge, slammed beside him. His hand reached out to Yngvar's. Their fingers brushed, but the crewmen swept along the deck and vanished into the wave breaking over the side. It blasted Yngvar back. Rather than stand, he crawled.

He pulled forward to reach Thorfast, who was clinging to one of the chests of gold. It had not moved yet.

"This is not safe enough," Yngvar shouted to him. "Tie off."

He pointed to the mast, but found it was gone. His heart flipped with terror. He had not even heard it snap. Then he saw four heroic crewmen setting the mast down while two others stowed their sail.

He pushed the rope into Thorfast's hands, then went to join the crewmen.

Together they tied down the mast and secured the sail. Rigging had snapped and lashed at them as they worked. No one spoke. Every face was bright with fear. But they knew their duty and had risked their lives for it.

So the storm pummeled them. The ship groaned and creaked. They crested waves then sped down into troughs. They screamed in terror, begged God for their lives. Most had tied off. Some still had not. Yngvar at last had tied his ankle to the rails alongside Alasdair, who sat as if he had just awakened from a dream. Waves and wind did not seem to rouse him.

The ties did save some lives where they held. Yngvar helped haul a man back aboard the ship once he had been washed over the side and dragged inverted through the water. For another, his ties were not well made and he vanished into the sea when a wave scoured the deck.

The terror of a violent storm gripped them for what seemed days. But as quickly as the violent storm had struck them, it just as quickly left them.

The waves subsided. The rain eased then trickled away. Clouds broke up to clumps of gray smudges. The ship rocked and creaked.

Throughout the madness, the covered gold at the center of the deck remained mostly unmoved. A single chest had slid from beneath the seal-skin tarp.

Oars and broken wood scattered the deck. Men lay facing the sky, their clothes stuck to their bodies and the boards underneath them. Some raised their heads, looking around as if they had just awakened from a nightmare.

Bjorn and Gyna had huddled together. As he unfolded his massive body from her, she popped up and looked across the deck to Yngvar. Her eyes were wide with fear and she blinked at him. Her nephew, Ewald, clung to her. He did not look much like the future king of the Saxons and more like a scared boy clinging to his mother's side.

Thorfast had survived. He had scrambled to Hamar, who had probably helped to tie him off. They both rested against the steering oar that had been taken aboard.

Valgerd and Rida were gone.

He looked back to Alasdair, who sat staring at nothing. A fire flared in Yngvar's guts. He reached a tentative hand to Alasdair's shoulder, but he did not respond to it. Rather than force him to speak, he instead worked out the knot tying him to the rails. Once it fell free, Yngvar turned to his own rope. The waterlogged rope fought him, fraying his fingernails as he dug at the knot. But he worked it out, and it fell away to let relief flood his left foot. Needles seemed to prick at his soles. He removed his boots to dump out water then rub down his tingling skin. He studied Alasdair as he did.

"She's gone," Alasdair said. The words were spoken so softly Yngvar first thought it the stirring of the wind. But his unfocused eyes had shifted to Yngvar.

"I am sorry," he said. "She was a good woman. You will see her again, you know. Your god has called her to his side."

"My god," Alasdair repeated. His hand formed a fist over his chest where his cross used to hang. His brows pulled together and he gritted his teeth. "My god has never listened to a word of my prayers."

Yngvar could not deny the truth in that. Yet he was wise enough to keep silent. He lowered his eyes, then stood.

"We will remember Valgerd for all she has done for us. We would never have survived without her."

Alasdair remained frowning, his white-knuckled fist clutched over his heart. As much as he wished to comfort his friend, others had been swept out to sea as well. He had his whole crew to consider.

"Hamar, do you know where we are now?"

Square-faced Hamar shook his head. He struggled to his feet as the ship continued to rock with the subsiding waves. To one side, a black storm ran away to the horizon. To the other side, a blue strip of mountainous land emerged.

"Somewhere we don't want to be," he said.

Yngvar nodded. If they had been driven north and now faced land, he could not imagine they were anywhere safe. Most likely they had traded the Arab threat for Byzantines. He lowered his head and pinched the bridge of his nose.

"Somewhere we don't want to be."

14

The rain continued to patter against the deck. It seemed almost apologetic as if gently nudging Yngvar for acceptance. The crew had recovered enough and now assessed the damage to the ship. Foremost was Hamar, leaning over rails to examine the hull, inspecting the destroyed rigging, all while tossing broken wood and other debris into the dark sea. A line of crewmen followed, mostly Franks, and all shook their heads.

"We just fixed all our rigging lines," Thorfast said. He stood with Yngvar, soaked like everyone else.

"We damaged some strakes," Yngvar said. "We need to bail. The ship needs repairs."

Thorfast gave a sharp nod. "Better than the ship being broken scraps on the waves."

"Depends who you ask."

They both looked to Alasdair. He stood gripping his hands on the rails. An empty scabbard hung by his side. His sword had been lost along with the woman he had planned to marry.

"It's my fault," Thorfast said. "I'm dreading to speak to him."

"It was fate," Yngvar said. "You did nothing wrong."

"Then why do I feel so guilty? I'm not one to feel much guilt. But look at him. I wrecked his life as surely as any storm. It was my dagger."

"Wasn't a dagger that took her. It was the sea. Fate sent a wave to collect her." Yngvar drew a deep breath. "Collect her and four others."

"Fate was kinder than it could've been," Thorfast said.

"We're not home yet."

Thorfast snorted. "You're seeing things my way now. It's the gold and the curse. We'll never get home until you end it. We need magic, not weapons, for this fight."

Yngvar bit his lip. The conversation made the band around his arm feel heavier. Yet the king had thus far only helped Yngvar. He had saved him during the earthquake. He had warned him about Rida, though Yngvar had misunderstood that message. To his mind, King Agamemnon was his ally as long as he promised to bring his glory to the north.

Yet he lost so many lives since taking the gold.

Yngvar ordered the bailing to begin. The fittest men gathered buckets, emptied them of the rain and sea water, then formed a bailing line.

"We can make landfall," Hamar said. "But we must plug these leaks. Strakes have cracked and I'd like to be sure there's nothing worse beneath the waterline. Hate for us to break up in the next squall."

"Agreed," Yngvar said. "We just need a place to beach. But repairs will need things we can't find ourselves, at least not quickly."

Hamar agreed, then scrubbed his square face with his strong hands. "I'll set a course. Once we learn where we are, maybe those maps might help us figure out where to go. You know how to read them?"

"As good as anyone else here. I am not sure how to use them to navigate but we could at least determine the closest settlement. Keep a sharp eye for sails, too. If anyone learns we have this much treasure aboard, we'll never see home again."

Yngvar ordered the men to their tasks, promising a time for remembering the dead. Alasdair did not appear to hear and remained alone and staring out to sea. Even Gyna did not approach him. "Words won't help him," she said. "He will speak to us when he is ready."

The renewed purpose helped the crew recover from the horrors inflicted on them. They reset the mast, but with the rigging lines destroyed they were still better sailing under oar power. Hamar guided them along the coast until they found a suitable shoreline to beach.

Whatever storm had blown them north had not touched the shores of this place. The beach was empty and free of debris. After beaching the ship, the crew spread out on the beach to stretch and relax. Hills of brown sand covered in dull green shrubs surrounded them. Yngvar felt every shoreline looked the same. The green sea was at high tide and the black clouds on the horizon were parting for the sun. Deeper inland, rocky mountains rose above the hills.

"Ewald, take some men and scout the area," Yngvar said. "And this time be thorough."

The young Saxon thumped his chest. "I will find any danger."

As Hamar and his assistants, Franks who understood basic ship-building, inspected the damage, Yngvar did not want to see it himself. If he looked at it, he thought, somehow it would become worse. So he spread the cloth maps on a flat rock and sat to examine them. Two of the freemen joined him, along with Thorfast. Gyna had gone with Ewald, and Bjorn followed Hamar, inspecting the hull. Alasdair remained alone on the ship.

"Which way is north?" Thorfast asked.

Yngvar pointed, letting his finger linger over the rough canvas. He squinted to all directions, not sure what he was looking for. He knew the position of the cursed island on the map. From there he guessed where they had landed in Africa. Based on what he knew now, he was on a large island which could be in Greece. He only knew this island seemed as large as Sicily. He could not estimate its size because of the storm. He had only seen it within sight of its shores. But there was one large island on the map. He could not read the word printed there. None of the freemen could read it either. But one spoke a name.

"Crete," he said. "That must be Crete. Is that where we are?"

Yngvar rubbed his head. "I have heard that name before. The commander spoke of it. If Valgerd was here ..."

Thorfast hissed through his teeth. "Better not let Alasdair hear you thinking aloud. But what about this island? You look worried."

He repeated the name. Commander Staurakius had spoken of another island just like Sicily, one the emperor thought was more important to his empire. It was an island full of Arab pirates that clung to the belly of the empire like a leech. One day soon the emperor would devote all his might to reclaiming that island, which Staurakius had feared would divert reinforcements for Sicily. That island's name had been Crete.

"That's where the Arab fleet headed," Yngvar said. "To Crete. They have defeated the Byzantine emperor in Sicily. But the Byzantines want Crete more. So his armies must be here to fight the Arabs, who are coming to aid their kin. We've landed in the middle of war."

Thorfast smiled at him.

"Well, then this can't be Crete since this beach is at peace."

Yngvar collected the map, standing up to look to the hills. The freemen stood with him, each looking worried as if an army might sweep down.

"Even if it is not Crete, we are close enough to it to be in danger. The Byzantines must come from the north and east. The Arabs from the west. We need to sail south and skirt them."

"Our ship needs repairs," Thorfast said. He shielded his eyes against the glare and scanned the sea. "There's nothing coming that I can see. My eyes are better than yours. So I think we have time."

Yngvar rolled up the maps and slipped them back into their cases. The two freemen looked to him for direction. He patted their shoulders.

"Until we know more, fear nothing. We are as flies to these armies. As long as they do not know what is on our ship, they will let us scatter just as flies do."

An hour later, Hamar concluded that besides the rigging, three loose strakes had to be replaced before the ship could face a long sea journey. He judged the ship had weathered the storm better than he might have guessed. "She's flexible," he said. "But sturdy-made. I have never known a finer ship. It was worth all the sacrifice to bring her back to us."

As the sky darkened with the close of day, Ewald, Gyna, and their small scouting party returned.

"There is a town with some farms surrounding it north of here," Gyna said. "Ewald could get to the farms. They're Arabs. I thought we'd find Byzantines here."

They had all joined on the beach, even listless Alasdair. They sat around the spot they had planned to build a fire if there was no immediate danger. Yngvar looked at the pit and circle of stone as he spoke.

"We are in Crete," he said. "This is a dangerous land. Those Arabs won't deal with us and the Byzantines are sure to arrive soon. Maybe they are here already. It is a large island."

"We can try to sail farther west," Hamar offered. "There may be better chances of finding repairs away from the danger. But if another storm hits us, well, the ship will not hold together."

Yngvar waved the suggestion away. "One Arab village will not like us more than another. The Byzantines will want to press us into serving in their army. I'd rather not risk breaking up at sea. Besides, we need more than repairs. The waves have swept away supplies or spoiled them with sea water. We must try these towns. If we cannot get what we want by peaceful trade, we will take what we need."

They camped without a fire that night, eating the last of their preserved fish and pickled vegetables. Yngvar had never acquired a taste for the food of this land, but he could not afford to eat well. He had to eat full. The last of their ale went down sour, but no one complained. Alasdair drank more than his usual fill, and while not drunk, his face was flushed and his eyes drooping.

With men finding a place to bed down and a night-watch rotation set, Yngvar had dispensed with his duties. He plucked Alasdair by his shoulder.

"Walk with me," he said. "I need your advice."

He led Alasdair away while the rest of his Wolves looked on, half in their sleep sacks.

They tottered along the beach until they were away from anyone else.

"How can I serve, lord?" Alasdair laughed. "I have no other distractions now."

"I am sorry about what happened," Yngvar said. "It's my fault."

"How so, lord?" Alasdair backed up, frowning. "You didn't push her off the ship. That was God's work. He's mysterious, as I've been told. So mysterious I cannot understand anything God does. I am not sure I want to understand anymore. He's not talking to me currently. Maybe never did."

"Don't say that," Yngvar said. "You should respect your god. I know we've had our differences. But sometimes I think your god helps you. And that helps me. So I need you to forgive your god and be the old Alasdair I trust."

Alasdair's eyes grew wide. "You want me to forgive God?"

"Why not? I forgive Thor for nearly wrecking my ship and throwing me to the Arabs again. It's only practical. I will need his help before this is all done. So we can't be fighting, can we?"

"You can fight with Thor?"

"Didn't say I could win the fight. But Thor needs me. He needs all of us if he will defeat the Christian god, who seems to be winning everywhere I go. So, I forgive him, and I'll still honor him. We need each other, so he'll probably aid me if I bring him enough glory."

"Well, God does not need me," Alasdair said. "And He will soon throw me into hell, for I am a sinner. I have had blasphemous thoughts, lord. All day I have been thinking to turn away from Him for the old gods."

"Don't do it," Yngvar said. "Don't look so surprised. We need all the gods we can get working for us. If your god gets mad at you now, maybe he'll try to kill all of us. Besides, your god is all about love and peace. So if he took Valgerd, it's probably because he wanted her to avoid the worst of what's coming. Maybe he feared she'd become a pagan like me. Come on, I've learned that word. Don't raise your brows at me. That's what you Christians call us."

"I never called you a pagan, lord. But it is what some say, and it is not a kind word."

"Of course it's not. Most Christians aren't kind to begin with. Anyway, Valgerd is safe now from all danger. No more suffering for her. And I'm sure if she's gone to your heaven, she'll pull you up to her side when you're dead. That is a pity, for I wish you to fight alongside me until Ragnarok. But we're going different ways, it seems."

Alasdair rubbed his eyes and stared at his feet.

"Thank you, lord. I had not thought about it this way. God has given her eternal peace and taken her from the suffering of this world. This gold would've been a temptation to sin for her. But now she has gone to heaven, preserved at God's table."

"Sounds right to me," Yngvar said. "It doesn't make it any easier to have lost her. You will see her again, but not too soon. Be brave until that day comes."

Alasdair nodded, and though he was drunk, it seemed to Yngvar the stranger had left him and old Alasdair had returned.

"Now, we sleep. Tomorrow we go to find the Arabs and test our luck. Before we do, though, you and the others must pray to your god, and I will pray to mine. I think we will need boons from both to get off this island and away without harm."

15

Petronius was sailing for Crete.

He was not alone, but part of a convoy of ships all swept up at port back into the reforming Byzantine navy. The emperor was conquering Crete, it seemed, and it required every fighting man. Nine other ships sailed with him along the rolling waves of the Mediterranean Sea. The air was thick with the scent of a storm that raged along the horizon. He watched it now while Isaac shouted orders on his behalf. These tasks were more to keep the men occupied than to help speed them along their way.

For he planned to slip from the convoy at the first opportunity.

So he peered at the storm as sea mist flecked his face from waves breaking across the prow. All the sails were full, but that would change as they neared the storm. Such sudden and violent storms have terrorized sailors of the Mediterranean since the time of the ancients. He wished one would catch them, providing excellent cover to slip south and away from his commander. Yet he chased off the thought.

The Norsemen had fled south. They must land in Africa somewhere opposite of Greece. They would have searched for resupply, probably raiding coastal villages to take what they needed. By now, they would be following the coast west toward the Strait. All of Petronius's gold and his oath of vengeance would slip right past him as he sailed in the wrong direction.

"Sir, the men are wondering when we will make our run."

Isaac had stepped beside him, speaking discreetly over his shoulder as if the officers aboard the other nine ships might overhear. Petronius caught the scent of wine on his breath.

"We are at the center of the convoy, if the crew has not noticed. We'll peel off as soon as we can."

"Sir, the crew fears the Norsemen will escape."

"I prayed to God that He will let us be His sword against the pagans. We will avenge Cyril and be granted the reward of the Norsemen's gold. I am certain."

Yet he was uncertain, and with each hour that passed he felt less certain he would ever seize the gold his cousin had died for.

"Perhaps we could make it seem we've had an accident," Isaac said.

"I've thought of that," Petronius said. "But short of accidentally ramming another ship, I cannot think of what we could do."

They both stood in silence. Buying bows and arrows at port along with identifying themselves as the Byzantine navy had proven to be a poor decision. While they now had bows and enough arrows to handle a Norse ship, the Navy had also caught them. He had spent too long out of touch and did not realize it had been reforming after Messina.

"We will make port in Greece tonight," Petronius said. "On the southern tip of Laconia. That would be the only time we could think of making an escape. The others would pursue us, and if caught I needn't tell you what will happen to us."

"Sir, are you saying we will give up?"

Petronius met Isaac's stare. He saw a resolution there he had not expected. A fire of greed smoldered there. Petronius had seen it a thousand times in other men over his career.

"You think I am weak, do you?" He drew closer to Isaac. "You wonder if I've lost my heart now that we're back in the navy."

"The men wonder," Isaac said, raising his chin to the challenge.

"You did such a good job convincing them to claim that gold. Now it seems you've changed your mind. It is confusing, sir."

They remain locked in a stare. Petronius wondered what would happen when they claimed all that gold. Would Isaac turn on him? He believed Isaac was a better man than himself, but did not depend upon it.

"Now that the men are back under the discipline of the navy, they are willing to fight for the freedom the gold will give us. I would've saved my breath had I know we'd get dragged back into this." Petronius patted Isaac's shoulder. "Don't fret. I will get us away from this convoy and back on the Norsemen's trail."

Isaac stepped back, saluted, then returned to the crew. Petronius noted two men looking between him and Isaac, probably wondering what Isaac had determined.

So as they sailed, Petronius considered all the possibilities of escape from this convoy. He would need to set himself at the edge of the convoy and be prepared to break before reaching Crete. His other choice was to sail off during the night, which might be safer.

By nightfall they reached port in Laconia where they would wait to rendezvous with the emperor's fleet heading for Chandax, Crete's main city and seat of the self-styled emir of Crete. His ship would be in the vanguard and engage any Arabs threatening the landing. From there, they might assign him to patrols, which would be another opportunity to escape but likely too late to catch the Norsemen.

The end of a day at port was a welcomed relief for his crew, who had spent too long at sea. They filed into the town to find drink and women. Petronius completed his duties aboard ship, then questioned the locals in hopes of any news of the Norsemen.

To his great surprise, a fisherman had spotted a Norse ship.

"Just got news today, master," the fisherman said. He was storing his net for another day of fishing, standing in his small boat with two men who looked like younger versions of himself. "I've not seen it with my own eyes, but a trader did. A Norse ship came out of that storm from last night. Heading to Crete. The trader had just fled there, and expected the Norsemen might be mercenaries."

"Where's the merchant?" Petronius asked.

"Gone into town, master. I expect his ship is anchored here somewhere." The fisherman swept his hand over the spread of the port. There were scores of ships at anchor, and his own ten ships had crowded the port. The western horizon was an orange blaze, turning the crowds of people into a jumble of shadows. A dozen ships could be traders, and he would waste half the night searching for the right one.

"You're certain it was a Norse ship? Why would he mention this to you?"

The fisherman looked Petronius over as if deciding how rude he could make his answer.

"We were trading news, master. A strange sail is news, especially with the war coming. Though from what I heard, the ship struck no sail nor had any mast. I think he knew the ship's outline well enough from his own experience."

Petronius thanked the fisherman, who seemed relieved at his departure. He strode down the length of piers back to his own ship. As he did, he bumped with sailors from the other ships now making their way into town. Some saluted, others mumbled obligatory apologies. But Petronius's mind was far out to sea.

He bounded onto the deck where he found Isaac and the two others who seemed to be his constant companions. His excitement must have been obvious, for all three turned to him with expectant faces. They failed to greet him as an officer, but Petronius did not care.

"I've news of the Norsemen. They are in Crete."

The two crewmen looked to Isaac, who clapped his hands together. "God be praised. He has delivered them to us as I knew He would. It is God's will that such treasures not fall into heathen hands."

"It's God's will," repeated the two crewmen.

"Yes, it is," Petronius said. "But they have not handed us the treasure yet. I'm not sure where on Crete they've landed. If they made it out of that storm, then truly God is preserving the gold for us. That flimsy ship should've been wrecked. But if was not wrecked then their supplies are ruined. I'd wager they're also taking on water. I can't see it being otherwise."

"They would have made the most direct landfall they could," Isaac said. "Probably on the southwest tip of the island."

Petronius rubbed his beard. His eye was drifting out of focus, he could tell. The left half of his vision grew fuzzy. But his mind was on revenge, thinking of poor Cyril and the spear sticking from his chest. He remembered the cold terror at seeing his cousin's handsome face twisted with the agony of death. His killers were within reach.

"Sir, we need to find an excuse to sail to where the Norsemen have landed," Isaac said. "We'll be headed to Crete but not the right shore."

"I'm aware of that," Petronius said. "Give me some time to think. But whatever the plan, I need all men back on this ship. If an opportunity presents itself tonight, we must be ready. Can you round them?"

"They've only just left a few hours ago, sir," Isaac said. "They can't have gotten into too much trouble yet. They'll be at the inn, getting drunk with half the other men. Seems every captain let their crews ashore."

Petronius grunted. "Well, by rights they're sailing to war. Better let them have their fun now. But that also means there'll be officers near them who aren't drunk."

All three nodded. Petronius would have the same responsibility to ensure his men did not desert the navy before a key battle. Most men would not do such a thing, for a deserter's life was horrible and likely ending in either slavery or life as a boot-licker in a bandit camp. Still, tonight some young men will be told horror stories of battle and get drunk enough to try fleeing. Officers would haul them back to ship and if they were kind would let deserters work off their fears scrubbing the deck. Less understanding officers might whip them as a reminder to others who forgot the price of disloyalty.

He smiled at the thought of leading an entire ship in desertion. That would get him the notoriety in the navy he had always lacked. There would be a bounty on his head, but he would be hard to reach atop a mountain of gold.

"We can't call them back too early," Petronius said. "Or else we'll arouse suspicion. So go monitor them as best you can. Try to keep them sober and bring them back so we can shove off in the night. We'll have to make a run for Crete, or else the Norsemen will get away while we're dragged off to fight Arabs."

A few short months ago, Petronius would have enjoyed nothing more than to fight Arabs. Now it was no better than a nuisance to him. He watched Isaac and his two assistants disappear into the darkening streets. The arrival of a large naval force pumped life into the town. Torches fluttered to light. Prostitutes, con men, traders, and just bored locals flowed out of their homes to find the sailors and seek advantage from them. In another life, he might have been among those numbers. Tonight, instead, he prepared to defect from the navy forever.

As he waited for darkness, he dreamed of chests of gold and silver. Of jewels that sparkled like stars and ancient cups carved with the designs of forgotten craftsmen. He would be richer than any man alive, and Cyril would not have died for nothing. Petronius would find a way to donate some of his wealth in Cyril's name to a church. It needed to be far from here, but a donation would ensure his cousin's place in heaven and perhaps ease some of the many sins Petronius had accumulated over the years.

But his reverie was cut short.

He sat on a barrel in the ship's bow, leaning one arm over the black rigging as he stared at the stars over the sea. But he was drawn back to the dock where a group of men clomped down its length toward him.

Slipping off the barrel, he put his hand on his sword and called out to the nearest crewmen. He nodded toward the approaching figures. When Petronius confronted them at the gangplank, he had four others behind him.

"Captain," Isaac said, saluting. "Captain Leo Lascaris is with me. He'd like to speak with you, sir."

Isaac and his two assistants seemed more like they were being escorted back under Leo's two guards. Leo's dominant posture raked Petronius's nerves. He didn't like Captain Leo, especially since he was one of the three captains who found him and hooked him back into the Navy. His presence could mean nothing good.

"A private word," Leo said. He was a sturdily built man with a round head and tight curly hair cut short. He looked like a cousin to the ancient stone statues of senators in Rome. He had the same predatory, superior expression as those timeless statues.

"Then welcome aboard," Petronius said. He was as welcoming as a desert snake, but this did not bother Leo. He smiled and inclined his head to Isaac. As he bounded up the plank, his guards went with him. Petronius held up his hand. "Private means just the two of us. It's my ship, Captain."

Leo seemed to darken, but then laughed and waved off his men.

The night filled Leo's eyes with black shadow. But the gleam was clear to Petronius. Leo knew something. His lips were tight, like a secret might blurt from them at any moment.

"So, Petronius, my friend, let's talk freely if there is no one else to hear," Leo said, whispering and craning his head around.

"We're alone here," Petronius said. He had returned to where he had been sitting on the barrel.

Leo stared at him with a wicked smile, then licked his lips.

"Your men have been enjoying their time ashore. It seems they haven't lived like this for a long time. They've missed good wine and have partaken in quite a bit of it."

"If they're in trouble, I'll pay for whatever mess they've made."

Leo turned his head to fix him with a single eye.

"Ah, Petronius, I'm sure you can pay. In fact, it seems any of your crew could pay for all the others. They've been throwing around a lot of coin. In fact, I saw one and it wasn't like any coin I know. Certainly, it's not the meager drachmae a sailor should keep in his purse. It's more like the coin from a king's treasury."

Leo smiled, his eyes shifting left and right.

"An ancient king."

Petronius felt his face heating. He had such faith in his men, yet it had all been misplaced. He had thought them all with him, understanding the need for discretion. But once sodden with wine and women, the men had come apart like frayed rope.

"What are you saying, Captain?" He hoped Leo knew less than he was letting on. But the captain sharpened his smile and drew closer.

"You've found gold, dear Petronius. Lots of it. It only takes one hole in the hull to sink a ship. You have a leak, Petronius, and it's a bad one. Your more sensible crew have beaten him into silence. But I know you're after Norsemen who possess more than double the gold you all carry among yourselves. My guess is you're planning to sail tonight in search of it."

Petronius's hand itched over the hilt of his sword. But he could never draw it in time. Leo seemed unarmed, but he had not checked first. Petronius's face blazed with rage and shame. How had he let it come to this?

"You needn't answer," Leo said. "Right now me and my crew are the only ones who know your secret. And we can keep it that way."

"For a price," Petronius said.

"For a price," Leo confirmed. "But I don't want payment. I want in on this hunt. If what I've heard and seen is a good estimate of what treasure is out on the water in a lone ship, then a pouch of coins won't satisfy me. Not when I could have a chest of coins."

"You can't have an equal share," Petronius said. "We've done all the work to get that gold, and the Norsemen stole it from us."

Leo pursed his lips. "Then it is the Norsemen's gold and yours no longer. You lost it. Well, I can help you get it back. Two against one are better odds. Seems they have slipped you once already, and now you have a final chance to recapture it. You bought all those arrows. But what will happen if you don't stop them with arrows? If you're alone, they'll sail right past you. But if you have me, then we can herd them. We can board them and they will have to defend port and starboard. We'll earn an equal share. Because otherwise you may have no share at all."

Petronius closed his eyes. How much had the men revealed? He could punch a hole through the hull himself. But he drew a breath and faced Leo again.

"You'll be a deserter."

Leo snorted. "I don't want to die in Crete. We barely got out of Messina. Do you think me mad enough to follow the emperor into another disaster? No, tonight we can make our escape. You know what we are looking for, so I need you to guide me. You need me to ensure you win the fight against the Norsemen. We have come together for a purpose. We will both be richer for our cooperation. What say you? Companions of convenience? We go our own ways after we divide the gold."

Petronius stared at Leo's outstretched arm. He could use the extra swords against the Norsemen. He risked losing it all if they escaped him again. But now they were at their most vulnerable. They were likely trapped in Arab lands, struggling to recover from the storm, and had no idea Petronius was about to pounce on them.

He had to seek very advantage.

And another warship against the Norsemen only stacked the advantages on his side.

He accepted Leo's arm and the two shook.

The Norsemen were about to feel the strength of a Byzantine navy driven not by duty, but by revenge and greed.

They had no chance against it.

16

Yngvar wrested the last of the barrels aboard the ship. Sweat ran down his naked back, soaking the edge of his pants. He tied back his hair, but it still clung to his skin. The thick scars from Erik Bloodaxe's violent lashing drew silent stares from the Franks. The freemen had seen his scars before and most knew the story. The Franks, however, never heard the tale of his lashing at Erik Bloodaxe's hands. The sun was behind gray clouds, but its heat still prickled along those scars.

"Good business," shouted a wizened Arab trader. He wore a gray robe with a faded purple head cover. He differed from other Arabs he had seen. There appeared to be as many tribes of them as there were people of the North. This one wore a long white beard and had skin as dark as pine bark. His Greek was thick but understandable.

"Good business," Yngvar waved back. Thorfast was slipping the pouch of gold coins into the trader's hands. His guards and assistants, seven strong men, wiped their hands on their thighs and also waved back.

"Who'd expect this from Arabs?" Bjorn set down his cask beside Yngvar's.

"Best hospitality we've had in these southern lands," Yngvar agreed. "Prince Kalim feasted us before trying to kill us. These folk just feasted us."

"But we're not away yet," Gyna said. "And they know we've got gold."

She and Ewald were stacking rope they had purchased at the Arab town.

"And we're not repaired," Yngvar said. "But still we've been granted a rest from greedy men."

The crew took to their work with vigor. Each was excited to have supplies enough to sail straight home. They would have to ration their food carefully and pray there would be no more storms. Yet everyone knew they were set to escape and could row past any danger and not worry.

All for Arab generosity.

For despite this land slipping into war and the Arabs here having a reputation for piracy and evil, they had welcomed Yngvar's careful approach. When they found he could speak Greek, it was not the mark of an enemy to them. They invited all the crew into their homes, fed them, and traded news as they could. The women served them and averted their eyes. But they giggled among themselves when they thought no one watched. They were particularly fascinated with Thorfast's white hair and more than one feigned an accidental brush against it. The trader who now collected his gold and rounded up his empty carts on the beach had dealt fairly with them. He sold all they needed except the ship-building supplies. Yet he kept a good supply of rope suitable to repairing the destroyed rigging.

The gods, or perhaps the Christian God, had seen to aid them for a change.

"The only stain in the snow now is plugging our leaks," Thorfast said as he climbed aboard. The Arab traders now headed toward the scrub-covered hills, their carts trailing behind their tired horses. The afternoon haze painted them in flat shapes of gray, purple, and blue. Their cheerful singing was still audible as they faded away.

"Hamar thinks the trees here can serve for replacement strakes," Yngvar said. "He's got a crew out now felling timber. It will take a few days to make a new strake. We've already traded for pitch and fur to caulk the hull. Things are finally looking good for us."

While they all nodded, Yngvar noticed both Bjorn and Thorfast sneak glances at Alasdair, who was already at work on the rigging.

"It's a hard time," Yngvar said. "His god tests him, but I think he will be fine."

Gyna stood and brushed her hands on her thighs.

"He's the strongest of us all," she said. "I am sad for what happened to Valgerd and I liked her. But I did not like her drawing Alasdair away from us."

Yngvar nodded and looked to Ewald, who was spooling up rope that had fallen over. Perhaps Gyna did not see how Ewald was the same distraction to her as Valgerd had been to Alasdair. But he did not wish the Saxon ill. He wiped the sweat at his brow with the back of his arm.

"We should celebrate tonight," Yngvar said. "We must sample one of these wine casks before trusting them to the open sea."

The crew welcomed the plan. Hamar returned with logs from a nearby stand of trees and shouted praises to the gods. He had found oak in that cluster. He and his assistants spent the hot afternoon splitting the logs, then quartering them, then splitting them again. They worked with axes which had rusted after the storm but were still serviceable. Hamar obsessed over keeping repair tools at hand. While he could fight, it was not his expertise. He was a man who knew the way, and who knew ships. As such, his role in Yngvar's crew was perhaps the most important. Putting him in the shield wall was always Yngvar's last choice.

So they planed and scraped boards. They collected the shavings for fire-building. Had time allowed, they might have used the wood from the back of the bark to fashion cord. They used different axes for different tasks. The fine work of cutting the strake grooves fell to Hamar himself. Once he had settled on this, he had to shape the strake to fit the hull which required him to tie the fresh wood into the right shape and allow it to dry. Before this, he bored holes for the nails that would secure it to the hull.

By nightfall they held their celebrations and the wine disappointed no one. Even Alasdair smiled. They recounted the names of their fallen, with Ragnar and Valgerd being the most recent. They drank to their memories. Then they slept on the beach and dreamed of home, for it must be within their reach now.

The days passed as they waited for the strake to dry and set. Hamar tested it with a fussy pull on its length multiple times a day. After three days he declared they could set the strake the next day, caulk it, and be ready to sail. Their cheers echoed over the hills.

Talk of curses and bad luck had faded. While they had seen ships on the water, these were never more than fishermen at work before the dawn and returning when the sun peaked in the sky. A promontory to the west blocked their view from that direction. But they commanded clear views of the south and eastern approaches. For the first days, Yngvar had posted lookouts on the promontory. But when one man was nearly bitten by a snake, he decided not to risk it. They were leaving the next day, and though war was coming, it had not found this tiny corner of Crete.

Nor had anyone else, it seemed. To Yngvar, this was the most perfect place he could imagine beyond his own home. He now stared out at the crystal waters of the Midgard Sea and experienced regret for leaving such beauty for the gray and dreary north.

By midmorning Hamar stepped back from the strake with a mallet in hand. His brow glistened, and sweat matted his hair. He wiped his face, flicked his hand, then proclaimed the strake repaired.

"Let me rest before we caulk it," he said. They set a bucket of pitch out for the task. Hamar and his assistants sat on the white beach in the blue shadow of the ship. Gyna delivered a skin of water, which Hamar gratefully accepted.

Such a perfect moment. Yngvar felt warmth in his chest. He was taking his gold and friends home, and nothing could stop him now.

Yet the gods heard his thoughts, and Loki chief among them must have mocked this hope.

Two Byzantine patrol ships slipped around the western promontory. Their sails were full and bright in the dazzling sun. Their hulls were black and leaning into a sharp turn.

His stomach flared into heat. For he recognized the distinctive shape of one ship. Just as one recognizes the shape of a familiar man against bright light, so he recognized this shape.

"Petronius," he said. He shielded his eyes and strained to confirm what he knew approached the beach.

Others also noticed. Alasdair, who had been down the shore to be alone with his thoughts, was now running along the surf and screaming.

"Enemies! Byzantines!"

Hamar, Gyna, and the others hidden in the ship's shadow, now leaped up to see what others were already staring at.

"Get the ship on the water," Yngvar shouted. "Launch!"

Hamar stepped back in shock. "We'll be taking on twice the water we were before the strake cracked. It's not caulked."

"We'll outrun them. Hurry!" Yngvar was already herding his men toward the ship. But they had spread out along the beach. They had begun their stay vigilant, but after days of isolation they had grown lax. Their gear was far from them.

Bjorn and Ewald had taken Yngvar's orders without thought and were dragging men toward the ship. But Hamar was blocking their way.

"Do you want to sink? If we can't caulk the strake then water will flow in like it's not there."

The two ships now spread out so that Yngvar would have to pass between them if he tried to reach the open sea.

"How did he find us?" Thorfast asked, rushing up to Yngvar with Alasdair close behind.

"How else? The gods led him to us. Punishment for getting lazy." Yngvar had gathered his gear. Their gold remained safely tied down on their ship along with supplies. But the men had left their swords and shields ready around the campfires.

"We can't leave without our weapons," Alasdair said, still huffing from the run up the shore. "We'll be wolves without fangs."

The crew instinctively went for their war gear first. Hamar continued to block men from nearing the ship. Yngvar grunted and charged across the loose sand to confront him.

"We can bail. We just need to outdistance them, then set ashore to caulk the strake."

Hamar's square face had flushed red. "The strake will open up enough under stress. I can't make hard turns while it's not caulked. Water will pour in."

"Get us to sea," Yngvar said, lowering his voice. "Or we'll lose the ship, the gold, and our lives in the bargain. What would you have us do?"

They stared at each other, but Hamar's eyes turned aside and he sighed. Yngvar clapped his shoulder, then returned to his crew. They at least had not wasted time. They had rearmed and gathered their shields, spears, and swords. One Frank carried a bucket of pitch and a freeman companion carried the sack of fur.

"Get it all aboard," Yngvar waved them forward. "Bjorn, you lead the shove out to the waves. Hurry!"

Bjorn grunted, smacked Ewald's back, and they set against the hull to push the ship into the waves along with a half-dozen others. Yngvar leaped onto the deck, helped Gyna and Alasdair aboard, then went to the prow.

The two ships were drawing apart. There would be no way to the open sea that did not put them in striking range of either. He wondered at their plans. They seemed to offer him a chance to pass through and gain the sea. With the wind in his favor, they would never catch him even with a leaking strake.

"What is the trap, Petronius?" he asked himself. He stumbled, then grabbed the ship's neck as it shoved into the surf. Alasdair arrived beside him, holding the wooden beast head.

"They must fear us, lord," he said. "We rarely remember to set the beast head these days."

Despite his own fears, he smiled at Alasdair, and together they set the snarling beast head on the block made for it. Yngvar had thought it looked like a wolf, but Bjorn had insisted it was a bear. It was all vicious snarls and jagged teeth and wild eyes. Whatever it represented, it was fury carved in wood.

The first waves rolled beneath the hull. Yngvar cooled in relief at the familiar sensation of being lifted into the water. Bjorn howled behind, the ship hardly diminishing the strength of his bellow. The crew aboard the ship set their long oars, prepped the sails, and readied shields and swords by their sides. Rather than fear, he heard their anger and irritation at having their idles ruined. Yngvar grinned at them.

"That's right! These bastards are still chasing our gold. They're jealous thieves. Aren't those two sins to the Christian god?" The Franks called back in anger, while freemen shouted alongside their companions. "Well, let's hasten them to their judgement."

The crew roared in answer. The ship lurched into a swell, then Bjorn clambered over the rails, followed by Ewald and the rest.

Alasdair gave Yngvar a sly look.

"A call to the Christian god? Between you and Gyna, I'm not sure who is changing most."

"Don't get hopeful. I need the men ready for a fight, and it seemed the right thing to say."

Yngvar walked the deck shouting encouragement, yet ever watching the two ships spread out to block them. He felt like a boy playing a game of break-the-shield-wall. One boy would charge and the others would array against him, arms linked to prevent a breakthrough. Bjorn had always been best at that game. It seemed the Byzantines had a similar thought and must have played a similar game as children.

But they had not built his ship to break through anything. They built it to evade, to speed, to slip up a shallow stream to strike then retreat. They built it to fly over the waves toward a distant shore with glittering treasures waiting to be plucked.

When he completed his rounds, he carried his own shield on his arm. He could not guess the Byzantine's plan. To attempt a run around one of them would surely lead to capture. While the Byzantine ships were far larger than his, they were still lithe in comparisons to the main ships of the Byzantine navy. These were agile patrol ships and turned tighter and gained speed quicker than their larger cousins.

Petronius was also a good sailor. He would know Yngvar's tricks, or at least the obvious ones.

"What's the plan?"

Thorfast gathered the other Wolves around Yngvar. Their shadows flowed over him as he thought.

"We can't go between them, since that's the bait they're offering."

"It's the surest way to escape them," Thorfast said.

"You know Petronius better than that. He won't surrender advantage. If that way is open then it's a trap."

"Let's board 'em and the fates will decide," Bjorn said. "I've seen enough of this maggot for one life."

"I thought about that," Yngvar said. "But then we'd be boarded by the other ship."

"Not if we boarded on the far side of one," Thorfast said. "At least not right away. It would be enough time to clear a single deck before reinforcements arrive."

"So fresh men fighting against tired and injured men?" Yngvar raised his brow at Thorfast. "As reckless as I am, I'm not taking those chances."

Yngvar stared at the deck, and the ring of booted feet circled with him. He listened to men shout out reports of the Byzantine movements. Hamar ordered men to bail.

Yngvar caught the stinging note in that order. For men bailing were men who could not row or otherwise help the ship maneuver. They pried up the boards and began dipping buckets into the hull. Yngvar heard the planks clatter and the curse of the men bending to the arduous labor.

He looked up, and everyone else followed. Bjorn's one eye was wide with fury. Thorfast's were hooded and cautious. Alasdair's were dutiful and expectant. Gyna seemed on the verge of laughter. But her nephew Ewald hovered behind her, straining to listen to what he must only half understand.

"The best plan is the one even we do not know. It can't be guessed or anticipated. It is neither a feint nor a test of luck. It is the plan that comes when sword rings on sword, when shields smash together, and men cry out in pain."

Thorfast cleared his throat. "So you'll figure it out when we get there?"

A wave rolled the ship and Yngvar set his legs wider to steady himself. He looked to Thorfast, who smiled wryly. Then he looked toward the two Byzantine ships on the horizon.

Hamar had set their course for the obvious pass between the two enemies. He watched them even their distance, then turn so that their broadsides would face him as he passed.

The golden circlet of Agamemnon, now bent into a band clasping his arm, felt as if it tightened of its own accord. His skin tingled beneath it.

Then he smiled. Yngvar turned back to Thorfast.

"As it turns out, I have a plan. You will hate it."

17

Yngvar's heart pounded against the base of his throat. His hand tightened on the pommel of his sword. The green jewel pressed into his palm as if begging him to draw it. But not yet. His ship skimmed over the waves. They had caught the wind and the sail now snapped and the mast creaked overhead. He clasped his other arm around the neck of the prow, leaning forward as if leading the ship.

He had ordered the oars shipped. The crew sat ready with shields in both hands. If the gods loved him, then they would only need shields. Bjorn and two others eschewed shields for axes, and all three of them crouched against the gunwales. Though no gunwale was high enough to conceal Bjorn's head and shoulders. He had to trust the fates not to cut the thread of his life this day.

They sped toward the ship on the far left, which was Petronius's. The wind drove them with force enough for what he planned, which required absolute precision or else he would smash his entire ship to splinters.

"Lord, shelter behind your shield like the others." Alasdair stood beneath him and tugged on the hem of his shirt. He pointed to the rest huddled in the gunwales.

"No, I will shield Hamar," he said. "He must steer as he never has before."

Petronius's ship drew closer. The far ship was already turning as expected. It would try to stem Yngvar's escape. Its oars were beating the waves, but the wind did not help them as they turned. It was the advantage Yngvar needed.

He stepped from the prow, adjusted his shield on his arm, then plucked a spear from the rack. He looked to Gyna, who smiled at him.

"You want me to cast it again?"

"Stay down," Yngvar said. "You'll just fall overboard when we clash."

Ewald pushed his aunt's head lower and she shoved him away with a growl.

Now Yngvar stood beside Hamar, whose sweat must be as much from worry as heat.

"You can do this," Yngvar said. "We have done before it."

Hamar grunted and leaned on the tiller.

"But to a ship that big from one such as ours? You might as well ask me to ram it straight on."

Yngvar patted Hamar's back, then set the shield over the rails to guard Hamar.

"We're almost there, old friend."

"We're almost swamped," Hamar said. "We'll need twice the men to bail after this."

Yngvar scanned the line of his crew. They had overlapped shields like the scales of a giant snake running the length of the ship's side. Alasdair slipped into it and set his own beside Thorfast's. The axmen gripped their hafts with both hands.

Petronius's ship loomed now.

Yngvar's ship sped forward with a full sail.

The gamble he took was all based upon Petronius's desire to catch him. At this speed, he would pass the Byzantine ship and likely evade the other. Once on the open water, he would speed beyond reach of either. Petronius did not know about the leaking strake and would expect Yngvar to continue without stop. If he let Yngvar pass, he was giving up forever.

Petronius could not catch him by wind power alone. He would have to row and use the wind. His trimmed sails were already being lowered for when the moment came. They were facing as if expecting the need to pursue.

So Hamar guided the ship as if planning to pass at full speed.

Petronius's crew slid their oars into the water and stroked. They had to gain the momentum to keep pace.

"Now's our moment," Yngvar said. "Cripple the bastard."

Hamar nodded and eyed the spear Yngvar held. He said nothing. No one wanted to curse this cast with a prediction.

The ship jinked hard toward Petronius's. Hamar leaned over the rails to judge the distance.

The Byzantines shouted threats. Yngvar saw their heads over the sides. As expected, the crew not on a rowing shift pulled up bows and set flaming arrows to their strings. Yngvar had not expected flames, but had expected arrows. Why else present a broadside for him to pass through? Petronius had found bows and knew Yngvar had none. They planned to strafe the ship, grapple it, then finish the crew.

The Byzantine ship was black and solid as it moved through the water again. The oars lifted and fell.

"Brace!" Hamar shouted.

The beast head on the prow seemed to grin as it pointed straight at the line of oars extending from Petronius's ship.

With expert precision, Hamar scraped the ship along Petronius's length.

The oars snapped as Yngvar's ship clipped them one by one. Byzantines screamed out in shock. The oars sheared away, flipping over to crash on Yngvar's deck or else spinning into the water. The ship rocked and water shot up between them to shower the crew huddled against the gunwale.

Yngvar glimpsed the shocked and angry faces glaring at him as they slid below.

But the shock did not delay the Byzantines.

Bowstrings thrummed, and arrows hissed across the gap. Grappling hooks flew, and rope uncoiled behind them. One hook thumped onto the mast and caught. Amid the rain of smoking and burning arrows, Bjorn leaped out with his ax and aimed for the rope.

Yngvar's shield shook as an arrow thumped it.

Hamar screamed as an arrow skimmed across the back of his neck. Yngvar's ears rang with the shout, as they pressed together against the volley.

"Keep us straight!" Yngvar yelled.

"Keep your shield up," Hamar answered.

The slide along the edge of Petronius's ship lasted a mere ten heartbeats. Yet to Yngvar it seemed as if they were snapping oars one by one with the speed of a bored child toying with a dead branch. Flaming arrows pelted the deck. Most ricocheted off the shields angled against them. Petronius might have been better served to shoot at their sail. But he seemed to want to kill rather than cripple Yngvar. Fire was not effective against his ship. He meant it to be terrorizing. Yet to Yngvar it was so much hissing and smoke as the arrows struck water instead.

He saw Petronius now. He too had come to rails of the ship, though he carried no bow. He instead carried a spear of his own.

His face was taut with fury. His teeth shined yellow in the midmorning light.

Oars broke and flew into the air between them. Petronius scanned the ship, likely searching for Gyna.

But his eyes met Yngvar's.

They both cast at the same instant.

Yngvar had readied his spear, hauling back and leaving Hamar exposed.

Petronius had been prepared to cast and now let the thin shaft fly.

In the same instant, a wave shoved Yngvar's ship against Petronius's hull. The ships slammed together with a heavy thud and a cool burst of salt water.

He stumbled back, never seeing where his cast landed. He slid past Hamar, who had the stability of the tiller to keep him upright. His left shoulder pounded onto the deck, sparking pain through it and down his arm.

Petronius's spear gouged the deck, bent at the head, then flipped away. Yngvar rolled with the violence of the crash. He heard his crew scream. Bjorn's curses were clear above the rest.

He scrambled to his feet. Arrows still chased him. Their iron heads studded the surrounding deck. They were no longer flaming arrows but just as deadly.

His crew had all been knocked back from the gunwales. They lay on their backs, shields covering them like a blanket of round scales. Blood flowed out in places where arrows had found a mark.

But they had sped past Petronius. The angle reduced the efficacy of bow fire, and already the arrows drizzled out.

Yngvar was about to let out a call of triumph.

"The strake!" Hamar called out. "Gods be cursed! That hit did us in."

Yngvar's eyes widened. He held his breath and heard the water gurgling beneath the deck. The ship was already sinking lower into the waves.

And the other Byzantine ship slid across their front, still distant but poised to nab them no matter where they turned.

"Bail!" Yngvar shouted. He grabbed a bucket and pried up a floorboard with the spear Petronius had cast at him.

Black sea water sloshed in the shadows, pooling in the ribs of the hull. Yngvar could not see the strake, but it did not seem broken. The impact must have wrenched it out of place. He strained to adjust his eyes to the darkness. Water was sheeting into the hull.

Men pried up boards all around, while others dipped buckets into the opened deck. Yngvar did not wait, but dipped his bucket into the dark. When bailing, the hardest part was remaining bent over long enough to fill a bucket. Now it filled too fast. He handed it off to Alasdair, then shouted for another bucket.

As many men who could bail did so. Yngvar stared into the shadowed hull and smelled the tang of saltwater. He felt the ship slowing. He imagined it sinking and the enormous treasure sinking with him.

Then he stood up.

That was the answer.

"Pull in the sail!" He shouted. "Forget the oars. Slow your bailing. We're surrendering."

Despite their desperation, every crewman stood up in surprise.

"We fight!" Bjorn shouted, raising his ax. "Give me Byzantine blood! Make a necklace of their ears to bring home!"

But no one other than Ewald, who had already drawn his sword, joined him. Gyna shoved her nephew down.

"Lord? We're sinking."

"Of course we are," he said. He pointed at Petronius's ship as it drew closer. "And those fine men want what we have. So they'll keep us from sinking, won't they?"

"We're making a hostage of the gold?" Thorfast asked. "Won't we lose it?"

"Probably."

"So that's it? We just give up."

"Yes."

"This is not a jest. You're serious."

"Most serious."

Yngvar smiled placidly at Thorfast. One of the crew returned to bailing, and another joined him. The ship was already sitting lower in the water and listing on the side of the replaced strake—which had been on the opposite side to where they had struck. He had planned to protect the strake. He just never guessed such a hit would loosen it to this degree.

"Lord, you seem remarkably calm." Alasdair offered him the empty bucket. He gently pushed it aside.

"Let the others bail for now. I need to speak with Petronius before the other ship arrives. I have another plan, one I was hoping would not be necessary. But that moment has arrived."

Thorfast sighed. "Could you have really thought of something riskier than what we just did?"

"Riskier and more reliant on luck." He rubbed his armband, feeling his skin tingling beneath it. "But one that should please the gods—and the king whose gold we carry."

He didn't wait for their reactions. Confidence was half the art of leadership. Though his heart pounded and his knees felt weak, he tipped his head back and gazed toward Petronius's ship.

They had lost half of their oars, which had things gone to plan would have ensured they could not catch Yngvar's ship under any circumstances. Yet now they used the wind to close the brief gap. He expected to see Petronius in the prow, cursing and launching. But the black ship approached with an ominous calm.

"Bjorn, put down your ax and get those chests of gold. The rest of you form a shield wall around him. When I give the word, you will throw the gold into the open deck and smash it through the hull. Use all your strength. You alone have the muscle for this."

The crew gasped. Bjorn fixed him with his one eye, but then pulled up the tarp over the treasure. A flaming arrow had burned a section, and smoke puffed as he lifted it.

"Lord, can he lift such weight?" Alasdair looked skeptically at Bjorn. But in answer to the question, he growled and hefted one of the massive chests off the deck.

"His face will turn blue," Yngvar said. "But he can do it if he's mad enough."

Yngvar repeated his plan in Greek for the benefit of the freemen. He expected them to balk, but they seemed to better grasp the ploy. Byzantines and their subjects were craftier people.

The shadow of Petronius's ship slid over the deck. Men with arrows nocked lined the rails. Their shadowed faces were grim and slick with sweat. Yngvar set his jaw against them and drew his sword. He raised his shield in case Petronius intended another cast. Yet the solemn approach of the black ship seemed more tired than aggressive.

"Get your shields over Bjorn," Yngvar called. "And keep men on the buckets or we'll go under before I can save us."

Boarding hooks flew across the gap. No one opposed them this time. A hook with a dangling rope remained embedded in the mast. The ship lurched as the Byzantines hauled them to their side.

"Well, now we'll just tip over into the water," Thorfast said. "You know they'll just take the treasure and kill us. I'm hoping you plan an ambush."

"I am planning on greed," Yngvar said, still scanning the rails for Petronius but found nothing. "He shouted a lot about that man Gyna killed. His bother or whatnot. But Petronius has wanted all this gold and more from the very start. I liked him. He was a good sword-brother against the Arabs. But he is a greedy bastard who'll turn himself inside out to justify what he does now. So let's use that to pin his arm behind his back."

The bailing continued with Hamar shouting for the men to go faster. The Byzantines were more interested in the shield wall built around Bjorn, who squatted beside a chest filled with gold. Ewald and Gyna both sat with him, ready to help.

"Petronius," Yngvar called. "Your god loves you best. You have caught me. I am taking on water and cannot last another moment. Come claim your gold."

Yngvar turned to the other Byzantine ship. It was turning into the wind and struck oars into the water.

"Hurry now, before your friends come to claim it all."

Still Petronius did not come to the rail. Instead, another man shouldered his way to the front. Yngvar recognized him. He was one of Petronius's closest men. That was all he knew of the man who now set both hands on the rails.

"You bastard," he shouted. "You put a spear through him and still call for him to stand before you?"

Yngvar raised his brows. He murmured to Thorfast, "My spear hit him?"

"So it seems. I was suddenly looking at the sky the moment after you released."

Yngvar shrugged, then turned back to the man addressing him.

"So he is not dead? Who are you? I need a man to make a swift bargain with me. We both have little time. I am sinking and a ship comes ready to take half of the gold I carry."

"I am Isaac," he said. "With the captain gravely wounded, I am in command now."

Yngvar thought he heard a protest from the ship. But Isaac gave no hint of recognizing it.

"Here is my deal to you, Isaac. Tow us back to shore. In trade you take all the gold for our lives. It is truly cursed. I've had nothing but misfortune since taking it. I would be free of it. It's yours."

Isaac smiled, glanced past Yngvar at what must be the approaching Byzantine ship, then shook his head.

"There's time enough to load that gold and take it aboard my ship. Let your ship sink, and we'll carry you to safety."

"I think you misspoke. You will carry us to slavery." He emphasized the last word. "No, you will tow us to the shore. We will surrender the gold, not a sword drawn if all you'll do is take treasure. Otherwise, we'll fight you till the death. Dead men don't enjoy gold as much as the living."

Isaac laughed. "I'm taking the gold and leaving you to drown, then."

Bows creaked as archers prepared to strafe the deck.

"Bjorn!"

Bjorn howled as he lifted the chest off the deck.

"Hold your arrows," Yngvar said. "Or he'll drop that chest of gold through my hull. We'll cut your lines and take it all with us to the sea bottom. And I swear my revenant will haunt you till Ragnarok."

The shield wall parted for a moment to reveal Bjorn grunting with the effort to hold up the chest. He had lifted it as high as his waist and every cord of muscle stood out on his arms and neck.

"Put up the bows, or down we go," Yngvar said.

The shield wall closed around Bjorn, who expelled his breath and set the chest down again.

Isaac had raised his hand and the bowmen pulled back behind the rails. His face reddened and he glowered.

"And what of the other ship? That gold belongs to us alone. Those are freeloaders who have earned none of it."

"You shouldn't have invited them," Yngvar said. "You'll have to deal with them."

"You clipped half our oars!" Isaac shouted. "We can't out-speed them!"

Yngvar shrugged. "We're sinking. Hurry now. Do we have a deal or not?"

Isaac slammed his fist on the rails, conferred with two men beside him, then vanished. The rest of his crew looked behind, then they too melted from the rails.

"Keep bailing," Yngvar shouted. "But we've got a tow to shore. Remain around Bjorn and keep those shields ready."

"That chest is heavy," Bjorn said, plopping to the deck beside it. "Why'd it have to be me? Couldn't a couple of the lads done the same?"

"And let the Byzantines forget how strong you are?" Yngvar folded his arms as if chiding Bjorn. "They need to remember stepping on our deck means they've got to deal with you."

The explanation lit up Bjorn's face. He slapped Ewald's arm, who sat beside him, and laughed.

Petronius's ship began to turn. His crewmen dropped more hooks to Yngvar's ship. His own crew voluntarily secured these to the rails. The ship listed to the side, but the bailing was keeping them afloat. Shore was not far. However, the crew would be exhausted by the time they reached it.

"That other ship won't be far behind." Thorfast stepped to the rail with Yngvar. He flicked his pale hair from his face. "What are we going to do about them? I don't see your full plan yet."

"It will take days to see my full plan," Yngvar said. He remained with his arms folded, staring after the distant Byzantine ship trailing them. "But for it to work, we have to remove this other ship. If we do that, then I'm certain we can get Petronius or Isaac or whoever is running that Byzantine pirate crew to follow my plan."

Thorfast cocked a brow. Yngvar smiled.

"My plan is simple. We properly repair our ship, sail back the way we came, and Petronius will come deliver all the gold he took from us. As long as we rid ourselves of this other ship, I am confident the rest will fall into place."

"You are mad," Thorfast said.

Yngvar nodded.

"Only madness will lead us out of this trap."

18

Yngvar's ship had to row the final distance to shore, for the Byzantine ships could not get directly to the beach. In any other circumstance they could have slipped past their captors. But with the severe leaking, it took all the crew to bail and row.

Leaping into the wet beach sand never felt more comforting to Yngvar. He now stood by the ship as the crew flopped to the ground in exhaustion. Hamar staggered past him, his square face red and shining with sweat. Yngvar too had soaked through his shirt. Immediately upon reaching land, gnats and flies found them.

The midmorning sun pricked his flesh. Clear weather and a strong breeze made for an excellent day at sea. The fishermen now far off were skittering away toward the shore. Doubtless they would report Byzantine ships to whoever ruled these shores.

Yngvar was counting on it.

"Don't get too restful," Yngvar said, walking along the line of his men. He tapped Alasdair, who walked with him. He would translate the Frankish into Greek for the benefit of the freemen.

They propped up on their elbows, their faces taut and squinting in the bright light.

"For a time, we will let this treasure out of our grasp. I cannot promise we will see it again. But I have a plan to do so. You see the Byzantines loading up their rowboats behind me? They are the ones to take this treasure. We cannot let the other Byzantines grab it. For then I am sure we will never lay hands on this gold again."

The men stared up at him in confusion. One freeman cleared his throat, then spoke up.

"Is there no other way? We've gone through so much for the treasure. And we've let ourselves become cursed. You see how many have died since we touched it."

Other freemen rumbled, and once Alasdair had translated, so did the Franks.

"The curse is not what has taken these lives," Yngvar said. "The ancient king waits for me to keep my promise to him. I will bring his name and glory to the north, where men have seldom heard his name before. For this, he stays his hand. The deaths have been the work of fate and not a curse."

"How can you know this?" The same freeman sat up straighter now, as did his fellows.

"Because I wear the crown of King Agamemnon." Yngvar slipped off the armband and held it up. "I carried this from his tomb, and through it I know his will and he knows mine. I swear to you, he has protected me from death because I made a sincere oath to him when I first trespassed on his grave."

He let the men gaze up at the circlet he had cut to create an armband. Some men frowned, but whether in doubt or confusion Yngvar was not sure. No one protested further.

"We have little time before the Byzantines come ashore," he said. "Follow what I say. Do not fight with them unless we must. I will bring the treasure back. But first we must chase off the other ship."

With this, he turned to Alasdair.

"You're the only other one to speak Greek that I trust. The merchant and his people are not far. Fly as fast as you can and warn them of the Byzantine's arrival. I will delay them here on shore. Take a horse and ride to that Arab town on the coast. Tell the pirates there that an easy bounty awaits them if they hurry. We will hold the Byzantines in place as long as we are not attacked. We will fly a white flag so they understand we will remain out of the fight. They are not to harm the ship we shelter, and that will guarantee them an easy trophy and reward from their lords."

Alasdair's smooth face wrinkled. "Lord, why not let the Arabs destroy both Byzantine ships? We would keep all we own and be free."

"They're deserters. They've no duty to fight to the last man. The Arabs will take prisoners and discover the gold on Petronius's ship. They would soon learn what we carry and we'd have more than two Byzantine ships after us. We'd have an Arab fleet. We must keep this gold a secret if we are ever to pass through the Midgard Sea unharmed. So we enlist Petronius's aid. He will want it to remain secret for the same reason."

"But the other Byzantines might reveal us to the Arabs."

Yngvar smiled. "They might. But they do not carry ancient gold on their ship. The Arabs will think the accusation is mere bait for a trap or a ploy to save themselves. It is a risk, but one I think unlikely. The Arabs here are pirates and will want to turn in an easy bounty on a captured Byzantine ship. They won't want to chase after sailor stories about gold they can't be sure is real."

Alasdair looked to the others. Bjorn and Thorfast both nodded. Gyna was whispering to Ewald, who nodded and grinned.

"You've no time to waste. But there were plenty of swift horses in that merchant's stables to make up time. Take Ewald with you. He's as fast and crafty as you, and good in a fight. Better to have eyes to watch your back."

"I will run as fast as I can, lord. Ewald must keep up."

Ewald understood enough to thump his chest in defiance.

With Alasdair and Ewald dispatched, Yngvar turned to the rowboats coming ashore. Petronius only had two of these small ships. Getting the treasure into his own hold would require both. He waited with arms folded as the rowboats glided along the waves. Bjorn and Thorfast flanked him, and other crewmen hovered behind. No one drew a weapon as the Byzantines pulled their boats ashore.

Isaac led the contingent. He had stuffed the boat with so many men Yngvar wondered how they intended to get the gold aboard their ship. Two men reached into the last boat and carried an injured man out between them.

It was Petronius. A broken spear shaft had lodged in his thigh and his pants were dark with blood. He screamed and groaned as his two bearers stumbled through the surf. But eventually they got him up onto the shingle and away from the water. They set him down and he let out a long moan.

Yngvar watched with folded arms. Isaac had drawn up a scant distance, yet close enough for swords to clash. The waves purred behind him, and the warm breeze fluttered his shirt across his sturdy frame. Yngvar looked to Petronius.

"He's dying. Why did you take him ashore?"

Isaac's face reddened and he scowled.

"He's still the captain. He wanted to be part of this deal."

Yngvar shrugged. "I thought I was making a deal with you. Who leads, after all? Your friends are breaking their backs on the oars to get here before you can grab all the gold. But I wonder how you plan to take it all aboard your ship before they arrive."

"We can't do that," Isaac said. "They'll be here too soon. There has to be another way."

Yngvar's heart thudded. Could the gods finally be working with him?

"In fact, there is another way," Yngvar said. "But I will not speak it until I know who leads you."

"Petronius is still captain," Isaac said. "But he cannot lead. So I command in his place. He's here for a personal reason."

Yngvar looked again to Petronius. He lay flat on the ground, his chest heaving. The broken spear shaft jutted out of his thigh. If removed it would be like unplugging a wine cask. He would bleed to death. Unless the Christian god blessed him, Petronius was dead. He just had the unfortunate luck of not realizing it yet.

"He wants revenge for his cousin's death," Isaac explained. "We're to take the woman who killed him."

With no one to translate for him, Bjorn just stared with his typical frown for anyone not of his clan. Yngvar glanced at him and was glad he could not understand. He also scanned over his shoulder for Gyna. She watched him with a flat expression.

"It's a pity we all didn't get to know each other better when we were friends," Yngvar said. "But you were always aboard your ship. Had you spent time with us, you'd know Bjorn here is her lover. Do you want to ask Bjorn how he feels about that idea?"

Isaac's stern gaze did not change, nor did he look to Bjorn.

"He's still the captain," he said. In a lower voice he added, "And some men still follow him."

"Those men are fools," Yngvar said. "You've no time to negotiate with me. You can take the gold. We'll step back and let you claim it. You touch the woman, then we'll kill the lot of you. And you know your friends will sit back and watch. They'll want to take the gold from whoever remains standing. So we can either make a deal now or let's draw swords and have done with it. On land, I say we will fare better than you in a fight."

Petronius, despite his deathly pallor, began shouting.

"I must avenge Cyril! Bring me the woman. Let me see her killed for what she did!"

Some Byzantine crew stirred, but they looked sheepishly to Isaac, who remained glowering at Yngvar. He curled his lip and held his hand up for peace.

"We should've left him aboard the ship," he said. "We have no time to bother with Cyril's revenge. It was a fight and he died. Nothing to be said for it."

"Nothing to be said?" Petronius raised his head to say more, but began coughing. He felt flat again.

"Forget him," Isaac said. "It was my mistake to bring him here. What is this plan to get us all the gold?"

"It is a simple plan," Yngvar said. "You were probably intent on towing us and making certain we did not try any tricks. So you might not have seen the fishermen heading for shore to warn of your arrival. Maybe their news will not travel. But I have made my own precautions and sent my fastest men to warn the Arabs."

"You did what?" Isaac and his crew all reached for their swords. But Yngvar remained passive with his arms folded.

"We made friends with them while we camped here. Turns out the common folk can be friendly. There is a seaside town near here and there must be Arab warships at anchor with the battle coming. These will speed here to capture you, but I will fly a white flag. I believe that means peace in these lands? My man will ensure the Arabs know we are working with them to hold you here. If you will remain with me, then only your friends will be attacked and captured. You just make sure the gold stays on shore and keep them here until the Arabs arrive. Then step back and let them die."

Isaac's nose wrinkled as if smelling a rotten squid.

"You want us to abandon them to the Arabs?"

"Make your choice soon. For your friends are nearly here."

"Then you'll turn on us once we've got rid of the others," Isaac said. "Your plan is as transparent as glass."

"I've seen glass once, but it was colored. Definitely not clear," Yngvar said. "I'm in no position to threaten you. My ship is still a wreck. Plus, we don't want the gold any more. It's all yours. The curse is too heavy. Perhaps your god will protect you from it. But mine do not. We have suffered as never before since taking that treasure. The ancient people hunt us at night. I have seen their ships following in the dark. They are pale things in starlight, barely visible. But whenever I see such a ship, death follows. I saw one on the water before you arrived. Truly, I only hope to rid myself of the treasure and send the ghosts after you."

Isaac's frown turned thoughtful, but it snapped back.

"Why do you want me to have it?"

"I am done with cursed gold," Yngvar said. "Some of your men at least worked to take it from the island. And we were once allies. Those other Byzantines might want a fight. They might see us as slaves to be used or sold. I just want peace and to go home. We have our treasure from Prince Kalim. That is enough. The Arabs are coming regardless of what I've done. The fishermen saw you. If we stand together, they will probably let us alone. But if the Arabs defeat both of you, then they will find your original share of gold and soon learn I have the rest of it. I don't expect they'd believe me if I offered to surrender it peacefully. So I'd rather you take it all and dispose of these others who you should never have involved. I can go home with some gold and my pride, rather than losing all of both."

Isaac again seemed to reflect on the situation. Yngvar saw the greed in his eyes. He would believe anything if it meant he could claim all the gold for himself. He wanted to believe it was possible, and Yngvar was happy to tell him it was. He could have it all—for a time.

"Be quick," he said. "Your friends are getting into their rowboats now. Your task is to keep them ashore. I suggest you claim to have negotiated a peace and that you celebrate victory before dividing the spoils. That will allow enough time for the Arabs to arrive. Then you join me under my white flag. When all is done, you take the gold and leave me to repair my ship in peace. We shall not meet again."

"What if they win against the Arabs?" Isaac asked. But now he was stroking his chin, and his eyes seemed to be calculating his next move.

"Then we attack them together. Even in victory they will be weakened. They're not expecting us to cooperate. Though if you want my help, we would expect a share of treasure as payment. You'd be hiring us as mercenaries. We could sit back and watch you kill each other, if you preferred. But it won't come to that if you cooperate now."

Isaac looked to sea, where two rowboats bristling with spearmen headed to shore.

"We have an agreement. But you'll not get anywhere near your ship. That ship is my hostage against you. I'll keep it and its treasures to be sure you don't attack."

"And we will watch to be sure you do not damage it more," Yngvar said. "For just like a living hostage, if you hurt my ship we will reap your heads and pull out your guts. And you, Isaac, will have your lungs cut out while you still live. For blood and killing, the Old Gods are stronger than your Christian God. Don't doubt me in it."

Isaac narrowed his eyes at Yngvar, but he turned away. He pointed to one of his crew. "Get Petronius out of here."

"I want him," Yngvar said. "I cast the spear that felled him, and it grieves me to have killed a man I once called a friend. Let me ease his last hours."

Isaac stopped on his left foot, then turned back.

"Are you serious? He wants to kill the woman."

"He is mad with grief," Yngvar said. "He will want peace before he dies. Only I can give it to him. Besides, if he lives I will restore him to you."

"He'll not live."

The tone of Isaac's voice informed Yngvar all he needed to know. Even if saved from his terrible wound, Isaac would kill him. Gold lust had a way of turning brother on brother. At least such illness had not infected Yngvar and his crew, possibly because they had not yet divided their treasure. But more likely because King Agamemnon sailed beside them, just like the story Yngvar created about the ghost ships.

Petronius gathered his men to discuss their plans. The Byzantines cast glances over their shoulders at Yngvar. He instead explained his exchange to Thorfast, Bjorn, and Gyna.

"You want me to take care of the man I tried to kill?" Gyna laughed. "Maybe I'll just finish what I started. We owe him nothing."

"He'll likely die," Yngvar said. "If he sends Isaac to where we can find him, then he'll have done us a great favor. We will have our gold back, plus more."

Gyna tilted her head back. "Why are we just learning of this extra treasure now? Were you planning to return for it on your own?"

"I'd not return to these waters again for all the gold in the world. I felt it wise to keep it secret. You'll see why soon enough. But let me go to Petronius first. All of you can explain the plan to the Franks while I handle this last part."

Yngvar went to Petronius's side. One of the Byzantine crew stood over him, concern on his face. He glared at Yngvar. He seemed familiar, though most of these dark-faced, dark-bearded crewmen looked the same to him.

"You heard my agreement with Isaac. I want to speak to Petronius alone."

The man's nostrils flared. But Petronius groaned and raised his hand.

"Let the bastard have his fun. Go on, He's already killed me. What else is there to do?"

"Are you sure, Captain?"

Petronius lay stretched out in the crewman's purple shadow. The white sand around his leg was stained red with his leaking wound. He was pasty and sweating. Flies crawled around the broken shaft jutting from his thigh, dancing in the caked blood.

He shooed the crewman with one hand.

Yngvar crouched beside him after the man had stepped away. Petronius closed his eyes against the sun. Yngvar shifted so he cast a shadow over Petronius's face.

"You're dead," Yngvar said. "Unless someone helps you. Even then, you might not live. So let's not fight in what might be your last hours. We were not always enemies."

"We weren't fast friends, either," Petronius said. He opened his eyes, and one had drifted so out of focus Yngvar guessed he must be blind. Yet his good eye fixed him. "The woman killed my cousin. He was a brother to me."

Yngvar shook his head. "Gyna should've killed you. That's what she was trying for. You stepped out of the way, and you killed your cousin. If you were so intent on protecting him at all costs, you should've stood and died."

"Gyna, yes, that's her name. Strange woman. If you want to be friends again, then set her head on my chest so I can look into her dead face before I go to heaven."

"You're not going to heaven," Yngvar said. "You should swear your life to Odin and Thor this moment. Put a hand on your sword and beg them to take you into the feasting hall of Valhalla where you can still prove you are a hero. Otherwise, your god is throwing you into his hell."

Petronius laughed, then groaned.

"I'm not here to speak of gods. We were allies once, and perhaps even friends. Gold has ruined that, as it often does. I'm about to lose my gold. You are about to lose your life. But neither must come to pass."

Petronius snapped his head to Yngvar. Even his drifting eye shifted to focus.

"Is it magic you offer me? Black magic from the north? A devil's bargain to keep me alive?"

"A bargain for certain. But not magic." Yngvar patted Petronius's shoulder. "Some crew still follow you. But Isaac wants all the gold and your ship. So if I leave you to him, you will certainly die. I expect he'll just throw you overboard before you bleed out. In any case, you're in his way and my spear didn't do the full job of killing you."

"I don't see how you can save me. I am already weak and my leg ruined."

"We tie off your leg for one. Isaac has not done even that much and no one else has thought of it. We pull out this spear and burn the wound shut. The woman you so desperately want to kill has learned to heal. She will nurse you. Then if the gods will listen to your prayers, you will live. Or you will die. I cannot say which, but I will do all I can to aid you and grant a merciful death if it comes to that."

"Why?" Petronius asked. He lingered at the verge of death, and Yngvar could see the hope in his face.

"Because I cannot take this gold alone. I need help in ridding myself of two Byzantine ships. So I will grant you a share of my treasure, plus a share for any man you bring to my side. But these outsiders and this Isaac bastard will ensure I lose it all. My ship needs the repairs we did not complete. Once that is done, no one will catch me. I will not stop until I reach the Seine River. But I cannot repair and I cannot afford to fight your crew plus a fresh crew of Byzantines. I have to surrender my gold so Isaac will leave me to fix my ship. He doesn't want a fight either. Dead men can't spend gold on wine and whores."

"I can ask the few who will follow me to join you, but that is it."

Yngvar shook his head. "Say nothing. The fewer people who know my plans, the better. For now, agree to join with me. If the Arabs arrive and destroy the others, there may be a chance to attack Isaac. If we can and there's no need for my plan, then I will still grant you a share. But otherwise, all I need you to do is to tell Isaac that there is more treasure on that island. Far more than what I led you to believe."

"Is that true?" Petronius's eyes widened.

"It is," Yngvar said. "And I'm going back to fetch it. All I need is for him to be at that island with my gold. Just let him sail ahead and await me there. Tell him it's your dying wish that your beloved crew gets all that treasure. Say anything you feel will convince him to deliver me all the gold he'll take today. Then I'll handle the rest."

"I might not live so long," Petronius said.

"We'll get to work on your leg as soon as we can. But I'll tie off the bleeding now. I'll give you some time with Isaac. Plant the seed and if you live you will be rich. So fight against death like you would fight against Arabs."

Petronius closed his eyes again and sighed.

"I feel so cold that I may die before I can speak. Bring Isaac to me, and I will tell him your lies."

"Not lies," Yngvar said. "Just don't warn him of what is coming. The rest is the truth."

Yngvar took Petronius's baldric, then used it to tie off his leg. As the leather strap clamped down on Petronius's flesh he cried out. Others looked on, but few seemed concerned for his suffering. Then Yngvar gestured to Isaac that he was finished.

"I will try to spare him," he shouted across the gap, hoping those loyal to the captain will hear. "I might have a use for him."

Isaac shook his head. He was watching the Byzantine rowboats gliding ashore and releasing their loads of spearmen. Petronius called out to him, and he eventually approached.

Yngvar stepped back and smiled at his plans. Now to wait for the Arab ships and pray for Alasdair and Ewald's success. If they failed, all might face the slave pens again.

19

Yngvar sat around one of the four campfires they had set at twilight. They ate well, having been allowed provisions from their own ship. Bjorn belched after he downed a wooden cup of wine. Gyna laughed, but her eyes glinted with firelight as she scanned the hills for signs of Alasdair and Ewald. Neither had returned. While Yngvar did not expect them yet, he too could not help worry for them. Thorfast sat to his right side, and only once looked up from his bowl the whole meal.

The rest of the crew sat in stony silence. No one spoke since all their gold had been off-loaded onto the shore. It remained in a pile, still covered with a tarp held down by stones and casks. It seemed nothing more than a supply cache for a campsite. They also piled up their other supplies there and only carried their shields and weapons.

Isaac and his fellow captain set mutual guards around the treasure. The new Captain Leo was a sturdy man with short curly hair and a face like one of the stone busts Captain Staurakius had kept in his war room. He wore both his impetuousness and his scars on his face. It made Yngvar feel better to know he was the one being set up for an Arab slave ship.

Isaac sent men back in a rowboat to his own ship under some

pretense. Yngvar did not know what. But when the crewmen left, he gave Yngvar a meaningful look. They would let the remaining crew know when to fly the white flag and the rest of the plans.

At last, the only other excitement for the day was tending Petronius. As promised, Gyna helped, but there was only so much to be done without the right herbs and supplies. Bjorn used his tremendous strength to pull out the spear shaft. The trick was in not splintering or breaking it, which required sustained strength and a sensitive touch. But he succeeded. Petronius passed out from the blood loss and agony. Yngvar had heated Petronius's sword in a fire, then burned both ends of the wound shut.

He was likely to die from a fever brought on from the wound. But he had given his word to his old ally. Whether Petronius lived or died was up to fate now. He was unconscious and covered in a blanket. His leg was wrapped in thick cloths that were now bloody brown. If the flesh around the wound started to stink and turn green, then Yngvar would let Bjorn decapitate Petronius. It would be the swifter way to die. There would be no saving him otherwise.

At least he had already spoken to Isaac in private. Before he passed out from removing the spear, Petronius swore he told Isaac of Yngvar's plans to return to the island for a hidden cache of treasure. Isaac was a greedy coward and would be glad to let Yngvar gather it all for him on the beach for easy taking.

He was certain Isaac was one coward who had remained on the ship while Petronius and his loyal crew excavated the gold after the earthquake. That would be Isaac's undoing.

The fire cracked and threw golden light around the circle. Between Bjorn and Hamar, Yngvar saw the sea. The sun vanished behind the horizon, but light still stained the sky. The Arabs would either attack at night or else with the rising sun. Both had merits, but he guessed a night attack. In the morning the Arabs would attack into the sun. So, he sat and ate even though he had no appetite. The battle must begin soon.

Then he would know if the gods were pleased or they thought him a fool.

Yet by nightfall, no attack came. Captain Leo was eager to split up the gold and leave with the dawn. However, he and Isaac seemed to have come to some terms. Whatever happened between them, Yngvar caught Isaac's looks. He was red-faced and his lips taut in a flat line. But Captain Leo had been convinced that they should eat before the hard labor of loading out the treasure. This was further aided by the hangovers Captain Leo and his men had from a night of celebration.

Yngvar kept his eyes down, or else he would look to the sea or the hills for Alasdair. The Byzantines on both sides were on constant watch and would know he expected something. Anytime he caught the others doing the same, he growled at them until they stopped.

At last, the Arab ships slipped around the promontory. Yngvar never expected to feel such relief at the sight of their triangular sails and sweeping profiles.

They were not much larger than the Byzantine ships, but moved with the speed of seagulls swooping down on their prey. Three ships bristled with Arab pirates.

Isaac's ship was the first to unfurl a white flag. It also predictably nosed toward the shore, having already pulled up its anchor. Captain Leo's ship, however, had not been ready. Nor had they been warned. Isaac's ship, either deliberately or not, must have obscured the Arab approach.

None of Yngvar's men made any warning.

Captain Leo did not seem aware of the approaching danger.

Isaac, however, had been as nervous as Yngvar. He and his men saw the ships. Their agitation drew attention and soon Captain Leo was running to the shore.

"By God! We're at anchor!" He held both hands to his head. "Fuck! Isaac, you goddamned fool! I told you we should have--"

But Isaac had already run a spear through Leo's back. He was about to whirl around, but slipped off the end of the spear and splashed face-first into the water.

"Get the white cloth," Yngvar said to Bjorn. "And raise it high over our ship. But be ready for anything."

Yngvar and his crew ambled toward their ship. No one hurried or even worried. In contrast, Isaac and his crew had launched a surprise attack on Leo. His men were only just fighting back and would not prevail.

On the water, the Arab corsairs had surrounded Captain Leo's ship.

"And like that it's all over," Yngvar said. They reached their ship, and Bjorn stood on an empty barrel to set the white flag on the mast. The sail had been stowed, so there could be no mistaking it. He shook it out and the wind caught it.

"A strange sign for peace," Thorfast said, arms folded and looking up at the flag. "Do you think we should attack Isaac now? They're busy with the others."

Yngvar looked back to sea. The Arabs were boarding Leo's ship, likely tying it to their own ship to tow it to shore. The crew would be killed if they resisted or bound hand and foot for a slave market. The ship was too far off for Yngvar to hear their screams. Isaac's ship already headed toward them but could not disembark enough men to aid those already ashore.

"Isaac was a bit too trusting," Yngvar said. "And I went to such lengths to plan ahead. But I say, let's kill them."

He drew his sword, and his crew rallied to him. They leaped from the ship to face the rear of Isaac's crew. They were killing the last of Leo's men.

Then he saw the men emerge from the hill.

Scores of Arabs flowed down from the rocky slopes. They wore nothing but their plain gray robes and head covers. Curving swords flashed in their hands. They let out a war cry that echoed across the water.

"Arabs?" Isaac shouted. "Is this your treachery?"

Yngvar blinked and shook his head. "Not mine. They've taken this upon themselves."

Yngvar guessed there might be fifty men swooping toward them.

"We fight together," Yngvar said to Isaac. "We'll be an even match. Quick, join your men to mine. We have to fight them off or else we both lose everything."

Isaac did not answer. Instead, he drew his men alongside Yngvar's.

"A proper battle." Bjorn raised his ax. "I hope the boys are all right."

Yngvar knew he meant Alasdair and Ewald, who still had not returned. The white flag flying from the mast meant nothing to these men. They were running amid a cloud of dust toward them. Their eyes were bright with greed.

With the sea to their backs, Yngvar knew he must fight to the death.

And kill Isaac during the battle.

The lines of men clashed together.

Yngvar and his crew held heavy round shields against the charge. The Byzantines fared worse and crumpled back against the onrush.

They could not form a shield wall with men who did not have the discipline for it. Sailors were brawlers who fought man to man on their decks. They did not join shields and grind an enemy back until their corpses formed a tidemark on the ground.

Yngvar's sword clanged on a wild-eyed Arab's helmet. Not all were unarmored. This was no organized force. Some Arabs were kitted for war and others looked as if they had just run from their fields to join the frenzy.

The Arab toppled away and his helmet fell over his eyes. Yngvar kicked him down, then whirled away to stab another man in the leg.

He had long been out of battle form. Yet he had fought so many that his body reacted beyond his conscious thought. His shield found the swords, and spears poised to impale him. He stepped over fallen bodies without looking down. The smell of blood and sweat roused him to the battle lust he had so long forgotten. Now he thrilled at every cut. At every chop of the sword. Men fell before him and cried in agony.

Bjorn howled in delight as his ax spun in a mad circle. Heads and arms flew around him as he walked through what seemed a storm of blood.

As furiously as the Arabs had struck, so did they retreat.

They had expected a distracted and injured group of castaways. Instead they had clashed with trained fighting men. The few braggarts among them who had likely encouraged the group to violence must have died. For the Arabs turned and fled along the paths they came. Some fell as they fled, but did not rise again. Others moaned on the ground. Yngvar's men staggered through the wreckage of battle. Any enemy still moving received a quick jab through the throat or into the eye.

He did not find Isaac in the battle. But he was not ready to attack the Byzantines yet, for the Arab retreat might be a ploy. He stared after them to be sure they ran into the hills and did not wait in ambush.

"They are truly retreating, lord. They are cowards."

Alasdair stood over a dead Arab, his face dirty and covered in blood. Ewald stood beside him, leaning down to cut a wounded Arab's neck.

"What happened?" Yngvar asked as he ran up to Alasdair. "Are you all right?"

Alasdair waved aside the concerns. "The merchant was not as friendly as we thought. He scented our gold and was organizing pirates to come for it, but we left before he could. When I arrived, I told him the plans, then he lulled us into thinking he would do as we asked."

"He did," Yngvar said. "The ships arrived and captured Leo's ship. They ignored Isaac and ours."

"Perhaps it is luck, lord." Alasdair shrugged. He was still winded from battle. "I think those ships are other pirates working on their own. They took us captive, but they were a disorganized lot. Ewald escaped, then freed me. He's a good man."

"I'm glad he kept up with you," Yngvar said, smiling.

"As am I, lord. We had trouble leaving that town, but recovered our weapons and followed them down to this attack. I'm sorry we could not warn you of it."

Yngvar shook his head. "You did better than I could've asked. I'm glad you both escaped."

Ewald rose from his handiwork, faced Yngvar, but his smile turned to horror. He was looking past him toward the shore.

Yngvar whirled to follow his line of sight.

Isaac had gathered the remains of his crew near one of the four rowboats lining the shore. His ship had now come in as close as it was able and framed the Byzantines against its black hull. There were only a dozen Byzantines remaining. The beach was littered with dead from all sides. Yet they clustered together with swords pointed at Yngvar's men.

Yngvar was not sure what they were huddling so triumphantly over. It seemed a tremendous mass, like a beached seal.

But then he realized they were standing over Bjorn.

He lay on his side, blood running from his head. Isaac's men were already trussing up his arms and legs.

"Petronius warned me of your tricks," Isaac shouted. "So we've caught a fat prize even if it wasn't the bitch."

Gyna stood with a bloodied sword, staring at Bjorn's prone body. Thorfast stood beside her, dumbfounded.

"You harm him and you will suffer as never before," Yngvar said, raising his sword.

"You're all surrendering your weapons and coming aboard my ship. Say one word against it, and I'll poke out his last eye. Act against me, and he'll die. Now, throw down your weapons and line up to be taken aboard. You're taking me back to the island and fetching me the rest of my gold!"

20

Confusion swept across the beach with the speed of a racing wave. Yngvar and his men had been expecting to attack the Byzantines prior to the Arab attack. Now at least four of them were dead and the same number on their knees and bleeding. Isaac's men had fared worse, either from poor luck or just not being accustomed to fighting on land. Yet now they seemed to have all the advantages, and both Franks and freemen wavered between rushing them and throwing down their weapons.

"Don't make me wait," Isaac said. He put one foot on Bjorn's shoulder as he lay unconscious on the sand. The waves were lapping just short of his prone and bound body. Were it not for the blood trickling from his mass of black hair, he would seem asleep.

"How do I know he's alive?" Yngvar asked. He could see the rise and fall of Bjorn's side. He never breathed easily in that position and even unconscious he worked harder for his air. But Yngvar wanted time to think.

"You'll take my word for it," Isaac said. "Or I can ensure that he's dead. We've no time to waste before the Arabs return, either on land or at sea. Worse still, both."

"What about my ship?"

"I don't give a fig about your ship!" Isaac shouted. "Throw down your weapons now!"

Yngvar lowered his sword, then turned to the others.

"We've no choice. Surrender your swords."

"What?" One of the freemen rushed forward. Sweat plastered his short, black hair to his head. His face was flush with anger. "We outnumber them still. We're winning. We're not surrendering now."

"Drop your sword," Yngvar said. "You are sworn to me and will do as I say."

"Fuck that! I'm not becoming a slave again. Anyone with me?"

He raised his sword and pointed at the Byzantines.

Yngvar plunged his sword through the freeman's chest. The blade was sharp and balanced. The freeman staggered back and dropped his sword. He croaked and tugged back. Yngvar released his sword and let it fall. The green pommel gem waved with the shaking blade sticking from the dying freemen's heart.

"There's my sword," Yngvar said. "Anyone else who threatens Bjorn will die the same way. Don't think I can't kill you with my own hands. I will. Now drop your weapons."

Isaac laughed. "An excellent show. Now, pile them up on the beach then get to work loading that treasure on these boats. Hurry."

Sword and spear clanged into a pile. Yngvar stood to the side. Having surrendered his weapons, he let Gyna and Thorfast encourage anyone who seemed to hesitate. The Franks, who were nominally here for Bjorn's sake, never wavered. Of the freemen, several glowered at him as they tossed their weapons away. They were fewer now than the Franks. The injured were all freemen and far less willing to fight than their companions. They threw down their swords and limped off to tend their wounds. One man fell and his companions rushed to him.

"Let him die," Isaac shouted. "You men get to moving the gold. Hurry!"

The three other injured freemen pulled back from their companion. Yngvar watched, wishing he could do more but knowing he dared not risk Bjorn's life.

Isaac carried Petronius's body into a rowboat. He groaned and screamed, but they set him down out of sight.

"You were a fool to trust him," Gyna said. "People stick to their own kind, even if their own kind treat them worse than dogs."

"How did Bjorn get captured?"

Gyna sighed. "Too confident. Lack of practice fighting with his one eye. One of those reasons. I think Isaac and his men hit him from behind to take him captive."

"You seem calm," Yngvar said. Gyna stared after Isaac and his men.

"I am tired," she said. "It does not mean I'll not cut Isaac's balls off and feed them to the gulls. There will be a time to make him pay, and if Bjorn does not avenge himself, I will gladly do it for him. But not now. We cannot help him with rage."

Yngvar turned to Thorfast, who stood beside him with Alasdair. Both blinked in wonder.

"She's right," Yngvar said. "And I'll find a way out of this trap. We've lost our ship and our weapons. But there must be a way out. The gods test us."

"How many more tests?" Thorfast asked. "Bjorn has the simple task. He gets to take a nap while we figure out a plan."

With both Petronius and Bjorn now aboard the same rowboat, Isaac departed with five men to his ship. Those left on the shore stayed back from Yngvar but interposed themselves before the pile of weapons. Yngvar regretted losing his sword, carried from Ireland and through scores of battles, impossibly returned to him in Prince Kalim's treasure hall. But now it would rust on the beach. The fabulous blade would become a prize for some Arab scavenger.

"I think the Arabs watch us still," Alasdair gasped as they both recovered their breath on the shore. Five chests bursting with gold had been loaded and now they had a pause before rowing it to the ship.

"Let them watch," Yngvar said. "Then they will come down and gather weapons and pull apart our ship for scrap."

"And I went through such efforts to bring it back." Gyna rested her hands on her knees and dripped sweat onto the sand.

"Enough rest. Now get to the ship." Isaac's crew ordered them into the boats. Dragging them into the waves was like trying to shove over a mountain. The rowboats nearly swamped with the weight of the gold. But they reached Isaac's ship and after arduous work got all five chests aboard.

"You clipped our oars," Isaac said. "But I'll have all of you rowing still."

Bjorn remained unconscious and three men stood around him with spears readied. They raised their chins at Yngvar as if defying him to attempt a rescue. Yngvar looked away.

He made a careful count of Isaac's crew. He had nineteen men left. Yngvar had twenty-four, a mild advantage. Yet for all that advantage, they had no weapons and were ringed by spearmen. Isaac leaned over Petronius where they placed him in the ship's fore. They kept Yngvar and his others in the center.

After a terse exchange, Isaac glared at Yngvar.

"He has words for you," he shouted across the deck. "You alone may come."

The deck seemed to stretch forever as he walked between the Byzantines. They had been former allies, but now none of them seemed familiar to him. Had he never paid them mind, or had his hatred for these bastards caused them to become faceless enemies? He only knew he would kill them all if given the chance.

Isaac had his sword drawn and leveled at Yngvar. "I won't be far. So don't think to try anything foolish."

Yngvar held up both hands for peace, then when Isaac stepped away he kneeled beside Petronius.

His face had withered in the space of hours. His flesh was like wax and bright with sweat. He smirked at Yngvar.

"Come closer," he said.

"So you can stick a hidden dagger in my neck?"

Petronius's voice was husky and hollow. He frowned and pulled his two hands up to his chest.

"I'm dying. You tried to save me, but I will not live to the end of this voyage. So we must speak now. Closer."

Yngvar leaned closer, pinning his right arm with his own as he did.

"Isaac is not a fool," he said in a throaty whisper. "He knew you plotted something and knew I had a hand in it. Now he thinks I will try to kill you with a hidden dagger."

"I thought you would try that."

Petronius chuckled, then coughed. When he recovered, he looked up with his bad eye drifted out of focus.

"He doesn't want the blame. He thinks as long as you are alive, you keep the curse with yourself. But if I kill you, then the curse becomes mine and he is free. Look, I had to tell him what you planned."

"And it cost me my ship, my weapons, and the gold."

"But he's still going to where you wanted him to go."

"You did not help me, Petronius."

"I did, but you must make do with what I've set before you. And I want you to keep the promise you made. If I live, as unlikely as it feels, I want a share of that gold."

"You'll have a hard time convincing my crew."

"They follow you because you are strong and clever. And you keep them close to the treasure. They'll share with me if you command it. So it is not all lost. Here, we've not much time before Isaac suspects something. Know this. He is superstitious even for a sailor. He talks about God and believes himself some sort of a saint. But he and those who follow him, which are the majority that are left, are terrified of the island. Only their love of gold drives them ahead. That and their belief you will take all the risks in bringing it to them. I don't know what you can do with this knowledge, but fear of the island is his greatest weakness. Otherwise, he is capable, and the men love him. It's why I made him my first mate."

Yngvar made to lean back, then Petronius struck forward. He had found the dagger with his left hand. The blade flashed, but Yngvar was prepared.

For an instant he feared Petronius was serious. Perhaps he was. The force of his thrust slammed into Yngvar's palm as he caught the dagger just short of his neck. He growled at Petronius, then twisted his wrist until he shouted in pain and dropped the dagger. It clattered to the deck.

Isaac burst into laughter. To him this was all a jest. If Petronius had succeeded, he would be glad. But he lost nothing in Petronius's failure.

"Be careful," Isaac said. "The captain bites. I should've warned you. Now, he's thanked you for saving him. At least saving him long enough to see you all pay for his cousin's death. Now get back with the others and wait your turn on the oars."

So they rowed, even when the sails filled with wind. Yngvar rowed alongside the others. But Isaac was keen to limit their speech. If they spoke anything other than Greek, a crewman beat the offender with an oar.

Bjorn had awakened long enough to groan then vomit on the deck. But he soon collapsed and fell asleep again.

Yngvar and the rest stared after him, no one daring to speak a word. To be knocked senseless for an hour usually meant a bad head wound. To be knocked senseless for a full day meant Bjorn might never rouse from his sleep. Men who slept for days after being struck on the head often could not remember things. Yngvar led a warrior once who had taken a hammer blow from a Dane. After he awakened a day later, he found he could not speak again. Another man he knew could no longer use his left arm despite the wound being to his head. Another still had never awakened and withered in his bed until he died.

He threw himself into the rowing to put these thoughts out of mind. He told himself Bjorn had a skull carved from the stones of the earth. He would recover.

Yet he did not fully awaken, and the surrounding guards toyed with him. They prodded him with spears and kicked him. But he only grunted if he reacted at all. To the guards, it was grand sport. But Yngvar's fury only mounted by the time night had come.

They allowed Hamar to guide the Byzantine helmsmen. He did so with great weariness. To Yngvar it seemed he carried an anchor stone on his back.

By nightfall they were all exhausted. The Byzantines permitted them a few hours sleep while the ship drifted. The weather was fair. The stars shined on the deck, and Yngvar sensed the brewing anger among his crew. They would revolt and fight with their bare hands. Isaac would kill Bjorn. If he was indeed senseless, then maybe it would be for the best. But Yngvar fought back that thought.

In the late night, he awakened to hear Byzantines whispering desperately among themselves.

"A ghost ship follows."

"I think that is a mast. It is not like any ship we've seen. It has no sail."

"King Agamemnon comes for his treasure."

These were the whispers he heard flitting from crewman to crewman. Isaac arrived to halt the spread. But he too went to the stern and stared across the water. Yngvar dared not reveal he had awakened and instead watched as Isaac crossed himself then spun away to return to his post.

The scene replayed a dozen times in his head.

He felt the warm gold armband heavy on his bicep. He looked to the pile of chests stacked around him.

He had made up stories of ghost ships.

Had the king heard his stories and granted him this revenge?

That did not seem possible. More likely his story had spooked the crew already fearful of the curse. Now they believed they saw things that existed only in their own imaginations.

But as Yngvar thought on their reaction and Petronius's advice, a plan formed.

Then the plan grew.

And Yngvar smiled in the dark starlight.

He rubbed the armband as his grin stretched wider.

"Thank you, King Agamemnon. You have given me a fine plan. I will keep my promise to you yet."

And so he rested alongside the others, waiting for the moment they arrived on the island. For then he would have his revenge and his gold in one swoop.

21

The island was as Yngvar remembered it. Under the springtime sun it seemed a mountainous paradise with palm trees and bushes dotting its breadth. The one beach suitable for landing sizzled like white iron. Gray gulls screamed overhead, chasing the Byzantine ship and scouting for unguarded pickings. Yngvar once had a desperate gull snatch a strip of meat from his hand just as he was ready to bite it. But these gulls were plump on the fish that flourished around the island. The gulls circled, then flew off in disappointment to their cliffside nests.

If only freshwater flowed on the island, it would make a fine home to a raider crew.

Except for the curse which ensured this island in the heart of the Midgard Sea remained off any sailor's voluntary path. Only the shipwrecked suffered it. And others who sought the cursed island died for their time upon it. This had also been Yngvar's experience, though he would defeat that curse.

The Byzantines swore a ship followed that ever vanished beyond the horizon. It had to be real, for more than one man would point and declare they had spotted it. But they never allowed Yngvar and his own men to see it for themselves. If they left their oars, Isaac would scream out for punishment. One of his sailors would take a shattered oar to the offender's back.

Yngvar was content that their fears should grow. It would only serve his plans.

Now they all forgot about the ghost ship as the island drew near. They had rowed day and night for two days, escaping Crete and skirting the Byzantines in Greece. Petronius's ship of deserters was itself like a black-hulled ghost. Though they spotted numerous sails along the way, none of the ships were interested enough to seek contact. With a war in Crete, all shipping was intent on either supplying the embattled forces or escaping them. A single ship was of no consequence to anyone.

Hamar was relieved of his steering duties. Yet the Byzantines forced him to an oar. Yngvar took his shift, and Isaac allowed it, though he sneered.

"Exhaust yourself, if that is your wish. You'll be leading the way to the gold all the same."

Now they had dropped the anchor stone, and the ship tugged to a halt in the deep water. Only two rowboats could fit on the deck, though they had towed the other two from Captain Leo's ship. Men now reeled these in and tied off ropes to let them descend into the rowboats.

Isaac gathered a spear and sword, as did his men. They ringed Yngvar and his crew, leveling spears. Isaac thumped his spear butt to the deck.

"We will go ashore and make camp. I will allow you five men. The rest will remain hostage aboard the ship. We will bind them hand and foot. If you delay, then I will throw one of them over the side for every hour you tarry. If you give me any troubles, I will throw them all overboard. Your giant friend remains unconscious. He will surely die without your aid, if not from his wound then from thirst. If you want him back, you will not delay."

Yngvar looked to the others. Gyna's face was red with anger. Ewald stood with her, his teeth clenched. Thorfast and Alasdair stared ahead as if they had lost their battle and awaited death.

"I won't delay," Yngvar said. "But five men can't do the work I need. The chamber I found was buried. I must dig out the passages. Give me ten men. I want to go as a fast as I can."

Isaac considered the offer. He scanned the tired crew. Yngvar now had just over twenty men, and Isaac had about the same number. He wanted to keep a numerical advantage over hostages, but greed decided for him.

"Ten men," he said. "But I will have the work done twice as fast."

"And what will happen to us when the work is done? Is that when you plan to kill us? I'll not agree to my men being tied. You can hide behind the length of that spear. But I'll kill you with my bare hands before I let that happen."

Isaac shook his head. "You don't negotiate with me."

"I do," Yngvar said, stepping up to the spearpoint. "Or you can go find that hidden chamber. You can go into the king's tomb and take the curse upon yourself. The ship that has followed you will find you at last. And my ghost will stand in its prow waiting to take you to hell. So if you kill me now, you take my curse and lose my knowledge. I do negotiate with you. All my men will be set upon the beach, untied. Then you will leave us the extra rowboats and flee with your treasure."

Yngvar grabbed the spear shaft and held it square to his heart. He raised his brow.

Behind Isaac, Bjorn opened his single eye and stared at Yngvar. He rested on his side. His ties had loosened from the kicking and prodding he had suffered from his bored guards. No one paid him any attention.

Yngvar had guessed by the second day that he was feigning helplessness. Now he knew it.

"I will still not allow more than ten men to accompany you into the tomb. The others will be under guard. So do as you are told and you will have your freedom."

"Swear this in your god's name. Swear that once we have claimed your gold, that you will leave us unharmed and with the two rowboats."

Isaac narrowed his eyes. Yngvar felt the spearpoint, still held to his breast, jab at his skin. His anger was quivering up the length of the shaft.

"I do so swear, before God in heaven, that once you have completed your work, you will be left to His judgement."

"That was a simple thing," Yngvar said, smiling. He released the spear shaft. "Now we can get to work. What of Bjorn and Petronius? Both are better off remaining where they are. But when we have completed our bargain, you will bring Bjorn to us."

Isaac looked to the two wounded men. They set both at opposite ends of the deck. Petronius had fallen deathly quiet during the journey, but they had fed him. He now lay out as if he had died. Yngvar could not be sure.

"I'll send the giant back to you," Isaac said. "You wanted Petronius before? Want him still? He tried to kill you."

"His fate is not my concern," Yngvar said. "Leave him with us if your conscience cannot bear killing him yourself."

With the tense negotiation concluded, they were herded toward the ropes to descend into the rowboats. All twenty of Yngvar's men filled two boats, sitting shoulder to shoulder. They rowed for the shore as Isaac's men filled their own rowboats. As they did, Isaac had bowmen cover Yngvar.

He had huddled in one boat with his Wolves, who now crowded with him.

"I have a plan," he said as they rowed. "We've only got this moment to discuss it. There is another treasure room. I believe after the earthquake there might have been other entrances into it that are now revealed to the surface. It is possible some of those passages Petronius originally found connect to it."

"Lord, what about Bjorn? I think he is awake."

"He's awake," Gyna said. "I think he awoke the first time someone stuck him with a spear."

"Auntie, why is he pretending like this?" Ewald looked over his shoulder as if to check Bjorn back on the ship.

"Because that hit on the head knocked sense into him," Thorfast said. "He's waiting for the right time to strike. They did not retie his bindings after they loosened."

"He'll know the moment soon enough," Yngvar said. "But I worry that he is still weak and unarmed."

"Then you don't know your cousin," Gyna said. "Leaving him aboard the ship means anyone left behind with it will be dead before sunrise."

"It's my plan that they are all dead before sunrise," Yngvar said. "I will take ten of us down into the tomb. Gyna and Alasdair, you two will remain behind. You are too obvious for what I plan. But I will need your stealth, so Ewald will also remain to help you. Just Thorfast and I will go into the tomb with eight of the Franks. We all need to speak the same language, and one the Byzantines don't know."

"Now comes the part where you tell us how we're all likely to get killed," Thorfast said. "It's always my favorite part of your plans."

Yngvar smiled, hauled on his oar, then looked toward the island.

"I made sure that we all got onto the island so that Isaac would be forced to join us there. He can't risk sending us unguarded. Otherwise, we might all climb into the mountains to escape. He and most of that crew did not come to the island the first time. Petronius confirmed that for me."

"You can't trust him," Gyna said. "He's a liar and only out for himself."

"It might be so, but I think he is right on this point. When the sun goes down I need you, Alasdair, and Ewald to get free of the Byzantines. Get up to those rocks that overlooked our camp, where Ragnar and Lucas the Byzantine had threatened to drop them on Petronius and his men. Thorfast and I along with the others will herd them to that spot. When we do, you crush whomever we've not already killed. We will do this by moonlight. So we will have to disappear for a brief time and Isaac will become suspicious. He might watch you closer then. But I'm counting on you. Isaac and the others won't realize there is a ready-made trap on the island."

They rocked through the waves, closing on the shoreline. His Wolves all shared skeptical looks. The Franks coughed and cleared their throats to express their doubt. But Yngvar laughed and shook his head.

"By sunrise we will sail home with our gold and more still. But trust my plan. Spread the word to the rest in the other rowboat. The ghosts of King Agamemnon's warriors will rise with the moon and avenge themselves on all trespassers. You need only be terrified and flee for your lives when they come for you. The Byzantines will follow. Lead them to that spot. Then crush them."

Questions flurried up from everyone in the boat, but Yngvar continued to row. He had explained their part of the plan. He would explain the details to those who went with him into the tomb once inside. He kept his head down and within a dozen strokes the questions faded. They pulled their rowboat onto the shore.

Yngvar splashed through the warm water, his naked feet pressing into the mud. He had removed his boots, as did the others, since they would need sure footing for the day ahead. Soaked boots might work against him and, given the humidity, might not dry until the next day.

All eventually gathered on the shore. Had a stranger come among them, he might think they were all companions and not prisoners and their captors. All secured the four rowboats, then proceeded peacefully to the remains of their old camp.

It was all as Yngvar remembered. He glanced up at the high rocks to his right as they entered the camp. Everyone who had been in his rowboat did the same. He worried Isaac would notice, but ordering his own crew consumed his attention.

The remains of their camp detailed the violence of its ending. Rocks still sat where they had fallen. Splinters of broken tent poles and their tattered cloths waved with the breeze. The remains of campfires formed black circles all around the foothills leading up to the original tomb entrance. That had collapsed. It looked nothing like it had before.

As they assembled, the scent of rot drifted on the breeze. It was not heavy, but the note of it was unmistakable. The dead had either not been buried deep enough or else it was Nordbert and the other's corpses rotting beneath the stones that had crushed them.

When this note of death circulated through Isaac and his men, they seemed to quail at it. They clustered together. Each seemed to expect a hand to seize them, bursting from the beach sand.

"They are frightened already," Yngvar said. "That is good."

"Lord, if ten of you go down into the tomb, then only about the same will remain here. If three of us vanish, it will be easier for Isaac to notice."

Yngvar considered this while he studied the Byzantines arguing among themselves. He tapped the side of his nose with his finger as he thought.

"I will signal," he said. "I will let out a howl. You will know it's me and that you should escape to the task I've set for you. It will create a distraction too."

Gyna explained to Ewald, though he waved her off as if he understood. She then looked up at the rocks.

"If they don't all fall together, the bastards will escape the trap."

"Then coordinate your effort," Yngvar said. "You've all day to look up there and figure a way to loose those rocks at once. I will drive them to you. If they run back toward us, then I will kill them."

"How?" Thorfast asked.

"Enough talking," Isaac said. He walked up behind Thorfast, causing him to wince in surprise. "We will set up camp and I want your people gathered in the center. Pick your ten men and begin. I want to see the treasure soon."

Yngvar nodded. He looked toward the black ship they left at anchor where Bjorn and Petronius remained. Only four men had been left behind, barely enough to set sails and steer the ship in an emergency. His treasure was all neatly piled on its deck.

"I will bring your treasure," Yngvar said. He rubbed the circlet on his arm and it caught Isaac's attention.

"Is that part of it? I'll have that on the treasure pile. Give it to me."

Yngvar sneered. He was actually relieved to remove the circlet and let Isaac hold it for him. He would have had to conceal it for his plan to succeed. Yet he pretended at anger.

"You must cut it off my arm if you want it."

"No games," Isaac said. "All treasure from this island belongs to me. Remember your giant friend is dying on my ship. If you play games, then he will surely die. Give me that gold band."

Yngvar stared at him, and Isaac's eyes faltered. But he worked it off and handed it to Isaac. He took it in both hands as if he had never touched gold before. He tittered and worked it onto his own arm, though it was too loose for him.

"Now," Isaac said, holding the band in place. "Pick your ten men and get to work."

Just like he had with the armband, he pretended to struggle with his choices. He selected both Ewald and Alasdair, but then returned them to the group.

"You are too small to carry the treasure," he said. "And you need to stay with your aunt or she'll do something foolish."

Gyna glared at him and was not pretending.

He selected Thorfast, Hamar, and seven others. All were from the other rowboat. He could better explain the entire plan to them if they were in the tomb together. After this process, he prepared torches and gathered tools. Many of the makeshift tools were still in the old camp. Isaac had brought a shovel. They also had iron bars and rope for removing obstructions.

These preparations consumed several hours, taking them closer to nightfall. But he could no longer delay without angering Isaac. He was already irritable and jumpy, as were all his men. By comparison, it would seem Yngvar's unarmed men were the captors rather than the reevers.

"Bring me a sample of the treasure first," Isaac said. "I want a taste of what we are waiting for."

Yngvar nodded.

"And to ensure you do as instructed," Isaac said. "I will take men in with you."

Yngvar stepped back. He had not expected Isaac to dare to enter the tomb. He could not complete his plans with him present.

Isaac stood straighter, as if challenging Yngvar to call him a coward.

But he inclined his head.

"Join us in the curse, if that is your wish. I will lead you to the treasure."

22

Yngvar's mind raced. He led his ten men, plus Isaac and his two favorites, up to the original excavated entrance. He did not want to speak of the cliffside entrance, for if Isaac knew of it he could dispense with Yngvar altogether. Isaac and his men brought up the rear of the long line with spears readied.

"Spears will be useless down there," Thorfast whispered. They picked a way among collapsed rocks to follow the original path in single file. Thorfast was directly behind him.

Yngvar scrabbled over a rock.

"His coming inside changes everything," he said. He grunted with the effort, then slid to the other side of the rock. The way forward was relatively clear now. The original crack in the hill was now a yawning gap. White gouges on the stones and heavy ruts in the dirt showed where Bjorn had cleared a path to rescue Thorfast and Alasdair.

The black hole was sizeable enough only for a man to fit through. The stench of rot permeated the air around the entrance. Yngvar had to cover his nose in the crook of his arm.

Thorfast gasped and cursed, as did Hamar and all the others who followed him to the tomb.

They stood outside as one of the Franks fumbled with his supplies, trying to extract a torch.

"By God, what an odor," Isaac also threw his arm across his nose. "Is this the way inside?"

Having been a coward, Isaac had never joined Petronius on the island and had no concept of the tomb's layout. His two followers seemed equally ignorant.

"This is the entrance," he said. "There may be another way, but it is the path I took out of the tomb."

"Well, how did we get all the gold out of that hole?" Isaac asked. He drew closer, and when the Frank had sparked flame to the torch, he grabbed it away. He then thrust it into the darkness and leaned toward with his hand over his nose and mouth.

"There are other entrances Petronius used," Yngvar said. "He and his men carried out most of the gold you have. Do you remember which tunnels he followed? Ah, but you stayed on the ship while others gathered your treasures. Strange how the situation has reversed now. I suppose you must trust me instead of doubt my every action."

Isaac turned back with a sneer. He brought the torch closer to Yngvar so that its heat licked his face.

"If you're playing a game with me, I'll know it. Your crew lives at my whim. So behave."

They locked eyes again, but this time Yngvar played the coward and lowered his head. Better Isaac think him defeated than plotting something.

"We can go look for other entrances," Yngvar said. "There is still some daylight. But I cannot say where those passages will lead. I know this way will definitely take us to the proper treasure room. Then you can shine your torch on gold and silver as you've never seen before, rather than burn my face with it."

Isaac chuckled but pulled back the torch. "All right, open up this passage and let's begin. We must hurry."

So they began the arduous work of widening the entrance. Ten men could not all fit around the entrance, which had the fortunate effect of pushing Isaac and his two friends farther down the path. So Yngvar could whisper to Thorfast and the others as they worked.

"Looks like Isaac wants to see what is down there himself. So we will not shake him. I had hoped the smell of dead bodies would frighten him off."

"He's doing a lot of praying," Thorfast said. "And this passage is thoroughly clogged. Alasdair and I came up through it and there's not much space inside. What is your plan?"

"I want to get back to the first chamber we found. The floor collapsed into the actual treasure room. I had a look around it, but I had only sparks and a makeshift torch for light. There is an exit that leads to a cliff face. But I am hoping there is another I did not find. I expect the earthquake revealed others."

"Or blocked other passages," Thorfast said. They both leaned over a large stone and worked together to heave it aside. When it cracked on the growing pile of rocks, Yngvar wiped sweat from his brow and continued.

"That may be. But at least there is one way out I am sure of. So, for now, we must get inside and get rid of Isaac."

"Kill him?" Hamar asked as he rested on the shovel handle. He had been digging around a stone at the base. "We've got iron bars, this shovel, rope, plenty to do the task."

"There is too much risk in that," Yngvar said. "He may have foolishly carried a spear, but he also has a dagger. All three do. And if any escape to warn their friends, they'll kill the others. In those narrow passages, it's an excellent chance one could slip off. I say we force a collapse between him and us."

"So this is the part of the plan where you get us killed," Thorfast said. "I knew there'd be a part like that. Are you mad? It's not like we can control a collapse."

"We can't," Yngvar agreed. "But I believe if we can all get down into the chamber, we can collapse the entrance behinds us and separate ourselves. That would be ideal. If not, we at least have the collapse to aid us in surprising them. A spear can thrust through the smallest spaces. So we are disadvantaged in a fight with them. Shovels and iron bars need space to swing and we won't have it. "

"Isaac will still know we fooled him," Thorfast said. "And the others will be in danger."

Yngvar shrugged. "We have to take some chances. We must not let him see us causing a collapse. That way he will believe it is misfortune. Even if he suspects we have fooled him, he still wants this gold. He'll drive the others inside to fetch it before he kills them all. And we will have time to carry out my plans."

"You must be finished to be chattering away like this." Isaac appeared, standing atop a stone to see over the low wall of debris they had excavated. He had tied a dirty rag over his mouth and nose against the stench. Yngvar and the others had already accustomed to it.

"We're ready now," he said. "There is a way in large enough to pass through if you duck. But the interior is still clogged. There will be tight passages."

"Let's find the treasure first," Isaac said. "Once I've seen it with my own eyes, I can decide how best to get it out."

Yngvar looked to the others and spoke as low as he could. "I will be at the rear and start the collapse. Just go forward to the main room. There is only one path."

Hamar, being accustomed to leading the way, took a lit torch and entered. The other Franks nodded to Yngvar. Each of them had dark circles around their eyes and sweaty faces smeared with dirt. Dust coated their clothes and sea salt formed white stains. Yet in their silent nods, Yngvar read their faith in him.

"When you find Nordbert and the others, pray for them."

Thorfast grinned at Yngvar, but the Franks seemed appreciative. They would pass the crushed bodies of their beloved captain and his companions. That was the odor that stifled them.

Once Thorfast slipped in, Yngvar followed. Isaac was behind him, and the final two followed. The last man in line carried a torch along with his spear.

They moaned and grunted with the effort of navigating the collapsed passage. Sections were empty enough to pass or blocked enough that only one man could squeeze through with effort.

The steep incline down led to cooler air. Yngvar might have thought it refreshing if it didn't smell like rotting corpses. At last, they found the place Nordbert and the others had escaped. Yngvar imagined Gyna slipping past them here. Now he understood why the

Franks resented her survival. The massive pile of rocks and earth seemed impossible to pass. Hamar and one other had to widen the passage, causing them to linger over the scent of decay.

"Tell them to hurry," Isaac snapped. He coughed and held the rag over his face tighter.

Clods of earth hit them like rain as Hamar grunted and cursed to clear the way forward. From his end, Yngvar could only see their heads. Many of the Franks had squatted along the wall to rest. The dim torchlight fluttered along the walls. Some smooth frescoes remained showing. But most had cracked and fallen away like giant snowflakes on the passage floor.

"I've opened the way," Hamar announced. His voice sounded weirdly flat in the confines of the passage. "Only one at a time may pass, but it'll do."

"Then get moving," Isaac said. He prodded Yngvar with his spear-point. He now held it so high up the shaft it seemed more like a dagger in his hand.

Each man slipped through the opening, having to shimmy sideways to step through. Yngvar leaned forward to Thorfast.

"Push everyone ahead once you're through. This is a natural spot for a collapse."

Yngvar's chest tightened and his breath grew ragged. This might be his only chance to remove Isaac and he might trigger a collapse none of them could escape. He imagined a dozen ways his plan could go wrong, but he had no better ideas. If he turned on Isaac now, grabbed his spear, he might wrest it away then kill him. But the man in the rear would flee, leaving the middle man to block pursuit. His crew would suffer for that failure.

So he stepped through the crack Hamar had opened. Thorfast's white hair was gray in the murky light. His eyes were wide with fear, but he nodded then turned to push the man before him. His hushed warnings sent them running ahead. The passage here was relatively clear. Most of the debris had clogged the point Yngvar now passed through.

He looked back to see Isaac waiting with his spear up and hand pressing the rag over his nose. He then looked to the pile of stones that made Nordbert's grave and whispered to it.

"A little help here, old friend. Come to our aid one last time."

As he slid between the cool, rough rocks his shoulder caught a loose stone. His mind seized on this, and as he pulled through, he shoved it behind so it shot toward Isaac.

Thorfast had left his metal bar for him. Yngvar had not even considered this and silently thanked him as he snatched it off the ground.

"Watch out," Isaac shouted as the stone thudded before him.

In that moment of distraction, Yngvar stood up in the darkness beyond the opening. He raised the bar in both hands and slammed it into the first crack in the ceiling he could find.

He bent back and rocks and earth fell away. A second time, he slammed into it.

It was as if he had slashed open a wine skin of earth.

Isaac screamed as stones and dirt rained down. Yngvar continued to dig and pry more from the ceiling, but Isaac and his men already recoiled from the opening.

"It's collapsing," Yngvar shouted. "Help me!"

But he did not want help. Earth fell into his eyes. Bitter dirt bounced into his mouth as he cried out. A stone struck his shoulder.

He ran back, and the ceiling around the entrance collapsed. A gray rock as big as a man slid through as if a thin sheet of earth held it in place. It slammed down across the opening, which had collapsed.

And it kept collapsing.

Yngvar grasped the iron bar with both hands. He sped down the corridor which billowed with plaster flakes from the walls and dirt from the ceiling.

He stumbled down the hall, and the right wall burst open, disgorging a wave of black earth. It swept him off his feet, then slammed him into the opposite wall. A spark of pain shot through his shoulder. But he still scrabbled to his feet even as more dirt poured through the breached wall. It was moist earth filled with stones that churned him as he tried to extract himself.

Falling onto the passage floor, he crawled ahead then regained his feet.

He sped headlong into darkness, knowing before him would be the entrance to the false tomb and the way down. Darkness was total. He could not see his hand before his face. He wondered if Hamar had lost his torch.

Or worse.

Then the ground vanished beneath him, and he tumbled screaming into darkness.

23

Yngvar's legs crumpled beneath him as he fell through darkness to slam onto rock. Bright pain filled his vision as he ricocheted away to crunch down into a pile of hard earth or stones. This at least cushioned his fall as he lay on his back.

The smell of rot had vanished, replaced with the odor of dust and ancient decay. All was still black until he realized he had squeezed his eyes shut. He blinked them open, forcing away the dirt that clogged the folds of his lids.

A thin yellow light flowed over him.

Thorfast's white hair and Hamar's square face were his first sights. He struggled to focus, squeezing his eyes to spill tears from their corners.

"Using the rope would've been better."

Thorfast extended a hand to him.

Yngvar now recognized the other Franks hovering around him. Hamar raised his torch high. Its low-burning flame lit all nine heads with an orange halo.

A rope dangled behind them from a massive crack in the rock ceiling. Cream-colored plaster covered it, though extensive sections of it had fallen away to reveal gray stone.

The black stone coffin from the room above impaled the real

coffin beneath it like a spear. He had struck it when he fell through and bounced away to land in—

He sat up and looked about himself.

Gold and silver coins spread out beneath him. He had landed in a bed of coins that had exploded from chests crushed by falling rocks.

"You're right," Thorfast said. "There's a lot more treasure in here. I'm shocked you kept a secret so long."

Yngvar blinked. Then he looked to his legs. Nothing had broken, but his left ankle throbbed. The rest of his body ached from the shock of impact.

"I am not sure I can stand," he said. "My ankle took the worst of that fall."

Hamar hissed and Thorfast kept his hand extended. Yngvar took it, then struggled to his feet. The ankle protested with a sharp pain that made him grit his teeth. But he slowly settled on it, using Thorfast for balance.

"If I go slow, I think I can bear it." He looked around. With proper torchlight the enormous burial chamber seemed so different from what he had remembered. He sniffed at the air. If one did not know to expect it, the notes of sea would remain masked underneath the scent of dust.

He stepped free of Thorfast and found he could walk, though with a limp. The stone slab that had fallen over him and protected him from being crushed remained as it had. Agamemnon's coffin had been smashed open, and Yngvar saw the gaping hole where the king's remains released his ancient crown to his care. The precious stones set into the coffin winked in the light, though some had fallen from their settings to rest beside it.

"There are more items than coins," Thorfast said. "It seems you had gathered them already."

Yngvar scanned the floor. There was too much to consider now. Gold and silver plates, fabulous sea shells, jewelry and rings, jeweled daggers. Animal bones that he had disturbed in his fumbling were scattered about. Oil from broken earthenware jugs remained pooled on the floor as he remembered.

But more important, and key to his plan, were nine corpses lying facedown on massive bronze shields.

"There they are." His voice echoed around the chamber, calling everyone back from marveling over the treasures.

"Corpses," Thorfast recoiled. "Nine of them."

"There were ten, but I burned one to signal Alasdair for help. They will aid us in defeating the Byzantines."

He stared admiringly at their ancient helms and stained but sturdy bronze shields. Their harness had fused to their bodies and their spear shafts were brittle with age. But their spearpoints were long and honed to a brilliant edge. Yngvar was certain they could cut fresh sailcloth as easily as cutting an old sack.

"Is that the king?" Hamar asked, pointing at the coffin in the center of the room.

"It is. And you should thank him for his hospitality. For he has set out all we need." Yngvar pointed around the room. "Jeweled daggers and ancient swords collected here. Hunting bows and quivers collected there. The helmets and shields of his picked men resting before the way out of this chamber."

He pointed to the nine corpses and their ten shields. The rack that had once held the ancient guardians standing against the wall still linked them together as they faced the floor.

Thorfast laughed. Yet Hamar and the Franks did not seem to understand. Yngvar gathered them close and spoke in a low voice. He could not be certain echoes would not carry his plan up to his enemies.

"Isaac and his men fear the curse of this island. They fear a ship full of vengeful ghosts follows them. They are mad with fear. But they do not know the respect we have with King Agamemnon. They do not believe he preserves us as long as we will bring his glory and name to the north."

"Did they get caught in the collapse?" Thorfast asked. He held a dagger with a gilt handle and turned it in his hands.

"A rock separated us," Yngvar said. "I do not know what happened to them after. The hall continued to collapse on me. It may have done the same for them. But we must plan as if he survived and returned to the others. We have little time to waste, or else they might begin to search the ruins on their own. Worse still, they may kill our men and leave."

"They can try to kill them," said one of the Franks. "But they underestimate who they are fighting."

Yngvar shrugged.

"Whatever is happening aboveground, I cannot say. My plan will finish them for good. We will take up ancient shields and helmets. We will take swords and spearheads. We will become the living vengeance of King Agamemnon. Then we will rise from the grave by starlight and howl for the blood of those who trespass on our island. We will swoop down on them, driving them toward the trap Alasdair and Gyna have set and killing any who stands against us. Then we will capture their ship, for Bjorn is alive and well there. His four guards will be a pile of so many entrails when we return to that ship."

The Franks let out excited and joyous shouts. Yngvar looked to the ceiling, fearing to hear Isaac calling down curses. But he only heard the celebration.

"I thought it odd he lay quiet for so long," Hamar said.

"His skull is made of rocks," Thorfast said. "They brought him low at least long enough to capture him. But he's been pretending ever since."

"So, our plan is simple after we take their ship," Yngvar said. "There is a passage out of this room that leads to what must have been an ancient landing. We can set our anchor there and load this treasure onto the Byzantine ship. We will be twice as rich as before and finished forever with these Byzantines."

The men again laughed and lauded the plan. Hamar, however, looked thoughtful.

"I'm not sure I know how to steer that ship. Its sails and rigging structure differ from what I know. And it's much bigger. I can't see the water as easily."

"A ship is a ship, no matter its size," Yngvar said. "There is a steering board and there are sails. If you are familiar with one kind, it is no challenge to learn another."

"A Norse ship is far easier to sail," Hamar said. "Even a fisherman could steer one just using oars alone. But these Byzantine ships are different. And we shattered half their oars to make matters harder on us."

"Well, it will be a better problem to have than our problems now." Yngvar looked around the circle of men gathered to him. "We must find another way out of here. Bring your torches to the walls and look for cracks and feel for airflow. I have learned that the ancient people sealed up rooms and passages and never left a way open that was too obvious. There must be another means out of here. If we must use the way by the sea, we can scale the cliff. I did it once, though not with a giant metal shield on my back."

"You scaled a cliff?" Thorfast cocked his brow, then set the dagger he had been admiring into his belt. "Is there anything you can't do? The heroes of old seem as children beside you."

"Be useful and search the walls." Yngvar spun his friend around, then pushed him ahead. "I must offer my respect to the king while you do."

He paused before the dark opening to King Agamemnon's stone coffin. Perhaps this was not the real Agamemnon. He had trusted the slave Theodoros to have been accurate in his translation. But working in the dark might have frightened or confused him. Was this king that glorious hero of legend? Yngvar had never heard of him and also doubted anyone beyond the Midgard Sea had ever heard of him. Could the corpse moldering in the darkness of this coffin be another king hoping to take credit for the great Agamemnon?

It did not matter. For whatever the genuine nature of this tomb, it was filled with gold and ghosts. The ghosts had chosen to aid him in trade for a promise to make them famous in lands beyond their reach.

He looked down into the opening. The withered skull stared up at him. Gray flesh as thin as onion skin clung to bone. Eyelids had formed to empty slits, the flesh of the eyeballs long rotted away. Yellow teeth like pegs peeked out behind decayed lips. Wispy strands of gray hair hung loose around the skull, and patches of broken skin showed where Yngvar had lifted away the circlet.

"Great King Agamemnon," Yngvar said. "I have surrendered your crown to my enemy, but only for a brief time. You have ever aided me since I swore my oath to you. Now, I am here upon your island at the mercy of my enemies. These men would make it so I never carry your name to the north. I beg you to lend me strength against them, and I will be forever in your debt."

Speaking to a corpse, even one he felt a strange kinship for, turned his hands cold. The eyeless sockets seemed to stare into his own. He felt as if his words were being weighed with careful thought. Perhaps, if the king judged his words poor, a skeletal arm would stretch from the broken stone lid and grab him by the throat.

He turned away in time for Thorfast to shout out.

"Here it is! Directly opposite the other exit!"

Within moments the Franks had set their bars to the crack Thorfast found. Plaster and mortar broke as bricks crumbled aside. Shortly after, Hamar pushed his torch into the darkness.

"It is a passage," he announced.

"Then gather your costumes," Yngvar said. "For we go ahead now as draugr of the ancient people. Learn your roles well. Speak no words, but raise the anguished cries of the dead. Victory is at hand."

Yngvar's ankle throbbed as he limped toward the nine corpses and their gear. Thorfast looked him up and down, but Yngvar waved him off.

"A limp will look fine for a draugr. Better to move as if my bones are brittle with age than like a healthy living man."

"Just don't worsen it," Thorfast said. "No one will fear a lame draugr."

They picked their war gear with care. The huge shields easily concealed most of their bodies. Their ancient designs showed snakes, octopuses, stags, and monsters of various shapes. Yngvar did not make a careful study of these. His shield showed a terrible hag with snakes for hair. Thorfast's showed the remains of a leering face, but most of the paint had worn away with time.

Their helmets were old and ill-fitting. The horsehair crests were rotted and thin. But cheek-pieces hid their faces. Nighttime shadows would do the rest. They wore shin guards of bronze, but wore their own boots.

"It seems their arms were revealed." Yngvar pointed to the many depictions of warriors painted on the walls or on huge vases. "So tear off your sleeves or else throw off your shirts. No one will look at our feet. But our ruse will fail if we do not otherwise appear as these ancients did."

"It seems they wore a cuirass," Thorfast said. "But these men do not have such armor."

"These shields will hide our bodies from Isaac and the others," Yngvar said. "Besides, they build a cuirass for its wearer and would not fit us. Now, you all look like frightening spirits of the ancient people. Are you ready to bring death?"

Behind their shields and in the pitiful light of Hamar's dying torch they seemed as warriors from a lost time. Shadows filled their faces from their huge helmets. Their swords were more for ceremony than killing, but each of them had taken a spearhead to wield like a short sword. Those honed edges were certainly intended to kill.

Yngvar led them down the new passage. It was narrow and heavily collapsed. Dust and earth drizzled over them as they worked along its length. It seemed it might lead to a dead-end or else blockage, but the torch now in Yngvar's hand wavered with a fresh breeze.

"The way out is near," he whispered. "We must soon extinguish this torch. Remember the plan. Use their fear to herd them. Kill whenever you can, but do not chase men who run off-course. We can hunt down stragglers later. The idea is to crush Isaac's fighting strength and force them to either surrender or else hide on the island until we are gone."

They arrived at a place that seemed to have started excavation but was then abandoned. Perhaps Petronius had been digging in this hall just when Yngvar had returned. Had he continued, he would have unearthed the real treasure on this island.

Again, Yngvar thanked the gods and most of all thanked King Agamemnon.

He ground out the torch into the dirt that had fallen back into the passage. The bitter scent of the smoke rose into the darkness. Gray light now spilled in to illuminate the exit. He then gestured the others to help him widen it. They now had huge bronze shields to fit through the opening. But so eager were they to escape the tomb and begin their attack that the exit was soon laid bare.

Yngvar stepped out, his ankle protesting as he did, into the balmy night. Compared to the stale and murky stenches of the grave, the sea air was a bright and sharp contrast. Moonlight draped the island and turned the distant beach to stripes of milky gray. Waves rolled in and lapped the coast. But this was not the shore of their campsite.

"I know where we are," Yngvar said. "We've just got to round the hill behind us and we will be back at camp."

The others ducked low out of instinct, each nodding his head. Yngvar had broken his own rule about speech, such was his excitement. Yet he saw no one near.

Now he lumbered along with the shield before him and helmet heavy on his brow. His limping caused it to slide forward over his eyes. If he had to fight, he feared the helmet would be more hinderance than help.

At last the group saw the glow of campfires over the small, rocky ridge. He had to signal Gyna and Alasdair, plus create the distraction they needed to slip away.

He turned to Thorfast and the others. He drew them close, then whispered.

"Howl and groan now. Let their fear grow as we draw near."

Yngvar led the call. He leaned back, letting out his version of a ghostly call from the grave. Thorfast began to laugh.

"A draugr or the ghost of a goose? Which are you?"

"Make a noise, you worthless shit!"

The Franks joined, though some calls cracked from the laughter at Thorfast's jest. But Yngvar remained steady, and soon they were all calling out as one.

No one answered. But they had to have heard the cries by now. Yngvar waved his men forward. He limped ahead with his shield covering from chin to knee. The shin guards were heavy and clapped against his feet as he climbed the shallow hill. But he never stopped wailing.

He was a draugr, after all.

At the top of the short rise, he met three Byzantines with spears.

They huddled together like as many frightened boys clinging to their mother's skirts. When he saw them, he raised his gold-gilt sword and pointed it at them. He let out a breathy moan.

Despite Thorfast's criticisms, the men believed him readily enough. They turned and fled toward the light of the campfires.

This success encouraged the others, who now joined him. They hid themselves behind shields and stalked forward, their voices hoarse from their shrill calls.

The camp ahead seemed to rise as one. They looked at what to their eyes must be ten ancient warriors sweeping from the hill.

One of his freemen ran forward, pointing at them. "Look, the spirits of the island have come for us. It is Agamemnon himself!"

Yngvar winced at the overacting and the proclamation of Agamemnon's arrival. None of them looked especially kingly. Yet the superstitious fear overcame them.

Raising his sword, Yngvar shouted a war cry and then signaled the others to charge. He could not join them, or else he would surely collapse.

Nine ancient warriors surged forward, rushing at the camp.

Shrieks of terror answered their rush. Thorfast was fastest of them all. With his hair tucked beneath a mighty helm, he was hard to distinguish for the others. Yet he was also first to bring down one of the three men who had fled their approach.

With the dying man's cry of pain, the camp scattered. Men ran in every direction, though his own men ran toward the supposed safety of the cliffs.

Now Yngvar relied on them to herd their enemies. His acting would not serve them long. Panic was their only advantage. Once moonlight and campfire light revealed they were merely Franks hiding behind ancient shields and helmets, their advantage would vanish just like the ghosts they pretended to be.

Yet the Franks spread out and swept their enemies ahead toward the high rocks. The flow of Yngvar's men in that direction was an unconscious guide to them. When men fled, they followed the nearest man rather than choose their own paths.

They left Yngvar behind because of his ankle. But it seemed they would not need him. In moments, most of the Byzantines would be under the rocks, and Yngvar's men would slip away to let Alasdair and Gyna unleash death upon them.

A glow of pride swelled him. He raised his ceremonial sword and added his wail to the others. Then he continued to limp forward.

Isaac and his two companions blocked his way.

They stepped out from behind a boulder. Dirt and dust covered them. Isaac's dust-coated hair turned iron gray in the light. A dark and shining line of blood ran from his crown down along his cheek. His companions had fared no better. But they all still carried their spears.

When they encountered Yngvar, they fell back in fear.

But Isaac barred his companions from fleeing.

"Use your senses," he said. "That's no ghost. He's wearing Yngvar's clothes."

Such a simple statement, but it rallied Isaac's men.

Yngvar pointed his sword at Isaac and howled, hoping to shatter his confidence. Petronius had said he was superstitious. Yet the canny Byzantine curled his lip.

"Fuck you. You want to play at a ghost? I'll grant you the chance for real."

Yngvar was alone on the hill, his ankle weak, his sword a mere prop, and his shield and helmet too big for proper use.

He smiled.

"The gods are with me. Bring your best."

Isaac and his two men lowered their spears and charged up the hill.

24

Amid the howling of false ghosts and the screams of terrified men, Yngvar shouted his own battle cry. Isaac and two men raced up the hill toward him with lowered spears. Moonlight shined on the spear blades. Yngvar clasped an ancient spear blade in his belt. The gilt sword raised overhead was more of a club than a blade.

He could not escape the lopsided combat. No one would come to his aid in time. For this battle would be decided in moments. He would either shove back three men or else be impaled on three spears.

Fate would decide the contest in as many heartbeats.

The mighty bronze shield covered him. As Isaac and the others charged up, he hunkered behind it to brace for them. A tiny gap between his ornate helmet and the rim of the shield allowed him to watch their charge. Behind them, men churned and fled from Thorfast and the other false ghosts into the darkness.

As Isaac and his screaming companions neared the end of their charge, Yngvar kneeled to the ground and sheltered under his bronze shield. He did not trust his ankle to hold him, nor did he trust his sword to do more than harry his enemy.

Instead, he trusted the strength of the earth and the advantage of being uphill. By shrinking before them and sheltering under the huge shield, he became like a stone.

Three spears slammed into his shield. He heard one shatter, and two screeched across the bronze. He imagined the hag face with her head of snakes staring into Isaac's stunned eyes as his spear rebounded. He heard him curse. One of his companions lost his footing and crashed to his knees.

Yngvar burst forward, shoving with the might of his enormous shield. The ancient people must have been strong to carry such heavy shields to battle. Combined with his height advantage, Yngvar sent all three men stumbling back down the shallow slope.

He snatched up the ceremonial sword. The Byzantine who had stumbled was already scrabbling away. But Yngvar was too fast. He rammed the blade into his enemy's throat. The sword flexed but pierced the skin. The Byzantine rolled aside and gurgled up blood that showed black in the moonlight.

"Two more," Yngvar shouted as he looked down at Isaac and his companion. He let the sword fall away with its victim. The blade had bent, and its edge was now spent.

Isaac's other companion had recovered already, crawling up with a spear in one hand.

Yngvar leaped forward and slammed the edge of his shield across the man's skull. Whether it killed him was unclear. But the Byzantine flattened with a cry muffled in the dirt.

Then Yngvar's ankle buckled and he collapsed.

His hand was already on the neck of the ancient spearhead. He had yanked it free even as he rolled down the slope toward Isaac, who was now rising to his feet. His helmet fell from his head, and he lost the grip on his heavy shield. The short skid downslope had stripped him of all defense but his shin guards.

"You treacherous bastard," Isaac shouted as he straightened with the aid of his spear. "You're a dead man!"

Yngvar pulled over a shield that was no longer on his arm. The miscalculation lasted only a heartbeat. But it only takes as long to thrust a spear.

And Isaac already poised to strike.

The blade flashed as it drew back under moonlight.

Yngvar braced himself to buck away from the strike.

Then a crash of stone and screams of horror rose behind them. The ground shivered underfoot.

Isaac's cocked arm locked in place, and he turned toward the sudden noise.

Yngvar had expected it.

He rolled forward into Isaac's legs. Coming from uphill, he easily bowled over the Byzantine. He slumped over Yngvar's body.

The keen spearhead slipped up between his ribs and into his heart. Yngvar's fingers pressed close to Isaac's flesh. Hot blood gushed over his hand. He could feel the mighty pulse of Isaac's heart as it burst.

He spasmed atop Yngvar's body but gave no shout of pain.

"The gold ... my ... gold ..."

Blood poured out over Yngvar's hand and onto his body. With Isaac crosswise over him, he could not easily see his face. He was unsure if his enemy still clung to life. Yet he gritted his teeth and cursed him.

"That was the sound of your men being crushed to death. Join them in hell, you piece of shit."

He twisted the spearhead, and Isaac jerked. A low groan escaped him, breathy and desperate. But as Yngvar twisted again, his enemy did not react.

Isaac was dead.

Sloughing away the corpse, Yngvar called out in triumph. His ankle had nearly cost him his life. But the good work of his crew had ultimately saved him. He rolled over, wicking blood from his hands and arms as he did. Then he struggled to his feet.

He stood over Isaac's body, then rolled it over to see his face. His expression was caught between shock and regret, but his eyes were unfocused and dead.

"Greedy little turd," Yngvar muttered. He grabbed Isaac's spear, then worked off the ill-fitting gold band from his arm. He shouted with triumph as he pulled it free, then replaced it on his left arm.

"As promised, great King Agamemnon, I will use your gold to bring your glory to all men of the North."

With Isaac's spear for a crutch and weapon, he resumed his limp down the slope toward the camp. He shook off the bronze leg guards, finding them heavy and pointless.

Ahead were cries of agony and fear.

But also of jubilation. He reached the edge of the camp where Thorfast and the other Franks in disguise now linked arms and howled in triumph.

Before them was a tall pile of rocks and earth. Dust curled up, orange in the light of the campfires. Atop the ridge where stones and dirt still crumbled, Alasdair and Gyna stood. Yet they did not look toward Yngvar. They instead called down to the pile of rocks, resting on hands and knees and straining into the rising dust.

"What happened?" Yngvar had limped up to Thorfast and his celebrating ghosts. His pale-haired friend looked him over head to toe.

"Did you fall into a barrel of swords? All that blood!"

"Isaac is dead," Yngvar said as he impatiently pointed Thorfast to the collapsed ridge of stone. "Why are they calling down like that? Did our men get away?"

"Our men fled," Thorfast said. Now the other Franks paused to consider.

"The crew has gathered over there," Hamar said, pointing at them all huddled together. Rather than celebrating, they stood mute and staring at the pile.

"It's a hard thing to have crushed so many," Thorfast said. "You can see the blood leaking between the stones already. Must have sounded horrible up close."

But Yngvar did not believe the gruesome deaths of hated enemies would sober his men. He redoubled his pace and headed for the pile.

The trap had not caught every Byzantine. Some had fled in other directions. If they had survived, they dared not show themselves. For a landslide of stone and earth crushed most of their companions.

Thorfast had been right. Blood leaked from around the stones and earth that had piled beneath the ridge. As he neared, he smelled the foul stench of burst guts. The stones had been heavy. They did not bounce as expected, but crashed deep into the ground to pulverize anything beneath them.

As he arrived at the pile, he could hear Alasdair and Gyna calling out together.

"Ewald! Ewald!"

Gyna now dangled from the edge, then dropped onto the stone pile. She began to dig and throw aside rocks. Alasdair, in comparison, leaned back on his knees and crossed himself.

"Ewald!"

Yngvar did not need an explanation. Though he had not witnessed it himself, he understood what had happened.

A fresh gap showed in the ridge where the Alasdair, Gyna, and Ewald had prepared the trap. Alasdair and Gyna had been at either side with Ewald in the middle. That boy had always wanted to be at the center of everything.

When the stones crumbled, the center gave way.

The collapse swept Ewald along with it, down to be crushed amid the brown rocks of this cursed island.

Gyna wept as she clawed at the stones, flinging them aside as she repeated her nephew's name.

"A king's life for a king's favor," Yngvar whispered. "A heavy price."

He lowered his head as tears threatened, both for the end of a hopeful young life and for Gyna's loss. She had wanted to raise him as a son. She had not spoken those words. But he understood now. That desire had been the reason for her change. She wanted to be responsible and to think beyond the next moment so that Ewald would learn the same. She wanted him to claim his inheritance and become the leader he dreamed he was.

And now all that hope lay smothered under stones.

Thorfast, Hamar, and the Franks joined him. They held their shields low and threw off their heavy helmets.

"Should we help her dig?" Thorfast asked.

"We should. But not for any hope Ewald survived. We should dig for her sake."

So they hauled aside stones. The smell of blood was thick here.

But no one caught in this trap had been injured. They had all been killed. No muffled cries came from the pile. No hand reached up to claw at freedom. Any hand they found was merely a hand and nothing more.

The rest of the crew joined, so much that there was no room for all to work. The excess returned to the campsite to gather weapons the Byzantines had abandoned. It was a practical decision, and one Yngvar was grateful to not need to command.

Gyna eventually collapsed atop the pile of stones, throwing her arms wide as if to embrace the whole of it. She set her cheek against one stone and cried.

"Lord," Alasdair had climbed down from the cliff and now worked at Yngvar's side. "He was the only one of us killed in what could've killed many others. Yet why do I not feel like it was a victory?"

Yngvar sighed. "Every time anyone I lead dies for this gold, I wonder if it is worth the cost. Too many of our men are dead on this island. Have I really avoided the curse?"

Alasdair sighed. Now that Gyna had surrendered her effort to find Ewald alive, the others drifted away from what was now a burial mound for friend and foe.

"Lord, there is much treasure. So there must be equal cost to claiming it. I have feared the curse. But now I have decided to trust God, no matter how strange our fates become. As you have consoled me, I will console Gyna when she is ready to hear it. We must believe that Ewald's death was to avoid something far worse in his future. He has been given mercy, and we sinners have been awarded the punishment of suffering the loss of the good. If the gold has been worth our sacrifice, I cannot say, lord. We have not yet secured it."

Yngvar clapped Alasdair's shoulder. "Wise words. The worth of this gold will be for us to determine. I once wanted gold and coin to flaunt my power over other men. I chased it because the heroes of song chased it. Now I know better the bloody cost of such riches. When this gold is finally ours, I shall use it so it will justify its cost."

"There is still a ship capable of sailing away and stranding us," Thorfast said. He wiped grit from his hands across his thighs. "And while the Byzantines who escaped are still hiding, we need to secure the rowboats to keep them from escaping in them."

The cold logic was right in Yngvar's mind.

"Hamar, see to the rowboats then pick a boarding crew. We must clear the decks of that ship and ensure Bjorn is well."

"And that Petronius is dead," Thorfast said. "Or else I think Gyna will cut him to pieces with a small knife."

They filled two rowboats with men, leaving a handful ashore to guard the remaining boats. Yngvar would have preferred they all return, but Gyna remained atop her nephew's grave. He could not ask her to follow now, even if it was to rescue Bjorn.

They rowed by moonlight, trusting their shadowy forms would mask their identities from the four guards Isaac left behind. One hailed them from the ship as they neared. Yngvar shook his head so that none of the freemen would attempt a reply. When the rowboats glided to bump against the hull, the four guards gathered close. One dropped a rope ladder over the side to make the scant distance easier to scale.

Yngvar moved to climb first. He had a Byzantine sword at his hip and clenched a Byzantine dagger in his teeth. He scrambled up the ladder, and in the gloomy light of a single lantern set on the mast he remained unrecognized. One Byzantine even helped him aboard. He removed the dagger from between his teeth and all four men stared at it in confusion.

"When you see Isaac in hell, ask him who sent him there."

He shoved the Byzantine who had aided him overboard. He screamed as he plunged headfirst into the dark sea. Without delay, he whirled on the next crewman to ram his dagger into his ribs. He groaned and collapsed forward, clawing at Yngvar's face. He wrestled aside so that Thorfast and the others could follow.

The remaining two had swords drawn and ready.

But a great black shape gathered behind them and they vanished. Only their screams of terror marked them.

Bjorn held a head in each hand, then smashed their skulls together. He roared with fury, repeating it until both hapless victims dropped their swords, clanging to the deck.

"You fucking bastards!" Bjorn screamed. "Kick me and stab me, will you?"

Both thumped to the deck. Bjorn raised his massive foot and stomped on one man's head. He then lifted the other off the deck with both hands. He held the sailor overhead and let out a massive bellow. Then he dropped to extend his right knee and slammed the sailor over it.

The hapless man wailed in agony as his spine snapped with a dull pop. Bjorn rolled him aside with disdain, then returned to the other whose skull he smashed.

"Dead already? What did you do with the other two?"

The rest of the boarding crew were still clambering onto the deck to back up Yngvar.

"They're dead," Yngvar said, nodding toward the corpse at his feet.

"You bastard! I've been waiting to rip their guts out, and you killed them. You got to take their place."

Bjorn rushed forward, throwing his arms around Yngvar. But it was no attack. His cousin crushed him in a bear hug but laughed as he rocked him in his arms.

"I knew you'd get the treasure. Just knew it! Damn foolish Byzantines, they can all rot. Every one of them is a bastard."

"I'm glad the freemen can't understand you," Yngvar said, finally shoving his way free. Jubilant Bjorn turned his affection to Thorfast, who was already backing away to avoid him. He did not.

"We're all richer than the richest king," he shouted. "Lost our ship. But we'll buy ten more better than her. Look, the treasure is all here."

He spun Thorfast from beneath his arm and pointed at the treasure. Thorfast wobbled as if he were drunk.

"Did that blow to your head make you forget your strength? Don't kill us celebrating."

Bjorn laughed and shoved Thorfast away. He threw his arms wide to display his massive body to the rest of the men.

"A lucky knock on the head. Hurts still and my one good eye wasn't right for a bit. But I've never been better. Never!"

Yngvar calmed Bjorn, then turned to his crew. "Dump the bodies overboard. Check them for treasure first. Then get this ship ready to sail. By daylight I'll show you where we will gather more treasure still."

Alasdair found Petronius beneath a cloak and had pulled it from his head. His face was blue and his unfocused eyes stared at the moon. Black bruises showed around his neck where powerful hands had crushed his throat closed. Yngvar shook his head over the corpse.

"A sad end. He was a strange man, both friend and enemy."

"As soon as you left, my four guards choked him to death. He couldn't even fight back." Bjorn mimicked hands choking him by the throat. "Just seemed like something they decided themselves. But it was really you that killed him. He wasn't going to live with that leg wound."

Yngvar replaced the cloak over Petronius. "Maybe they expected a reward for doing what Isaac feared to do himself. Bastard died on his ship, though."

Bjorn laughed. But no one else did. Alasdair crossed himself and walked away with a frown.

"What's with his long face?" Bjorn asked. "Lad looks more pale than usual."

"Come with me. I need to tell you some hard news." Yngvar led him aside from the others, then described what had happened on the island. Bjorn's merry mood faded with every turn in the story. By its end, his one eye leaked tears.

"Ewald was a dutiful boy. Brave, strong, willing to fight. I wanted to show him some things. You know, once we settled on land. Show him how to use an ax. Now he's dead, and Gyna's heart is broken. She was getting soft over that boy."

"I know she was," Yngvar agreed. "Stay close to her, Bjorn. In fact, you should marry her and get her with a child of her own."

Bjorn staggered back, putting a thick hand over his heart. His one eye was as wide and bright as the moon, it seemed.

"Marriage and a kid? You want to kill me?"

"Come now," Yngvar said, smiling. "You were talking like a father just a moment ago. Admit it. Gyna is a rare woman. Claim her before she decides on another. I don't understand why she's stuck on you, but she is right now. Don't worry about what to do. We'll be so rich we'll never need to go a-viking again. We can enjoy our spoils and grow old with our families. Then when we are toothless and gray-haired, we will sail away for one last adventure and die as heroes."

"No more fighting? Wife and children?" Bjorn turned his one eye to the treasure. "Maybe I should've dumped this overboard."

Yngvar laughed. "Fate has put you two together. No man can deny the three heartless goddesses who spin a man's fate to their whims. Besides, you love her. And you can foster your children with me. I'll teach them more than just the best way to split a skull with an ax."

"Yeah, and what about you? I'm not getting tied up with a family if you ain't. You got to marry, too."

"I will," Yngvar said. He tried to imagine this woman, but none came to mind. He had once fancied Thorfast's sister, Kadlin. But he had been a boy then, with a boy's dreams. The years had concerned him with oaths, ships, raids, and deeds of glory. There had never been any woman to last through all of that.

"To who, then?" Bjorn asked.

But the question remained unanswered.

Alasdair shouted from the rails of the starboard side.

"Lord, I can't believe it. But there really is a ghost ship out there. And it's heading for us."

Alasdair's warning halted all activity on the deck. Men looked to each other, then turned to follow his pointing finger. Bjorn and Yngvar did the same, but Yngvar could not see what Alasdair did. He rushed to the rails with Bjorn. Both strained to see into the moonlit distance.

"I can't see in the dark no more," Bjorn growled in frustration. "What is the lad talking about? What ghost ship?"

Yngvar strained to see. He leaned forward until he was so far over the water his nose filled with its scent.

At first he thought it was the glint of moonlight on the waves. But then he saw the thin, gray outline of a mast. Then he saw spidery limbs rising and falling aside a moon-painted hull. Oars.

He could not believe what his mind was telling him.

"Lord, it cannot be." Alasdair said.

"What cannot be?" Bjorn shouted. "I can't see a fucking thing. Tell me!"

"It must be," Hamar said. "But I can't believe it either."

"It is," Yngvar said.

"What? Tell me or I'll rip your eyes out myself!"

Thorfast blew through his teeth, then lowered his head.

"Tell me!"

Yngvar put his hand on Bjorn's shoulder, stared at the gray shape gliding silently through the moonlight toward the glow of their lantern.

"It's our ship. Someone is rowing our ship and I don't think they mean us any good."

25

Yngvar raced across the deck, scooping up the bows he could find. Others followed along. Some bows were unstrung, and their strings lost. Those with strings still attached to one end, he handed Bjorn to string.

"Lord, I've found arrows." Alasdair whispered across the deck. "There are few remaining."

"We just need a volley," Yngvar whispered back, "I want them to board us. I want my ship back."

"How is it here?" Hamar asked as he searched beside Yngvar. "She was sinking when we left her."

"Maybe it's a ghost after all." Yngvar picked the last bow off the deck.

They gathered eight bows with strings. They had more unstrung bow staves. The archers must have kept their strings on their person. Eight was enough to thin a boarding party.

Thorfast, who kept watch, now waved his hand for Yngvar's attention.

He now saw the clear outline of his ship. So he grabbed the lantern from its hook on the mast, then flung it overboard on the opposite side. He did not want to alert them too early or else they might turn aside. Now they were too close to avert their course.

"This is madness," he said. He handed a bow to one freeman. He preferred the sword in hand. "I'm defending against my own ship. Might as well kill me with my own sword."

His ship sat lower in the water than it should, indicating it was still taking on water. But whoever sailed the ship must have made basic repairs. The strake was buckled, and with no caulking it leaked too heavily for open sea sailing. He wondered at who would have done this.

But he did not wonder for long.

As the ship glided ahead like a silent hunting shark, he saw head covers on the crew.

Arabs.

The Arabs from Crete that fled into the hills had stolen his ship and pursued. They either suspected the Byzantines carried great treasure or one of the Byzantine wounded might have admitted to it. While Yngvar assumed he left none behind alive, it was possible some had only been unconscious and revived later.

Yngvar did not doubt the gold-hungry Arab pirates from Crete had patched his ship and set off after Isaac. They had trailed behind, waiting for a night when the Byzantines sat peacefully at anchor and unsuspecting. They had truly been as ghosts.

With the lantern extinguished, only the moon drizzled silvery pale light across the deck. Yngvar hoped it would better hide the bowmen spread out along the rails. But the Arabs knew they had been spotted. They turned the ship broadside and sent boarding hooks spinning silently through the gloom.

Yngvar raised his fist to signal a stay of arrows. He wanted the Arabs secured to his ship before unleashing their scavenged arrows. They numbered fifteen men to what he surmised were nearly thirty Arabs. But he did not fear a lopsided combat. The bows that the Byzantines had thoughtfully prepared for him would strafe away the Arab numerical advantage.

So hooks thumped onto the rails and deck. One hook slammed beside his foot, and he remembered how Lucas the Byzantine had died. He stepped back from the iron hook as it gouged the boards. He watched his ship intently, but from his sides he noted his men had drawn their bows and angled them down at the Arabs. Still, he held his fist high. The Arabs had not yet tied the ships together beyond hope of escape.

They were full of throaty curses. But for the moment it did not feel like the start of a battle to Yngvar. The Arabs worked mostly in silence. His own men prepared to meet the enemy and stood locked in place. They lacked shields, but held the advantage of standing higher than Yngvar's ship. It was a position he could come to enjoy, though he would always prefer his own ship best.

Bjorn and Thorfast flanked him. Bjorn held a sword taken from one of his slain captors, but it seemed small in his hand. He gripped it more as if asking what it was for than preparing for a fight.

Alasdair had gathered a bow and watched Yngvar for the signal.

When the ship drew near enough that teeth of the grinning Arabs waiting to board shined in the moonlight, Yngvar dropped his fist.

Arrows hissed across the short gap, and the battle began.

Even in the dim light, the tight range and the cluster of targets ensured every arrow struck a body. Some splashed into the water with a dying scream. Others howled as they collapsed from the rails. But more stepped into place.

A second volley sped across the gap and more men cried out in pain.

The two hulls thumped together and robed Arabs climbed the ropes trailing from the boarding hooks.

"Kill them!" Yngvar shouted. "Redden the sea with blood!"

His bowmen continued to shoot into the thicket of Arabs, who did not carry bows of their own. Watching the slaughter, Yngvar was gladdened he never had to board this ship. He intended to once, but the cost would have been great.

It was like scaling a wall. Though a man could leap the short distance and pull himself over the rails, this was not possible during a battle. With no pressure from the opposite side, Yngvar committed his men to defense against boarders. When Arabs made the leap, a sword hacked away their fingers and dropped them into the foaming sea.

The boarders gained footing, breaking through the thin line that blocked them at the rails. But Bjorn and Thorfast struck down these enemies. Yngvar, nursing his ankle, remained in the rear to watch for any tricks. He regretted not leading the defense as he should have. But a man who often begs fortune from the gods will soon consume all their goodwill. He consumed his share of luck for the night. To step into battle now was to invite a disaster.

But he did not need to battle. His preparation, bowmen, and superior height had already won him the battle. The Arabs had just not yet realized it.

They were desperate and had expected to sneak upon a sleeping ship. They had sailed far with no path to retreat. Their hands were locked in the wolf's jaws, and they recognized their deaths waiting.

Bowstrings continued to hum, and men on both sides cried out. When the last of the arrows were spent, so was the enemy's will to fight.

The Arabs had sent four men onto the deck, and they sprawled in widening pools of blood. The rest died on their ship or else fell into the sea. Yngvar could not see from his vantage, but he heard struggling from the water.

He learned something about his own ship from this attack. Her low profile made for speed and maneuverability. But she was a poor platform for attacking a higher-sided ship. He had known as much, but to see how easily such an attack could be repelled sealed the lesson. The Arabs would've been better served by having bows of their own and a means to set fire to the deck and sails. But the Arabs had wanted to take the treasure and could not risk sinking it along with the ship.

Alasdair, who stood high to the stern balanced in the rigging, pointed his bow at one final target then loosed his arrow. It was the final blow struck. For the Arabs who still lived surrendered.

Of the nearly thirty men he faced, now twelve remained. They threw down their swords and begged in their strange language. Yngvar had them taken aboard the ship.

"Hamar, make sure you secure our ship and be certain it can stay afloat without bailing."

Hamar wiped blood-spray from his square face and nodded.

The twelve Arabs huddled together at the center of the deck. None spoke Greek. They were all thin, desperate men with hooked noses and sunken eyes. He noted the dryness of their skin, their cracked lips, and their thin arms. These men had been starving long before they took to the sea.

"So you wanted my treasure?" Yngvar asked. "You should at least see it before you die."

They herded the twelve Arabs toward the chests of gold that remained where Yngvar and his crew had loaded them. He opened one so the Arabs could admire the gold filling it.

Each one seemed ready to dive headfirst into it. They looked to the men surrounding them, realizing they had nearly matched numbers. Yet they were unarmed.

Yngvar picked twelve gold coins from the top and bestowed them to each Arab. They accepted the coins in eager palms, bowing and thanking him.

"It's a reward for returning my ship," Yngvar said. "Use it to buy your way out of hell."

He turned to his men.

"Throw them overboard and make sure none live."

The first Arabs seized did not resist, but the remaining ones fought back. Some were run through before they could be tamed. But in the space of moments, the twelve Arabs were all thrown into the sea. Bowmen watched them drowning, and shot at any that might have otherwise survived.

Yngvar turned away from the murder. He usually showed mercy for captives. But both Arab and Byzantine had destroyed his tolerance. He would take no prisoners on his return voyage home.

"We cannot feed them, lord," Alasdair said as he returned to the deck. "Were you to keep them as slaves, they would turn on you one day. There was no choice."

Yngvar smiled and tapped the empty spot on Alasdair's chest where he used to hang his wooden crucifix.

"You will wear a cross of gold there soon. Though you will anger your holy men if you do. Only they can wear holy gold so openly."

Alasdair blushed. "I will not make a showing of my riches. I will give to the church to thank God for preserving me through these ordeals. But I would rather men think me poor and insignificant."

"That is wisest," Yngvar said. "And I have thought much about what bringing this much gold home will mean for us. As much as we would celebrate our return, we must conceal our wealth until we can defend it. But first, let's reclaim my ship. I want to present it to Gyna. Perhaps it will ease her mind to know it was not lost after all she did to bring it back to us."

Alasdair wiped sweat from his brow. "I'm uncertain, lord. It was in saving this ship that she found Ewald. Perhaps the memory will sting more than soothe. But I will be with her. Before Ewald, she favored me most."

Yngvar laughed. "I thought you never noticed."

"Of course I noticed, lord. But being her favorite is not an easy thing. I was glad for Ewald in that respect. I will miss the young king of the Saxons. He saved me from the Arabs back in Crete, and I never properly thanked him for it. It does not seem right that he should die in a pile of dirt. But God has His plans, and I cannot question them."

Upon boarding their ship, they first threw the Arab dead overboard. They counted only four arrows left of the sheaves Alasdair had found. Again Yngvar imagined himself buried among the corpses of his crew, all of them pierced with shafts as these Arabs were.

Hamar declared the ship would float. "They spread pitch and fur on the inside. That's backwards from what they should have done. Look where they tore up the deck. The boards don't fit back the right way. This was all done so badly, I'd rather they never tried. This terrible work can't last on the open sea."

"There is still pitch. You can fix the strake and make us seaworthy again." Yngvar stood on the prow where the beast head remained fixed. He had never taken it down. "There is no one pursuing us now. We have time."

Hamar grunted but turned away, cursing.

Thorfast and Bjorn both helped in cleaning the deck and dislodging arrows that had missed their targets. They often yawned. Yngvar felt the same weariness now that all the battle madness ebbed. He was about to proclaim their work done for the night and suggest they sleep on the Byzantine deck which though bloody was cleaner than his own ship.

But Thorfast straightened up as he pulled something from the shadows of the gunwale.

"Now I know this is impossible. But yet I hold it in my hand."

He raised a sword to Yngvar. Though only gauzy moonlight lit the deck, he could not mistake the green stone in the sword's pommel.

"My sword!"

Yngvar jumped down and rushed to grab it from Thorfast. Its shark-skin handle bit into his hand. He raised the unsheathed blade, feeling its exquisite balance. It was as if lifting a willow branch.

"There's some rust on it," he said, noticing the blotches along its length. "But this is my sword returned to me!"

"Fucking impossible," Bjorn said.

"You need to name it," Thorfast said. "That's why it keeps returning to you. It wants to know its name."

Yngvar held it toward Alasdair, who shook his head in amazement. The rest of his crew looked on in admiration and surprise. Some commented on how they wished the Arabs had also taken back their weapons.

"I think this one was sticking straight up," Yngvar said. He looked to the freemen and noticed that some seemed to understand him. Since he had killed one of their number with the sword, he set it point-down into the deck.

"Well, someone saw the green stone and probably picked it up, then learned it was a finely balanced sword. It only makes sense they took it."

"You are fortunate they dropped it on the deck, lord, and not into the sea like so many of the others."

He still had the sheath for the blade, but had discarded it on the Byzantine ship. No sense in carrying the painful reminder of its loss. Perhaps he might find it there still.

Once they disposed of the dead and his ship secured to the Byzantine's, he allowed his men rest. Bjorn and Alasdair took two Franks and returned to the island to see Gyna. Yngvar did not go. He knew Ewald had died because of his plan, and he dreaded seeing her.

He and the others found their places on the deck. The moon had traveled the sky and left a splash of sparkling stars in its wake. He stared up at these, but his eyes soon fell shut and sleep took him.

The next morning he awakened, and for a moment thought he was still a prisoner of the Byzantines. But the scent of blood irritated his nose, reminding him of the carnage of the previous night. He stood on his ankle, which was painful still but not as bad as the night before.

The following days saw a flurry of activity.

He met with Gyna first. Her eyes were puffy from tears, but she did not blame him. In fact, she embraced him and cried again until Bjorn peeled her away. At first she wanted to dig Ewald's corpse out of the pile of stones, but the effort was too great. Like Nordbert before him, he remained buried where he had died.

Hamar and his assistants hauled their ship onto the beach and improvised caulking with the remains of the pitch the Arabs had retained. In the meantime, others carried all the treasure on the Byzantine ship to the island for eventual transfer to Yngvar's ship. Some had suggested using both ships, but he disagreed.

"We can't sail Petronius's ship back north without attracting too much attention. We will have to take all the treasure onto our deck and pray we don't swamp."

They used the Byzantine ship to remove the rest of the treasure from Agamemnon's tomb. Yngvar clumsily sailed it around to the cliff entrance. The experience reinforced his decision to avoid using this ship, as he nearly wrecked it on the cliffs. Hamar had been right to say that a Norse ship was simple enough for an experienced fisherman, but this Byzantine ship was hard to steer. It seemed to sail according to its own will. It was a final boon of the gods that he steered it around the island without disaster.

They removed the treasure via the hall Yngvar had discovered. They widened the exit and spent nearly a week extracting all that they could and transporting it around to the beach. Only Yngvar and Thorfast were brave enough to enter where King Agamemnon's corpse rested. They carried the treasures to the exit where others picked it up. On the final day, when they had cleared all they could, Yngvar again paused by the coffin and kneeled before the king.

"You have my thanks for your protection. You have bargained wisely, great king. For now, I carry your name north, and I will spend your gold to proclaim your glory to the people of my homeland."

At last, Hamar declared their own ship ready for sailing.

The treasure was fully loaded on the deck and hidden as best as they could under tarps and sailcloth stolen from the Byzantine ship. They had doubled the size of their treasure, which set every man's face aglow with delight.

They buried Petronius on the island. Yngvar had wanted to dig him out and send him off on his ship. They had been allies, though his greed inflicted suffering on all of them. But after a week in the earth, he would be rotting. So he remained buried on the island alongside its many other victims.

They towed the Byzantine ship to sea, then let it drift. Perhaps other sailors would find it and wonder at what had happened. Being that the abandoned ship was near the cursed island, it would enforce the fears for the place. This would please Yngvar.

For he still left treasure on the island he could not carry away on his ship. He left it buried there, for the future. He wondered if he'd ever have the strength to come south again. But if he did, he knew where he would go first.

At last, they shoved off the cursed island. The ship was laden with gold and sat low in the water for its tremendous weight. They struck a course for the north. Nothing followed behind them and ahead lay nothing more than open sea and fair skies.

"We go home," Yngvar said to the ocean spread before him. "And I will keep my promise to King Agamemnon, so we may all live in peace with our spoils."

And so they sailed back to Frankia.

26

They arrived weeks later in Frankia on the Seine River, docking at Rouen.

Yngvar had not been to this country since his father's passing and he had sworn he would never return to it. Yet his Frankish crew deserved to go home to the families they had left behind. He also owed the families of the dead the life price of their men.

The sky was gray and the weather cool even at the start of summer. But the green pines and thick trees that crowded the banks were soothing to his eyes. His crew also celebrated their return.

The freemen, however, were lost. They knew no homes and had no place to return. By now he had seven former slave-soldiers who spoke seven unique languages, it seemed. Yet they all spoke Greek and had learned halting Frankish. They swore to serve Yngvar and remain in his care. For even with great riches they had no means to enjoy it.

So they docked amid a bustling Frankish port, the same port where Nordbert had received his command from Jarl Aren Ulfriksson, Bjorn's father.

Now neither Nordbert nor Aren lived. He had died after the murder of his lord and best friend, Jarl Vilhjalmer.

Frankia was in a state of chaos, with no ruler in Rouen. Vilhjalmer's son, Richard, was ten years old and Jarl of Rouen. Yet he was being held somewhere in northern Frankia. The lands of the Northmen, Normandy, were said to have been broken up. The new Frankish king planned to reclaim the territory once ceded to Hrolf the Strider in the time of Yngvar's grandfather Ulfrik. By extension, Yngvar's ancestral lands were now lost. He regretted choosing such a poor time to return to his birthplace.

The Franks went to find their families, not even fearing to leave their treasures behind. They were so pleased to return home, and trusted Yngvar so well, that they could leave it in his care. An evil man might have sailed off with all that gold. But Yngvar and his Wolves were not evil men.

Bjorn and Gyna both remained gloomy. Bjorn had never cared for his father. He never knew his mother. Yet news of Aren's death seemed to sadden him and he sat in long bouts of silence with Gyna, who had also been pensive throughout their journey home.

Once the Franks had found their families and the families of their fallen companions, Yngvar declared they should leave Rouen and find a place to divide their treasure in secret. He had been so used to his ship being conspicuous that he took careful but unneeded precautions to slip away in the night. Norsemen and Franks of Norse descent filled Rouen with their ships, each one nearly identical to Yngvar's.

They found a landing place on the Seine where they could offload then divide their gold.

The crew all got their shares. Yngvar and his Wolves retained greater shares for having led them to the gold. Yngvar, as leader, had a claim above the others, but he took only a modest portion of it.

They had gathered by a single campfire so as not to draw attention. Its golden light slid across all their faces as Yngvar declared his intentions.

"You are all rich men now. Richer than some lords of this land. I will not keep you in my service. But know this. You must be wise with your gold. You must not speak of it, show it, or otherwise use more of it than your station should allow. Melt these coins, which are strange and the cause of much attention. Keep your wealth in land and livestock. In fact, go far from this place and forget your brothers. The new King Louis says he will reclaim Normandy. He will gladly claim your gold if he learns of it. And do not donate to your churches. Priests gather gold faster than kings."

The Franks and their families looked to each other and then to him. None had considered what it would mean to become suddenly wealthy.

"How are we to protect ourselves?" asked one.

"I don't want to move away," said another.

"Why can't I just buy men to defend me?" asked one more.

Yngvar raised his hands for silence.

"We are all rich. We all share the same problem and same secret. I have promised you all that upon return to Frankia you should have your shares and go home. But now you see that it cannot be. My friends, we have become a crew. We have faced together what few men could understand. We have an interest in protecting what we have suffered so long to get. I have a plan for my gold. I have a greater share than you, but that is not because I am greedy."

"Yes you are," Thorfast said. Laughter rippled around the campfire. Yngvar inclined his head.

"Well, I like gold as much as anyone. But I want to build a place where my family and friends can live in peace. I have a claim to lands here. You should all know this. I grew up here as did Bjorn and Thorfast. Whoever rules in my father's old hall must be sent away. I will do that. I will claim my father's lands, and whatever other lands I need to have space for my people. And I have the gold to do it."

The Franks looked to each other. One of them stood before Yngvar.

"I will surrender part of my share if you will use it for protecting our families."

"We would use it to hire men to our service. We will use it to buy mail and swords, shields and spears, bows and arrows. Then we shall use it to build homes and halls. To set up walls and towers. We will have a land of our own, where we may enjoy our wealth and live our days in peace. Soon we will have no need to hire men, for they will come to serve of their own accord. This is what I would do with my gold."

His freemen understood enough Frankish to be the first to kneel before him. They were desperate men with no homes.

"You seven freemen will become my hirdmen. You will wear mail and carry round shields. You will learn to fight with spear and sword in a shield wall. My hall will be your hall."

This seemed to please them, for they smiled and bowed low.

To Yngvar, it seemed strange that men who had once shared a barracks with him now bowed at his feet. But their display of loyalty brought the Franks to him along with their families. Soon, all of his former crewmen kneeled. Hours before they were dreaming of vanishing into an idyllic countryside to rest on their pile of treasure.

But men needed certainty and safety in a time where there seemed to be none.

Thorfast rested against a tree, arms folded. He smiled at Yngvar. "And what shall we be to you? We have sworn ourselves first to King Hakon. Shouldn't we return to him? Maybe he is a greater lord than you. He has an entire kingdom to give out to his loyal men."

"Go to him," Yngvar said, barely disguising his irritation. "No one need follow me. But I will not yet return to Norway. I have broken promises to the king, and should be an outlaw in his eyes. Were he to discover how much gold I possess, he would have me killed. Then he would claim this treasure for himself. So go to him and see what your treatment will be like."

"Well, you're prickly tonight." Thorfast shifted from his tree. "So you are saying you will be as your father was, a jarl? Then I shall be as my father was and serve the jarl."

"No, you shall be a hersir and lead hirdmen of your own. Same for Bjorn and Alasdair."

Gyna lowered her head and looked aside.

"And you," he said. "Are a woman. But women can lead. My grandmother did when my grandfather was here fighting for Hrolf the Strider. You too shall own land and may raise a hird. Only if you so desire. Perhaps you and Bjorn may wish to join your homes."

"Let's leave that discussion for another time," Bjorn said.

Yet Gyna raised her head. "I'll consider the offer. But you make a lot of promises for a jarl of nothing. Right now you just have a pile of gold. Land is not as easily divided as coins, especially when other folk are living there before you."

"That is true," Yngvar said. "We will pool our wealth to raise forces to secure what we need. This must be done slowly and in secret. But when done, we will march to the hall of my childhood and demand it be returned to me. If the claim of my blood does not win the day, then my sword shall."

"I can agree to that," Bjorn said. He clapped his hands together. The others seemed less eager for more violence.

They divided their treasure over the course of the night, with everyone chattering about a new kingdom in Normandy where they would all be as lords. Yngvar did not wish to dampen their enthusiasm. He doubted they would do more than carve out a haven in the chaos of a now-dissolved Normandy.

The following weeks were full of covert activity by Yngvar and all his crew, including their families. They had spread out into the countryside to collect what they needed. They sent word north on merchant ships for fighting men to join Yngvar on the coast. They could also bring their families. Other men who were able-bodied but dispossessed of both property and future joined as mercenaries and adventurers. They came from Denmark, Norway, England, and within Frankia itself. Many brought their families.

Yngvar migrated his camp along the coast. He could never raise an army while there was order and peace in Normandy. But war had come, and greedy jarls snatched at their neighbor's lands. King Louis's men had not restored order after kidnapping the rightful Jarl of Rouen, Richard. In this lawlessness, Yngvar found a land already fertile with swords for hire and readying for war.

His Franks knew blacksmiths and weapon smiths eager for gold in a time of uncertainty. They worked in Rouen at great forges capable of meeting great orders. They were paid well by men they knew well, and so swords and spears and coats of mail left the city hidden in carts and in barrels. These journeyed along the Seine until picked up by Yngvar and his ever-expanding followers.

No matter the condition of the men joining him, Yngvar outfitted them as formidable warriors. As their numbers increased, he insisted they train together. This was a strange concept to his traditionally minded warriors. They understood locking shields and holding against enemy charges. But each fought as a warrior and not a soldier. Yngvar saw the value in the units and order that the Byzantines had taught him. While such a system could not last, he could use it to his advantage in the short-term. It made his new men cohesive and confident in their fighting prowess.

Provisioning his men was more of a challenge, for in uncertain times people hoarded their food. But he overpaid for provisions, and greed won out. He knew this would draw attention. The alternative was to set hungry spearmen loose on the countryside, which would have been a larger problem. He began to hear rumors circulating in the towns and in Rouen. He had not been named, but news of a wealthy lord seeking to invade Normandy was on everyone's lips.

Nearly a month after arriving in Frankia, and living a nomadic life up and down the coast, Yngvar had raised over three hundred men.

And he had the attention of Paris.

It was the heart of springtime when Frankish scouts pinpointed Yngvar on their shores. They had grown too large to move unhindered and had settled on the beaches. He had five ships and three hundred warriors, all in scoured mail and freshly painted shields. These carried the standard of his family, a black stag on a green background. He had many more numbers in the families of his men.

Gathering such an army had barely cut into the wealth he had carried back from the Midgard Sea.

Within days of their contact with the Frankish scouts, Yngvar was summoned to meet King Louis's men under a flag of truce. The meeting would take place on the coast, south of the Seine and in open ground. Yngvar's ships were to remain out of bow range and on the water.

Yngvar prepared to meet the king's envoys. He would take all his Wolves and his hirdmen to the meeting. They shined their mail and sharpened their swords. He polished the green stone in the pommel of his sword. Bjorn now carried an ax engraved with a dragon's head.

Thorfast had let his white beard grow to his chest and tied it with a gold ring. Gyna wore mail fitted to her and tucked her hair under a helmet with a gilt faceplate. Alasdair remained much as he had always been. But amid the grandeur of his companions his simple outfit made him conspicuous.

The morning of the meeting, Yngvar gathered his original crew to him. They stood on the shore where the camps of warriors stretched down the beach. Their campfires filled the sky with gray smoke.

"We go to see the speaker for the new king. Louis the Fourth is unknown to me. He had been a friend to Jarl Vilhjalmer, though he now holds his son a prisoner. The only truth I know is that kings are liars and their word is worth less than gull shit."

"And their ambitions are splattered just as carelessly," Thorfast added. The men laughed and nodded. Yngvar as well.

"But if we can have what we desire without bloodshed, I would do it. These swordsmen will still have plenty of work. There are Bretons to fight and fresh enemies to make, even with the king's leave. Still, I would negotiate for our lands in peace, and under the king's protection. Then we would have the time build up to a strength to rival Rouen's. Let us see what can become of this."

He knew his father's homelands would never rival Rouen, for it was still distant from the Seine, which controlled access to Paris. But he could build a fort that would stand for generations. He had the gold for it now.

King Louis sent twenty mounted men with long spears and shining helmets. They were beautiful, and their animals radiated health and power. Yngvar recalled Rida al-Ghazi's horsemen, which now seemed anemic compared to these mighty war beasts.

One rider sat at the fore of the others. His red cloak fell over his shoulders and over his horse's flanks. He had no spear, but wore a sword. His armor sparkled in the morning light. With the shadowy line of trees behind him, he seemed as if he blazed with his own glory.

Yngvar led his contingent. The golden armband of Agamemnon's crown felt as if it burned his left arm. He rubbed at it as he considered the Franks. They did not dismount but stared down their long noses. The leader in the blazing armor wore a full-brown mustache in the Saxon style. It wiggled when he spoke.

"And you are the one called Yngvar Hakonsson?"

"I am," Yngvar rested his hand on the pommel of his jeweled sword. Thick rings of gold and silver filled each of his fingers. He wanted them to understand his wealth. It would lend him power in negotiations. "And you must be the king's errand boy."

The blazing man shifted on his horse, and his nostrils flared. But he did not bite at the insult.

"You may call me Wibert. Let us dispense with titles for now. I have the full authority of the king to speak for him."

Wibert produced a golden seal which in another time might have dazzled him. But now he had seen such wealth that a small gold-inlaid piece of wood was a trifle. Wibert held it forward as if expecting Yngvar to kneel.

"Don't tire your arm holding it out," he said. "It means nothing to me. I will take your word that you speak for the king. I speak for myself and the three hundred men who have gathered to me so far."

"So far," Wibert leaned over his horse's neck. "You intend to bring more? You've already invaded the king's lands."

"Invaded? I am merely returning home." Yngvar looked to Thorfast and Bjorn, who both nodded dutifully. "My father was Hakon Ulfriksson, and my grandfather was Ulfrik Ormsson. And they both served Hrolf the Strider. You know him today as Rollo the Jarl of Rouen. I grew up here and left on an adventure. Now I've come home with my spoils and men and find my father is dead and his halls razed. There are others living where I walked as a boy. Now, I would seek justice from Jarl Vilhjalmer, but I understand a shit-eating coward murdered him on the way to a peace talk. Can you believe that, Wibert? So I would speak with his son, Richard, though he is but a boy. Yet what do I find, Wibert? Richard is away in the north as a permanent guest of some lord of your king's. There is no law here to appeal to."

"King Louis rules these lands," Wibert said, sitting straighter on his horse.

Yngvar narrowed his eyes. "There was a treaty signed. I know of it since my grandfather and father were there for it. These lands were granted to them. But your king does not remember, or chooses to forget. So I am forced to bring three hundred men to reclaim what should not need to be reclaimed. And make no mistake, Wibert, I can buy many more than what you see now."

"You dare to make threats to the king?"

Yngvar felt the pulse in his veins. Agamemnon's crown pressed on his veins, emphasizing every beat of his heart. This was the time for Yngvar to fulfill his promise and prevent the curse. Agamemnon's ghost had waited patiently. All three hundred of Yngvar's men knew his fame now, but it was not enough. Here was a chance to claim a land and become a legend. That is what would forever rid Yngvar of any worry for a curse.

"Wibert, I dare much." Yngvar stepped closer to the horse before him. "And if you do not come down from your horse I will dare to cut it from under you. You will treat me with respect and act with the dignity that represents your king. Or else I will remember the ways of my father and grandfather. You will regret that."

To his surprise, Wibert laughed. Yngvar's threats seemed to have the reverse effect on him. He slipped easily from the horse, then an adolescent boy whom Yngvar had not noticed emerged from between the other horsemen. He took the animal's reins and led it away.

"Very good," Wibert said. "King Louis needs powerful men in this land. It is awash in conflict, and he wishes only peace for his subjects. You bring wealth and power. The king has the concerns of a kingdom to occupy his attention. The king welcomes a firm arm in this land, one like yours that has gathered so much strength in so little time. If, as you say, you are coming home then this is all the easier to settle. Life in this territory has been confusing at best. But with the king's authority and your formidable force, I'm certain you could do much to end that confusion."

"You are promising me my father's lands?" Yngvar asked. "So readily? It must be worth very little now to give it away like this. You won't offer me a fight for it?"

"The king will not," Wibert said. "Not if you are restoring the land in his name. But others may have words or worse for your ambitions. In this, the king would agree to look elsewhere."

"You will want my oath," Yngvar said. "And to seed men among mine to report to the king. But if you would ask for hostages, then you can tell your king to look for me in his throne room. I'll be easy to find as I'll be carrying your head and a bloody sword."

Wibert's genial smile faded.

"We can discuss the details. Let us set a canopy so we do not stand under the sun all day. We are both in heavy armor and the same for our men. Show them some mercy and let them sit, shall we? We do not have to end this day with the promise of war. We can negotiate something that benefits us all."

Yngvar looked to Thorfast and Bjorn, who were claimants in family lands. Both inclined their heads, but Bjorn frowned at Wibert. He was just the sort of handsome dandy he despised.

"Then let us speak," Yngvar said.

One of the other Frankish riders cleared his throat. Wibert's forming smile vanished. He slowly turned to his horsemen.

It surprised Yngvar that one of the mailed men wore a surcoat with a blue cross stitched on it. He also hung a thick silver chain and cross around his thin neck. He was too old and shriveled to be menacing in war gear, but he sat his horse with authority.

"That is Father Leufred," Wibert explained. "He will also take part in our talks to represent the Church."

"I will," declared the priest. "And let there be no mistake, I will not advise the king to make bargains with pagans. If you are to become part of the kingdom, then you must first be baptized as a Christian."

27

One year later, on a spring day as fair and balmy as the day Yngvar had brokered peace with Wibert and Father Leufred, he stood at the entrance to his new hall.

Despite having grown up in these lands, so much had changed in his absence he was uncertain he had rebuilt the hall in the exact place. Even the graves of his parents had been lost to him. Whole woods had been felled. Yet he knew the hills and the streams well enough to be confident he was close.

After his father had died, Bretons once again struck north. While they again failed to expand their territory, they had left ruin behind. Jarl Vilhjalmer's last days were consumed with politics and king-making, and so his jarls and petty rulers took to fighting amongst themselves. This had lasted until Yngvar marched into Normandy with three hundred well-armed men eager to claim land for their families.

However, no blood was spilled in reclaiming his home. Seeing his strength and their own isolation, the squatters in his ancestral home either accepted his rule or else moved off.

He leaned against the wall beside the doors now. Beyond the opening, his hirdmen laughed in the hall. Greek curses wafted out of the smoky darkness. But they had learned to curse in Frankish and learned how to fight with longsword and round shield. They were his constant companions and possibly the wealthiest hirdmen in all the world.

Ahead of him he looked out at the progress being made on the stockade walls. For now, they were timber and earth defenses. While building in stone was not beyond his means, he could not spare the time for construction. Teams of workers hauled timbers, worked them, while others dug ditches and shored up ramparts. The walls had to be up before summer raiding season.

They had spent the previous summer fending off neighbors, Bretons, and bandits. The king's authority meant Paris would not send spearmen after him as long as he advanced the interests of the throne. He was on his own to make peace in his new territory. The petty jarls and hersir who had bickered under Vilhjalmer now had a common enemy in him. They had tried individual attacks that had petered out by the end of summer. Now, after a snowy winter, they had negotiated alliances with each other. One day soon an organized attack would come.

But he would be ready.

Alasdair emerged from the hall. He squinted into the midmorning light.

"Lord, will the others be here soon?"

"I'm watching for them now." Yngvar thought he saw Bjorn's head above the distant crowd of workers. He too squinted. Years of bright sun reflecting off the sea had ruined his sight, at least so he claimed. Hamar, who now oversaw all his ships, had spent twice as long as he and had the vision of a hawk.

"Though it has been a long year, it still feels strange not to see them every day."

Yngvar nodded. "Indeed. Though we see them enough. They have their own halls and their own men to worry for. No longer are we carefree raiders. We all have responsibilities. Except for you."

"Lord, I serve you, of course!"

Alasdair touched his cross. He looked up to Yngvar and fixed on the small silver cross hanging from his neck.

"Lord, you have been praying as I've instructed?"

"Every night, I get on my knees beside my bed and toady to God. I pray he does not blind me or throw the pox upon me. I thank Him for loving me enough to not blight my land and for not starving the children of my people. I'm very careful about this."

Alasdair folded his arms. "Lord, God will not be deceived. If you are not sincere—"

"I pray to God when others must see it done. I pray to Thor when I am on the sea and to Odin when I go to battle. Each god has a purpose. There is no trouble adding one more to the number of gods I must appease. And wearing this cross has earned peace for my people. All it cost me was a dip in a stream. It seems an easy price to pay."

Alasdair remained quiet.

Now Bjorn emerged from the crowd. Gyna and Thorfast walked beside him. Yngvar pushed off the wall.

"Well, they must have met on the road, or else they were drinking together again last night. They should have invited us. Ungrateful bastards. Come, let's meet them halfway."

They met in the wide field that spread from the base of the hill where they had built the mead hall. Houses and tracks lined the field's edges, more haphazard than Yngvar hoped. But they had rushed construction to be ready for winter, all while securing their land. Blacksmiths clanged away at their forges in the distance. Dogs barked and birds called. It was a fair day for remembering.

Yngvar embraced all his Wolves.

"You all were supposed to be here by dawn," Yngvar said, chiding them.

Thorfast flicked the cross at Yngvar's neck. "We thought you'd be praying all morning. So I stayed with Bjorn and Gyna last night. You're lucky we were awake before noon."

They laughed and walked together toward the rear of the hall. They passed men drilling together, teaching their sons how to hold a shield wall in place. Bjorn shook his head as they passed.

"These kids look weak. What kind of boys are raised here? When I was their age, I was twice as strong as them. We can't go raising weak boys. I should teach them."

"How do you teach someone to be as mad as a boar and fierce as a bear?" Thorfast asked. "We don't need too many madmen in our ranks. You'll serve well enough."

Again they laughed and at length gathered to the rune stones Yngvar had raised in sight of his hall.

They surrounded these tall stones, engraved with runes in the twisting and curving shapes of serpents. They stared solemnly.

Yngvar felt the weight of Agamemnon's crown on his arm. He always did when he looked upon the tallest of the three stones. He rubbed at it as he remembered.

"A year ago today, we returned to Frankia," he said. All five of them continued to stare soberly at the stones erected in the deep green grass.

"I never thought we'd return," Thorfast said. "So many dead remain in Sicily and on that island."

"I'm glad to be gone from that place," Gyna said. "I'd not return there for even twice the gold we claimed."

Bjorn grunted. "Thought I'd never see you all again. Now it's like it never happened. Ain't it strange? Like a dream, it was."

"Like a nightmare," Yngvar said. "But we woke from it. And I'd say we all woke up stronger than we had been."

Alasdair said nothing. Yngvar glanced to him. He stared at Valgerd's name carved in the left rock.

Yngvar stepped forward and touched the runes of her name. He read the inscription aloud, though in truth he did not know how to read. He remembered what he had paid to have inscribed here.

"Dearest Valgerd. Shield maiden and lover. Gone to heaven." He traced his finger along the rough edges, continuing to read what he had committed to memory. "Brave Nordbert, loyal hirdman, died in Sicily. Ragnar who loved his mother best died in battle."

Thorfast chuckled as he always did at the reading. Yngvar let a smile touch his lips and continued to flick his finger along the curves of the inscription.

"Ewald son of Waldhar. Honored nephew and mighty warrior. He died in Sicily."

Gyna rubbed away a tear. Even a year later, she still mourned the sudden death of her young nephew.

And so he continued to read from the stone. He knew the name of every one of his men who had died somewhere in the Midgard Sea. Their names and their praises were carved into two stones to stand until Ragnarok. At last he recited the last name, then stood back so that all could remember the cost of their riches.

Finally, he turned to the largest stone. He placed both hands on it. It was cold and hard. He searched the complex coils, trying to remember where the inscription began on this rune stone. His fingers pressed against the inscription, he recited anew.

"King Agamemnon, greatest of all kings, hero of the Greeks, protector and gold-giver, forever shall his name and glory be repeated until the end of days."

The inscription filled the massive stone. Every visitor to his hall had heard the name of the king from Yngvar's lips. He showed all guests this stone and made them repeat the name until memorized. Rumors of his eccentricity returned to him, that he forced guests to memorize unpronounceable names to humiliate them.

But it was for the glory of Agamemnon and to honor the promise made to his ghost.

"I'd say we've no worries for curses with this stone," Thorfast said. "We had a strong year. If the king cursed us, by now we would be dead."

Yngvar stepped back. He nodded in satisfaction, placing one hand on the pommel of his sword.

"I agree. The king is well pleased with how we've honored him. I fear no curse and speak gladly of his story to all who greet me in my hall. Even when I no longer have a voice to speak, this stone will proclaim him forever. I have done what I have promised and the gold is ours forever."

They stood admiring the craftsmanship of the stones. Yngvar had hired the best engravers from Rouen to create them.

"Are you going to tell him?" Gyna asked Thorfast.

"That you are pregnant and finally going to marry this one-eyed fool? Shouldn't that come from you?"

Gyna turned pale. Bjorn shoved Thorfast back.

"You white-haired bastard! This wasn't how we planned to tell him!"

Yngvar's heart raced. He stepped back with his hand on his chest.

"Is this true? A child? Marriage?"

"You fool, you spoiled everything." Rather than answer, Gyna shoved Thorfast, who stumbled back laughing.

"You shouldn't delay important news for your jarl. I'm just keeping order here."

"This is wonderful." Yngvar grabbed Bjorn and hugged his blushing cousin. He attempted the same from Gyna, but she pushed him back.

"Act like a jarl for once," she said.

But he embraced her all the same. Alasdair repeated the embraces.

"Praise God! And praise Freya, as well."

This brought laughter again to the group.

"This is best news I could hope for," Yngvar said. "But this was not the news you wanted Thorfast to share. Then what was?"

"Ah, well, I was at the river meeting with Hamar and arranging some things." Thorfast pointed north toward the Seine. "A merchant ship had arrived, and as we got to talking I learned he had come recently from the Midgard Sea. He'd been as far as Sicily and knew of the places we also knew so well."

"And what news did he bring? Was it for the war in Crete?" Yngvar asked.

"I've no care for that war." Thorfast stroked his beard, which he had since trimmed back to its normal size. "It was news of a great earthquake that shook Greece and sent waves to scour the coasts. Waves as high as mountains, he said, washed whole villages away. But he said that the shaking was so strong that small islands shattered and sank beneath the waves. From what I learned, I think that cursed island is no more."

Yngvar and Alasdair stared at each other in amazement. Thorfast, Bjorn, and Gyna were all nodding along.

"So the curse is settled and the last of the treasure gone," Yngvar said. "King Agamemnon has removed himself from the world forever."

He spit for good luck, as did the others, but Alasdair crossed himself.

"Well, there is much to celebrate today," Yngvar said. "We go to the mead hall, and I promise you we will open a new cask and finish it before supper."

"Speaking of promises," Thorfast said with a sly grin. "You've got to name that sword yet. We've been back for a year and you've put it to good use since. So what will you call it?"

Yngvar thrummed the pommel. "I knew you would ask. I've given it some thought."

"Are your thoughts so precious you cannot share with us?" Thorfast grinned.

Yet Yngvar grew quiet. He stepped back, then drew the sword. Its edge gleamed white and the blue sky reflected along its perfectly balanced weight. The four others stood around it, reflections dancing along their faces.

"When we left this land years ago, we were boys playing at men. We chased tales of heroes that by now we all know cannot be true. I went in search of my fate, as my father and grandfather had before me. I have found it. My grandfather carried a sword like this one, with a green stone in its pommel. He called it Fate's Needle. So I name this sword for my grandfather and for my fate and the fates of those who have died beneath its edge. I name this sword Fate's End."

They all stared down at it. With a name given to his prized sword, it seemed to become a new blade. Perhaps it was as Thorfast had once said. The blade returned to him so often because it needed to learn its name. He slid it back into its sheath with a hiss of iron and a clack against wood.

After more congratulations to Bjorn and Gyna, they drifted toward the hall.

Yet Yngvar lingered and looked back once more to the three stones.

Alasdair noticed and paused while the others continued ahead.

"Lord, is everything all right?"

Light spilled over the stones as the sun emerged from scattered clouds. It bleached them white. Yngvar's eyesight was already poor and perhaps a tear of joy had clouded his vision further.

Yet he believed in that pool of light he saw this father and another man, his grandfather, watching him go. They wore mail and helmets and their hands rested on the hilts of their swords. They smiled.

"Lord?"

He blinked and wiped at his eyes with the back of his wrist.

The stones remained as they always had been and nothing more.

"I am glad to have named my sword," he said. "I am glad for many, many things. Come, let us go celebrate."

Yngvar strode toward his hall, his hearth, and his friends. He was the richest man in the world.

AUTHOR'S NOTE

Agamemnon is an important figure in Greek mythology. He was king of Mycenae. He was also the leader of the Greek army in the Trojan War. Like all mythological heroes, his life was full of drama and tragedy. He offended the goddess Artemis. As a result, she prevented his army from sailing to Troy. She could only be appeased if Agamemnon sacrificed his most beautiful daughter. What had he done to offend the goddess? He shot a deer, sacred to her, and claimed not even Artemis could have shot so well. Later in life, Agamemnon's wife murdered him. Being a Greek hero was tough business.

Agamemnon's tomb and location as I have depicted it is a complete fabrication, as you may have already surmised. However, I based its design somewhat on a historical tomb. I took the Treasury of Atreus as my inspiration. This is located in Mycenae and is also known as the Tomb of Agamemnon. It is a grand structure and elaborately built into the side of a hill. Again, this actual location merely served as inspiration and I did not make a literal presentation of it in the fiction. The actual tomb likely had nothing to do with either Agamemnon or Atreus, his father. The naming of this archaeological find was likely more due to wishful thinking than the genuine discovery of a hero from the Trojan War.

Did Yngvar and his Wolves find the real Agamemnon's tomb? This question is never answered in the story but there are clues to suggest they did not. The biggest clue is the treasure itself. The first coins in the Western World date back to 600 BC. Agamemnon would have been buried many centuries before this date. So if not Agamemnon, then who was buried on that cursed island? Like Yngvar and his Wolves, we can only speculate. The lands surrounding the Mediterranean Sea did not lack for rich and powerful men in the ancient world.

Moving forward in history to the time of this story, we find the Byzantines focused on ending the threat from Crete. Shortly after the disaster of Messina, where the Byzantine Empire forever lost Sicily, a new effort focused on conquering Crete. The emirate of Crete had its roots in piratical Iberian Muslims who conquered the island in the 820s. From that point forward, it was a hub of piracy throughout the Aegean Sea. At last, the Byzantines sent a vast fleet to Chandax and besieged the city for over a year. When all settled, Crete was back in Byzantine hands, the surviving inhabitants Christianized, and Sicily turned into a distant bad dream.

Lastly, as the third movement in history concerning our story, we return to Frankia. Jarl Vilhjalmer, known to history as William Longsword, had spent his final years engaged in king-making adventures and fighting with the Count of Flanders, Arnulf I. King Raoul had died, and the sixteen-year-old Louis IV was living in exile in England. Vilhjalmer and Louis had previously met. After Raoul's death, William persuaded Louis to return as king and that he would pledge loyalty to him.

Things went well for Vilhjalmer for a time. Though he was later excommunicated for his attacks on Arnulf's estates. One might imagine this was more of a political setback to him than any threat to his soul. His father, despite his baptism, was a pagan and that sentiment must have lurked in Vilhjalmer's heart. Fighting between Arnulf and Vilhjalmer was at last settled in a truce.

They were to formalize the settlement of their differences in a peace treaty the following year. Vilhjalmer proceeded to an island in the Somme River during the last days of fall to meet with Arnulf. His good faith was met with hidden daggers, and he was killed in an ambush by Arnulf's men. As it so often seems in history, the wrong men are excommunicated and the evil ones laugh their way to success.

Further villainy ensued upon Vilhjalmer's son, Richard I. The Norsemen called him Jarl Richard. He was installed as the Jarl of Rouen upon his father's death. He was only ten years old. King Louis IV promised to preserve Normandy, but shortly after Richard's assumption of his father's position, Louis reneged. He seized lands in Normandy for himself, then broke up the territory. He granted lower Normandy to Hugh the Great and took Richard as a hostage, confining him to northern Frankia.

There is much more to Richard's story, as this is only the beginning of a long life of conflict and impressive achievement. Yet I leave his tale here for now.

I have taken liberties with the timeline of events in Crete and Frankia. The treacheries of Arnulf and Louis IV occurred perhaps twenty years prior to the Byzantine's recapturing of Crete. The arrangement I chose makes for more interesting narrative background rather than adhering to a rigid historical timeline.

As for Yngvar and his Wolves, they have found their gold and their glory. They have grown from youths into leaders of men. Their stories as descendants of Ulfrik Ormsson are finished.

As you see from the outline of events in Frankia given above, the future is hardly peaceful. While Yngvar and his people are fabulously wealthy and capable of holding their own, the world around them will remain unsettled for a long time. Richard will eventually return to reclaim his territory. Battles will be fought, and years of bloodshed will ensue. But there will be an expanded and stronger Normandy and a line of nobility that will carry far into the future.

Perhaps we will meet Yngvar again as he navigates his way through history. There are still obligations in Norway and a brewing war with Denmark. Erik Bloodaxe is king in York, and Yngvar's hated enemy. Bjorn owes him an eye still. But for now, the stories of their youth have been told and their stories as leaders remain to be written. One day we might revisit these three young men who dreamed of gold and glory and see what they became.

But for now, you have followed their circuitous road through dozens of trials. Certainly a lifetime of adventure by anyone's measure. It has been my sincere pleasure to tell their stories, and I offer my sincerest thanks to all those who have read and enjoyed them. Raise your drinking horns and remember heroes who trod the world with sword and shield seeking gold and glory!

NEWSLETTER

If you would like to know when my next book is released, please sign up for my new release newsletter. You can do this at my website:
http://jerryautieri.wordpress.com/

If you have enjoyed this book and would like to show your support for my writing, consider leaving a review where you purchased this book or on Goodreads, LibraryThing, and other reader sites. I need help from readers like you to get the word out about my books. If you have a moment, please share your thoughts with other readers. I appreciate it!

ALSO BY JERRY AUTIERI

Ulfrik Ormsson's Saga

Historical adventure stories set in 9th Century Europe and brimming with heroic combat. Witness the birth of a unified Norway, travel to the remote Faeroe Islands, then follow the Vikings on a siege of Paris and beyond. Walk in the footsteps of the Vikings and witness history through the eyes of Ulfrik Ormsson.

Fate's Needle

Islands in the Fog

Banners of the Northmen

Shield of Lies

The Storm God's Gift

Return of the Ravens

Sword Brothers

Grimwold and Lethos Trilogy

A sword and sorcery fantasy trilogy with a decidedly Norse flavor.

Deadman's Tide

Children of Urdis

Age of Blood

Copyright © 2020 by Jerry Autieri

All rights reserved.

No part of this book may be reproduced in any form or by any electronic or mechanical means, including information storage and retrieval systems, without written permission from the author, except for the use of brief quotations in a book review.